HEIR APPARENT

HEIR
APPARENT

A NOVEL

WITHDRAWN

JAMES TERRY

Skyhorse Publishing

Skyhorse Publishing books may be purchased in bulk at special discounts for sales promotion, corporate gifts, fund-raising, or educational purposes. Special editions can also be created to specifications. For details, contact the Special Sales Department, Skyhorse Publishing, 307 West 36th Street, 11th Floor, New York, NY 10018 or info@skyhorsepublishing.com.

Skyhorse Publishing® is an imprint of Skyhorse Publishing, Inc.®, a Delaware corporation.

Visit our website at www.skyhorsepublishing.com.

10 9 8 7 6 5 4 3 2 1

Library of Congress Cataloging-in-Publication Data is available on file.

Cover design by Erin Seaward-Hiatt

Print ISBN: 978-1-5107-3108-0
Ebook ISBN: 978-1-5107-3109-7

Printed in the United States of America

For Deana and Marlowe

1

THAT MORNING WHEN the cops came knocking, I was dreaming that a man had shot me in the head. I saw the flash. I heard the bang. But I didn't feel a thing. Who this man was and why he wanted me dead, I no longer recall.

I have also forgotten how I managed to make it to the door in a relatively presentable state, but I must have, for I distinctly recall Detective-lieutenant Randy Hicks of the 66th Street Division taking a long disdainful look at me before he and Detective Stiles swaggered into my apartment with the proprietorial play of the hips peculiar to their kind.

"Christ Almighty," Hicks growled, looking around with disgust. "Smells like an embalmers convention in here."

"Someone's been on a holy tear," was Stiles's contribution.

Hicks and Stiles: grace and gentility personified. Hicks with his fat fists stumped against his sagging belt, legs planted as wide as the Colossus of Rhodes, sweat lake irrigating his shirt. Bony Stiles, flanking his commander, rubber band nervously expanding and contracting around his right thumb and middle finger in time with his gum-chewing jaw. I had the distinct impression looking at them that I was watching a couple of bad actors who had been giving the same matinee performance to empty theaters for the past decade, so inured to the stale yawns which greeted their best gags that somewhere beneath their lines they managed to carry on a conversation about their wives or the price of cigarettes or some other banal topic whose ostensible purpose was to obliterate the silence which, if left intact, would all too eloquently convey the complete absence of any fellow-feeling between them. Everything about them was a sham, their spirits ossified by daily draughts of petty power. It was impossible to imagine them ever out of their wrinkled, sweaty suits. They were born in them, yanked from the womb in tiny brown gabardine suits—porkpies, ties, and all—sweat stains already in place around their armpits. "It's a cop!" the midwife must have exclaimed as she placed the newborn on its mother's panting bosom.

"Some wild party," Stiles quipped, picking up my *Bix Beiderbecke and his Rhythm Jugglers* LP and studying the front and back covers with evident disapproval.

Hicks was eyeballing me. "Do you know a man named Walter Morris?"

"I don't know my own mother at this time of the morning."

"He seems to have known you."

I scratched the right side of my nose.

"I take it he's dead."

"I'd say so," Hicks said. "Would you say so, Stiles?"

"I'd say so."

"Yeah, I'd say he's pretty much dead," Hicks said. "Not much chance of his brains being stuffed back into that hole in the side of his head."

"One funny little thing." Stiles removed a folded-up piece of typing paper from his inside jacket pocket, unfolded it, and handed it to me. It was splattered with dried blood. Down near the bottom, like the closing of a letter, was typewritten:

```
                    Yours truly,


                    Eddie King
```

I turned it over. Nothing on the back. I looked at Hicks, then Stiles, then Hicks again. They seemed to be waiting for my confession.

"Is this supposed to mean something to me?"

"You're Eddie King, aren't you?" Stiles said.

"One of them."

"There's only three in the book," Hicks said. "And only one has a license to carry a snubnose .38."

Stiles grinned at me. He had been waiting all morning to deliver his line. "The note was in the stiff's lap."

I glanced at it again then handed it to Hicks.

"That's not all," Hicks said. "According to the old lady someone showed up at the door three weeks ago with a gun. He was wearing a black suit and a black fedora." He stared at me for about five seconds. "Didn't say anything. Just flashed his gun, then left."

"That's your man," I said. "Find the guy in the black suit and fedora and you've got your killer. There can't be more than half a million of them out there."

"I'd like to take a look at your piece," Hicks said.

I nodded towards the hat rack. "Be my guest."

Hicks walked over and unbuttoned the flap and removed my revolver from the shoulder holster. He brusquely flicked open the cylinder, peered down at the chambers for a few seconds, then raised the butt of the barrel to his nose and sniffed. He frowned. He flicked the cylinder shut and reholstered the firearm, not bothering to rebutton the flap.

Turning to face me, he replanted his fists on his hips.

"Empty chamber," he said. "Pretty fresh by the smell of it."

"Good nose."

"You want to tell me about it?"

"Not particularly."

"I think you'd better."

"It's a long story."

"We're in no rush," Stiles said.

We all looked at each other for a while.

"I need a cup of coffee," I said. "Do you guys want one?"

"I'll have one if you're having one," Stiles deferred to his superior. Hicks shook his head, leaving Stiles no choice but to regretfully decline.

I went into the kitchenette and put on the kettle and dumped the remaining few tablespoons of my last jar of instant into my Wendell Willkie for President mug. Waiting for the kettle to boil, I opened the fridge and surveyed the cold void. The real mystery was why I always persisted in believing that somehow something edible might have materialized since the last time I looked.

The kettle wheezed. I poured the water, giving it a stir with the handle of a dirty spoon before returning to my guests. A wave of wooziness coming on, I sat down on the right arm of the recliner. Hicks had moved from the hat rack and was now standing half-in and half-out of a parallelogram of sunlight, his upper body in shadow, his trousers overexposed.

Stiles stopped snooping long enough to say: "We're waiting to be enlightened."

The sight of two of my neckties knotted around the uprights of the bed frame revived an image from last night that I would rather have forgotten.

I scalded my tongue, winced, and began.

"I'm not one of those rare individuals who can remember his own birth, but I'm pretty sure that my memory is reliable as far back as two years old. I have a vivid image of a woman's face looming over me, gazing down on me with eyes full of sweet pity. I always think of her as a nurse because she had a white cap of some sort on her head. She certainly wasn't my mother. I think she was Mexican. It's hard for me to remember anything else with any certainty until I'm about five. I'm in the back yard with my father. It's a sunny day. We're throwing the slobbery tennis ball to Rex   "

"All right, wise guy," Hicks cut me off. "If you want to play it that way we can play it that way."

"I told you it was a long story." I blew across the lip of my cup.

"You're lucky the gun was in his hand," Hicks said, "or I'd have you in the can faster than pigeon shit on a hockey puck."

I laughed. I didn't know what was funnier—his ridiculous metaphor, the dour look on his face, or the fact that he had waited all this time to inform me that the dead man had a gun in his hand.

"Don't tell me," I said. "Was it by any chance a snubnose .38?"

Stiles removed a handkerchief from his back pocket and noisily blew his nose. Neither of them responded to my query.

"Who was this guy anyway?" I asked.

"Some kind of ink slinger," Hicks replied.

"Suicide," I said. "Case closed. Ernest Hemingway. Hart Crane. Petronius. A long and illustrious history of writers offing themselves.

The guy has a .38 in his hand, and you're standing here sniffing my gun because my name is on some note in his hand. What am I missing?"

Hicks and Stiles exchanged a smug glance.

"We found a piece of dried roof shingle in the front yard," Hicks said. "Morris's study is on the second floor, with a window letting out to the roof of the porch. The window wasn't locked. A section of exposed wood on the porch roof matched the piece we found in the grass."

"And you're telling me this because . . . ?"

"The bullet's missing," Stiles said.

"Not there," Hicks expounded. "Someone removed it from the scene."

"There goes your ballistics report."

"Bullets don't just vanish into thin air," Stiles pointed out. "Someone was there."

"Did you look in his head?"

"There's a hole through his head that Ben Hogan could sink a putt into."

Hicks moseyed over to the bed and fiddled with one of my ties.

"Looks like you had some company last night," he observed.

"An old friend stopped by," I replied. "We had some catching up to do."

"More like tying up," Stiles grinned. His dentist was either blind or had a dark sense of humor.

Hicks dropped the tie and moseyed over to the recliner's seat cushion, presently marooned in the middle of the floor with a full ashtray resting on it, two glasses either side of it, one of them smeared with lipstick. Beside it lay an empty bottle of Old Grand-Dad.

"Where were you yesterday between two and three p.m.?" he asked me.

"Entertaining my friend," I said. "We go way back."

"What's her name?"

"I don't recall at the moment."

"If it were me I think I'd take soliciting a prostitute over murder," he said, giving me the old concerned father look. "But that's just me."

I took a long sip. It felt good going down.

"It's always a pleasure chatting with you guys," I said, "but I'm running a little late this morning."

Hicks was in no rush. He stood there looking at me, as if trying to impress upon my retinas the human incarnation of Justice. All I saw was a big, fat, sweaty crooked cop. He looked at Stiles and made a putt with his jaw towards the door. Stiles tugged at his jacket lapels and sauntered past me, treating me to a whiff of his cologne, an oddly feminine scent. At the door, which they hadn't bothered to shut behind them, Hicks turned and eyed me.

"Open your eyes, King," he said. "There's blood in the streets. It's up to your ankles."

What the hell that was supposed to mean, I had no idea.

2

MY OFFICE IS in the Mandrake Building, an unimaginative six-story affair that I can see from my apartment if I crane my neck far enough out the window. It's a ten-minute walk, but I prefer to drive. I share the floor with a couple of small-time lawyers, a tax guy, a dentist, a psychiatrist, various vague professional services firms and some kind of fly-by-night mail-order racket. I've been there longer than any of them, so the territorial instincts I feel when I push the button for the third floor aren't without some justification.

The steak and fries that I'd wolfed down at the diner before coming in hadn't done much for the hangover. My temples were throbbing and my skull felt as empty as my bank account. If I hadn't had some paperwork to catch up on, I wouldn't have come in at all.

Both windows were open, the quiet music of mid-morning traffic playing to the rhythm of the blinds tapping against the frames. I stepped over to the window behind my desk and stood there for a while looking out across the city, thinking about Hicks and Stiles and a dead writer named Morris. It looked like suicide. But what kind of a goodbye to the world was that? What was my name doing on it, if indeed I was the Eddie King he had had in mind? And what about the missing bullet?

I turned from the window and sat down at my desk. I opened the lower right-hand drawer and reached in. A wave of queasiness rolled through me as my fingers closed around the neck of the bottle. I released it and closed the drawer. I sat there for a while, staring into space, then I crossed my forearms atop the desk and lowered my head onto them.

I was just drifting off when three tentative taps sounded on the glass of the door. I raised my head to see a mosaic of a man behind the pebbled pane. I willed him to go away. He didn't. He stood there for a solid minute before knocking again. I sat up and tried to make myself look alive.

"Yeah, come in."

The door opened. He was a late middle-aged man of medium build, with a soft, squarish face that was hard to imagine ever being stricken with spontaneous joy. The round spectacles perched atop his clump of a nose lent him an expression of permanent confoundment. The clothes and how he wore them attested to his money—a slate-blue pinstripe wool double-breasted Kuppenheimer, wide lapels, green silk handkerchief sprouting from the breast pocket, a bluish green William Morris patterned tie, matching waistcoat with a silver watch chain dipping from the pocket, gray homburg planted squarely on his head with a dash of yellow plumage in the wide grosgrain band, sterling cufflinks—but it was the soft, doughy quality of his cheeks and his plump fingers that spoke most eloquently of a life far removed from exertion of even the mildest nature.

"Parking," he huffed as he closed the door behind him. From his left hand hung a maroon leather attaché case. If the expression on his face as he took in the state of my office was any indication, he was beginning to doubt the wisdom of the resource he had consulted.

"Are you Eddie King?" he asked, clearly hoping I wasn't.

"That's what's written on the door."

He stood there, silent, for about ten seconds, then, having apparently reached some inner compromise, he said:

"I need a detective."

I gestured open-palmed to the seat on the other side of the desk. He remained standing at the door for another few seconds, as if telling himself he could still turn around and leave. Then he unnecessarily cleared his throat and walked up to the desk, pinched the pleats of his trousers and sat down, setting the attaché on the floor beside him.

"My name is Gordon Fletcher," he said.

"What's your trouble, Mr. Fletcher?"

Frowning at that word, he cleared his throat again.

"It's about my wife."

I nodded earnestly. The slightest hint of an ironic smile tugged at the left corner of his mouth as he glanced downward, or rather seemingly backwards in time.

"It began when I was a child," he said as if there was a screen between us and I was his priest. "To this day I still feel the blood rush to my cheeks when I recall my mother and father embracing. I feel it now just thinking about it. I wanted my mother all to myself, you see. I used every power within me—at first with only my body, later with more subtle methods—to try to come between them. As you can imagine, this didn't make for a healthy relationship between my father and I."

"Mr. Fletcher," I interrupted about five minutes later. "This is all very interesting, but perhaps what you need is a psychiatrist. There's a cheap one down the hall."

He glowered at my impertinence, but resolved to have his say he resumed his pathetic narrative, explaining in tiresome detail how he had destroyed one relationship after another rather than admit to his pathological jealousy. Then he met his wife and everything changed. By his account, and by the photograph he produced from the attaché and handed to me, she was drop-dead gorgeous. She was tall. Thick blonde hair fell to her shoulders in metallic waves. How I knew from the black-and-white photograph that her eyes were blue I don't know, but they promised more than a patent medicine ad. Her breasts swelled over the top of her low-cut gown. Her legs were long, sensuously shaped. Full rounded thighs swept into high-set hips, converged into a narrow waist. The gown looked as if one deep breath would disintegrate the whole thing. It was a studio photograph, professionally lit, the world behind her reduced by her radiance to soft, velvety darkness.

I set the picture on the desk, and Mr. Fletcher, seeming satisfied by the tenor of my silence, went on with his story. By his account, when he had first met his wife-to-be four years ago, she was enjoying the last days of her youth, in the widest sense of the phrase. If you wanted to find the hottest party in town, all you had to do was follow the bouncing backside of Heidi Malone. In the ballrooms of palatial estates, in the banqueting halls of grand hotels, on the dance floors of smoky jazz joints, wherever you saw a swirling mass of the city's brightest luminaries, Heidi Malone was sure to be found spinning in the center of it. She was an enigma—no one knew exactly where she was from or where she lived, though it was rumored she had once been a Lord & Taylor runway girl— which made her the vessel of a thousand flights of fancy, many of which were less than complimentary. To put it bluntly, she was perceived to be a loose woman, and as such had to attend to the responsibilities of upholding that image when circumstances to her advantage called for it and trouncing it when they didn't. For every man or woman drawn into her orbit, a dozen theories as to who she was hovered in the air around her. Her beauty alone was enough to cause the most generous women to cast aspersions on her and the most principled men to get tangled up in their own lies.

How unlikely it was, then—by his own admission—that Mr. Fletcher, a man jealous of his own shadow, should find himself that rare object of her favored attentions. It happened one night at . . . No. I can't be bothered to reconstruct that tedious scene. What matters is this: within a month of meeting Gordon Fletcher she was married to him, and Heidi Malone was a thing of the past. She was now Mrs. Gordon Fletcher, with all the privileges and duties incumbent upon that moniker.

From that point in Mr. Fletcher's narrative he was less than forthcoming about the challenges his new wife presented to his congenital insecurity. I can only assume that he sat her down on some velvet wingback chair in his library, placed himself on the matching ottoman, looked into those indigo eyes of hers and told her the truth. It was probably the first time she had ever witnessed such sincerity in a man, and it must have moved her. I can see the scene all too clearly. Having married this man for money and found true love instead, she must have sobbed for joy. And Mr. Fletcher, to have finally realized after a lifetime of quiet suffering that so much pain could have been avoided by placing what he most feared directly into the hands of the one who could destroy him—what an awakening that must have been.

But he wouldn't have been sitting there meekly on the other side of my desk if all was well in paradise. Lately certain disquieting rumors from reputable quarters had been finding their way to Mr. Fletcher's ears, fanning his smoldering neurosis into flames. Her car had been spotted on several occasions in broad daylight in insalubrious parts of town. A slip of the tongue from one of the servants revealed mysterious telephone calls in the night. Worst of all, and hardest for Mr. Fletcher to admit, she had flinched from his touch yesterday morning after breakfast.

"I want you to keep an eye on her," he said.

I've worked plenty of jealous husband jobs and they aren't my cup of tea. It's hard work following a woman around the city, watching her spend two hours trying to decide which purse, the green tortoise shell or the black chenille, goes best with her peep-toe alligator heels; standing on the other side of a lamppost listening to her make mincemeat of her dear dear friends with a dear dear friend; or worst of all, doing nothing at all for unbelievably long expanses of time. They are bored and boring rich women because their husbands, the only sort with money to burn on a private detective, are bored and boring rich men. These Chairmen of the Bored, courting the romance of scandal, convince themselves that their wives are cheating on them and hire me to prove it. They get irate with me when I have nothing to show for it. The worst of them eventually get desperate and suggest that I test her faithfulness myself, an exercise in futility considering that they forbid me to follow through should she fall for me. The last time one of these jokers accused me of sleeping with his wife and threatened to break me I vowed never to do business with a jealous husband again.

Why then did I accept this job? Had Mr. Fletcher's openness about his jealousies somehow endeared him to me? Was it a desire to see this goddess in the flesh? Maybe it was just the money. Whatever my motives, I felt I had no choice but to take the job. He wasted no time providing me with the relevant details. I told him my rate. Unsurprisingly he didn't insist on doubling it.

After he had gone, I locked up, returned to my apartment, and went back to bed.

3

THE NEXT MORNING, bright and early, I drove over to Palladian Hills. After the great conflagration of 1904, the smoking ruins of what until then had simply been called the Western District were transformed by a cabal of politicians and businessmen backed by the Greek mining magnate Nicanor Stigmatias into a neo-Hellenic fantasy. Shepherd Hill was renamed Olympus, the old fort there demolished and turned into Cronos Park, replete with follies of temple ruins and statues of Hermes and Aphrodite prancing about the olive groves. To this day, among the potsherds around the duck pond, you can still find progeny of the rock snails Stigmatias imported from Naxos for his Epiphany feasts.

If not exactly with gold, the streets of Palladian Hills were paved with the silkiest tar and bitumen known to man. It wouldn't have surprised me in the least to have rounded one of the bends in that maze of mansions to find a covey of society ladies playing shuffleboard across the macadam. Where not walled and gated off from the hazards of such frictionless streets, the homes were buffered by lawns so immense that even the most tenacious salesman wouldn't cross them without adequate provisions.

The Fletcher estate was on Thebes Way, up past Corinth Drive. Add the columns and the pediment, and the house might have doubled for the White House. All the driveway lacked was an air traffic control tower. Welded into the arching cast-iron gateway over the entrance to the drive were the words: THESEUS HOUSE.

I drove slowly past the property, continued up to Argos Lane, turned around at what, judging by the savage glare of a three-headed dog, must have been the gate to Hades, then drove back beyond the turn-in to the Fletcher place and parked in the shade of the row of cypresses that bordered the property. There I waited for an hour and a half, thinking among other things about a woman who called herself Brandy. A few choice images returned to me. Chiefly, her standing before me in nothing but my holster.

It was nearly eleven by the time Mrs. Morris's car, a silver '39 Morgan Sphinx convertible, finally appeared in my rearview mirror. It was a stunning machine, all the more so for the way it slinked out from behind the cypresses like the stockinged foot of a showgirl teasing the limelight before taking the stage. True to its namesake, it tapered in bold curves from a regal front end to an almost comically diminutive rear, the muscular front fenders calling to mind the powerful breasts of that mythical winged lioness. The blue of the sky, the green of the trees, the warm gray of the street pooled and swirled over its opalescent silver skin. The top was down. As Mrs. Fletcher turned the plump whitewalls out into the street and drove past me, I watched from the cover of my tilted brim to catch a blur of soft cheek below a cream-colored cloche. I waited until she had rounded the curve before setting out.

She wasn't in my sights for more than a few seconds at a time until we were out of the labyrinth and cruising down the coast road. Traffic was sparse at that time of morning, so I kept my distance. Along the scrubby sandbanks off to the left, a few late joggers were comfortably outpacing death. Beyond them lay the granite slab of the ocean under a woolen haze. I couldn't remember the last time I had been over to the west side, and I had to admit, with the cool sea breeze blowing through my hair, that I was long overdue. I felt a million miles away from the dirty sheets and empty bottles of my apartment. It is in moments like these, under the spell of space and light and fresh air, that I often fall prey to the dream of a different life. In it I am normal, easy in the company of my fellow man. I am employed at something creative, part of a team producing useful things. I work regular hours, partake of wholesome forms of recreation, enjoy a diet consisting of more than steaks and fries. I don't drink. Of course there is a loving woman somewhere in the picture, with a curvaceous figure and dark eyes. Even fleeting visions of children— two of them, a boy and a girl, running in slow motion towards me across a field, sunshine haloing their heads.

She stuck to the coast road, past Shepherd Beach and the western flank of Prospect Park, in no apparent rush to get where she was going. As we neared the Seapoint grade, which curved steeply around the wave-battered cliffs leading to Preston Avenue and on to Spring Valley, I figured she must be on her way to the 15th Street boutiques. Instead, at the base of the grade, she turned into the parking lot of Clifton Baths. The lot was virtually empty. She could have parked right next to the entrance. Instead she drove on to the far end of the lot and parked there, facing the ocean. I put a little time between us then pulled into the lot and parked at the opposite end. I watched her in the rearview. She sat in the car for a while, staring out at the sea. Finally the door opened and she stepped out.

She was wearing a light tan cotton summer dress that ended just below her knees, no stockings, a delicate avocado green cashmere sweater, matching pumps, and the aforementioned cloche hat. From the crook of her right elbow hung a tote bag of some kind of woven reed material. Altogether a very modest, tasteful ensemble, befitting her social status, though something of her supposedly wild youth survived in the play of her hips as she made her way across the lot and to the doors.

I waited until she had nearly reached the building before I got out and followed her. I bought a paper from the box outside the entrance and made my way in.

I hadn't been to Clifton Baths since I was a kid, at least thirty years ago, but the moment I stepped through the door and smelled the salty ocean water and felt the wet blanket of humidity close around me and absorbed the heavenly sea green light of water and girders and glass and a thousand other things still the same, I was instantly transported back to my childhood. Less a specific point in time than a pervading mood of loneliness. The cries of children echoed enchantingly from the glass and girders, raining down on me from all directions. I looked around but didn't see Mrs. Fletcher.

The cashier was so old that he could very well have been the same surly chap who used to man the till.

"One adult, please," I said.

"Twenty-five cents." His voice was nothing but wind.

I placed the quarter on the counter and drifted in dreamy nostalgia down the Grand Staircase to the observation theater. I took a seat and had a look at the paper while I waited for Mrs. Fletcher to reappear.

HEIR APPARENT

You could hardly call it an obituary. Down below the usual cast of characters—the ancient local judge, the old baseball player, the former Broadway actress—was one Walter Morris, "a.k.a. Baxter Conway, crime novelist, 62." No mention of how he had died. He was survived by his wife, Imogen Morris. No mention of any children or grandchildren.

I glanced up from the paper to see Mrs. Fletcher in a white one-piece, with swimming cap and goggles. To what god did I owe the privilege of being paid to watch Mrs. Fletcher's long, shapely legs carry her out of the ladies changing room, down the sandstone steps to the Grand Tank, and propel her in a graceful dive into the water? After a few seconds under water, she surfaced and glided out to the middle of the tank with an effortless sidestroke.

By the time I finished with the rest of the paper, all of my initial nostalgia at being back in Clifton Baths had worn off, and I was eager to get out of that swampy cavern of diffused light. Mrs. Fletcher finally emerged from the tank around one o'clock, released her perfectly sculpted hair from the swimming cap, and dried herself off with a towel that, since I hadn't noticed her placing it there, seemed to represent the grace of some higher power. In a more cynical mood I might have thought that the towel wasn't hers at all, that she had merely grabbed the nearest one at hand, and that now someone else would have to emerge to a cold, towelless world. But I was feeling strangely peaceful, generous, benevolent even. I must have been coming down with something.

That evening, back in my apartment—Mrs. Fletcher went straight home and did not emerge for the remainder of the day—my earlier reaction to the serendipity of the towel returned to me. Now the towel itself, at the time too distant for details, expanded in my mind until all other thoughts were wiped away. It came to me in a state of purity no real towel has ever known. Dry, warm, fluffy, this towel was nothing less than a perfect abstraction of the very idea *towel*. So white was its whiteness that I can think of no similes to match it. It seemed to be absorbing every cell of my brain. I sat in the recliner for a long time, eyes glazed, meditating on the bathing towel.

As night began to fall, I got up and changed out of my suit and flicked on the radio and poured myself a glass of Old Grand-Dad. They were playing Tad Wilmott and the Chicago Five: the snarl of Ray Gutshank's trombone, the comedy of Dexter Hines's muted trumpet, the slurred speech of Freddy Ortega's banjo—these were my companions on the rare nights when I was home for more than a few hours. I was defenseless to the rhythms of this music. It would start as a tapping of my left shoe, always the left, while I sat in the recliner sipping my bourbon. Around the third sip my left hand, the one not holding the glass, would join the plodding bass line of my foot with the rat-a-tat-tat of eighths and sixteenths. At a less predictable point along the way, I would realize that my head was making half-circles, around and back, back and around. Downing the last swallow, I'd be out of the chair, propelled to the middle of the room, dancing with the slack limbs of a marionette. On fire. Burning up my humble abode. And then, somewhere near sundown, a cymbal roll would break the rhythm and all the horns would melt into the dreamy bog of a love song: "This is for all you lovers out there tonight. For all your yesterdays and all your tomorrows. . . ." Flick—off the radio would go, and once again I would be in my native domain. Solitude.

In through the window drifted the small sounds of the day's dying, the last honks of the office dwellers heading home in their Dodges and Fords, the melancholy call of the evening paper boy, the seagulls giving the sun a noisy sendoff, the low murmur of the tired city. The radiance of that first drink warming my face, I placed my hands on either side of the window frame—over the years the paint on the wall where I place my hands has grown duller than the surrounding paint—and gazed out at the city and the sky. I don't consider myself a spiritual man, but those few moments I spend at the window of an evening always give me a sense of the divine, for lack of a better word. I see myself standing there, perhaps as a pigeon on the ledge sees me. My face ablaze with the fire of the sunset. My five o'clock shadow an hour late. My eyes—which I'm told are sad—seem on the verge of penetrating the heart of some grander mystery than the identity of a killer. No longer distracted by a million tiny details, I am seeing pure geometry and energy. Squares and circles. Space divided into color and shape. Blocks of blue shadow wedded to swatches of tinted light. Broad flat swathes of earth and sky. Nothing static. Everything, even the bricks, radiating life. Clumps of dark specks swooping and circling through the air. Down in the channels below, orderly progression of rectilinear forms, moving, stopping. This accumulation of motive and motion seemingly and why this gives me solace I do not know—without purpose.

That night, around eight o'clock, I emerged from my porous trance with the odd sensation that I was in someone else's apartment, so unfamiliar did the objects of my own dwelling strike me. I stood up and looked around at this place I call home, this place, it seemed, I had always lived in and always would. On the back of the door hung a two-year-old City Zoo calendar, open to May, featuring an aqua-tinted Zebra. It had been so long since this calendar had registered on my consciousness that I had no recollection whatsoever of how it had come to be there.

Another forgotten item that puzzled me, over on the lamp table beside the recliner, was a King James Bible. The puzzling thing wasn't where it had come from—I had bought it from a traveling salesman several months ago—but why I had bought it in the first place. He wasn't a particularly good salesman. When I had finally answered the door after his third and increasingly louder round of knocking, he had scolded me for not answering more promptly. He was a squirrelly young guy in a threadbare collage of garments intended to pass for a suit. Hanging from a white-knuckled fist was a big brown case with a white cross crudely painted on the side. He recited rather woodenly a Psalm rewritten as a sales pitch for Bibles, and then said something like, "Want one?" I did not want one. Nor did I feel sorry for the guy. The only reason I can think of why I shelled out two bucks for the thing was to get rid of him.

I picked it up and opened it for the first time. There was an inscription on the inside cover: "To my son on your eleventh birthday. May you always be, above all else, a man of God. Love, Mother. December 7, 1952."

My first thought was that the salesman had sold me a stolen Bible. But I couldn't help but find the inscription touching. I wondered who this woman and her son were. Before I knew it I had imagined an entire scenario: tracking the mother down only to learn that she was dead, hunting for the son, finding him in some halfway house in the Silage, handing him the Bible in dramatic fashion, his tears of gratitude anointing his path to recovery.

That moving little matinee prompted me to skim through the Bible in search of further clues. Near the end (*Revelation*, chapter 6), I did find something interesting: an old photograph of a woman, two by three, head and shoulders only. She looked to be in her early to mid-thirties. There was something in her features—a hardness in the bones of her face, a tightness in the collar of her dark dress, a severity in the containment of her hair—which gave me the feeling of mild remorse one sometimes gets in museums when imagining a once-living hand holding the hairbrush relegated to a glass display case. My guess from her clothing and hairstyle, and from the apparent age of the photograph itself, was that the picture had been taken sometime in the late twenties or early thirties.

I turned the photo over, but nothing was written on the back. Of course she could have been anyone, but once an idea is planted in your mind it's hard to uproot it. For me, she was the mother. The Bible in my hands was her gift to her beloved son. Had he honored her desire and become a man of God? Considering the provenance of the Bible, it didn't look good. I stared at the photo for a while, wondering if she was still alive, then I returned her to the apocalypse and set the Bible back on the lamp table.

The discovery of these three overlooked objects—the calendar, the Bible, and the photograph within it—in the space of a few minutes indicated to me that when it came to my own life I wasn't very observant at all. This wasn't the first time it had happened. Every six months or so I would look up from my work and notice some object whose origin, for the life of me, I could not fathom. Lately it seemed to be happening more frequently. That this sudden perceptiveness to my immediate surroundings was somehow linked to my earlier ruminations, for lack of a better word, on the towel that may or may not have been Mrs. Fletcher's seemed an unavoidable conclusion. More perplexing was the fact that I was thinking about these trifling matters at all.

4

BEFORE HEADING BACK to Palladian Hills the next morning for my rendez-vous with the Sphinx, I stopped by the library. I wouldn't say I was a regular patron, but every now and then some niggling detail on a case would stymie me and I would swing by the main branch to avail myself of the reference section. Built in 1917 with Carnegie money, it was a monumental Beaux Arts building set back from Lincoln Avenue on a broad landscaped terrace, façaded with half a mountain of Calaveras marble. Two massive greyhounds, affectionately known as Hope and Despair, guarded the entrance, above which rose, as if in doubt of the allegiance of the dogs, four colossal pairs of Ionic columns flanked by life-size statues of local deities. From the steps of the library, exiting book lovers enjoyed an unimpeded view of the verdigrised dome of City Hall towering above its inverted twin in the Pool of Remembrance, the favored watering hole of the city's indigent and insane.

I took the stairs up to the catalog room on the second floor, where I waited ten minutes amidst the murals of ancient scriveners for an elderly gentleman with shaky hands to conclude his investigations in the *Authors Cl-Cz* drawer. There was only one card under "Conway, Baxter": a novel called *Guttersnipe*. I wrote down the call number—for good measure I also checked under Walter Morris, but it seemed unlikely that the three books on the North American firefly were by the same author—and continued my journey upwards to the third floor.

The main reading room, which a brass plaque at the threshold informed me had recently been renamed the Helen A. Griffith Reading Room as a token of gratitude for the sugar magnate's widow's generous support, was so vast it produced its own atmosphere, a compound equal parts sloughed-off paper molecules, binding glue and dust mites, which judging by the number of drowsing heads had a decidedly narcotic effect on its inhabitants. I say inhabitants because at least half of the regulars were homeless people who took advantage of the only place in the city where they could sit all day in peace and dignity. Gut the *Titanic* and line its hull with books and you would get a fair approximation of the magnitude of the Reading Room.

As I made my way up the broad central gangway towards the information and retrievals desk, the echoes of my footfalls rained gently down from the painted sky, accompanied by the dry rustle of turning pages, the muted clearing of throats, the thunder of thoughtlessly scooted chairs. The morning sunshine streaming through the high eastern windows spread sheets of blinding light across the enormous oak tables that spanned the room widthwise fore and aft, each table massive enough to have hosted a Habsburg marriage banquet. Eventually I did arrive at the counter, where I handed my slip to the prim middle-aged woman in a tartan skirt suit who, upon checking my selection for accuracy, smiled faintly to herself before sending it down the tube to one of the denizens who roamed the miles of stacks below.

I took a seat at a nearby table and wondered as I waited for the book what the librarian's little smirk was all about. Was she familiar with the novel, tickled by some recollected scene? Was there something inherently comic in me requesting that particular book? Gazing up at the painted ceiling, I felt as though I were floating upwards, drifting past the rosy-hued clouds that rimmed the portal, out into pure robin's egg blue, native domain of cherubs and seraphs.

Five minutes later the book arrived. It was a yellow clothbound hardback. No dust jacket or cover art. Black lettering on the spine: *Guttersnipe*. Baxter Conway. I opened it. On the title page, between the author's name and the title, was a small woodcut of a smoking pistol. I glanced over at the librarian, half-expecting her to be smirking at me, but she was lost in private contemplations.

I turned to chapter one and read a bit of it. About halfway down the first page I had the peculiar sensation that I had read this novel before, all the more peculiar as I don't read detective novels. Maybe it was the jaunty tone of the narrator, the clipped, hardboiled style that even an illiterate child can imitate. I read on, surprised to encounter on page two a fairly accurate description of West Grand Avenue, which the Mandrake Building happens to be on. I read some more, and lo and behold if on the very next page a man didn't enter my building and take the elevator to the third floor.

Then came this: "Stenciled onto the pebbled glass of the office door was his name and profession: Edward King, Private Detective."

"Sonofabitch," I muttered, a little too loudly. I glanced up. A woman with a face like a deflated football was glaring at me. I lowered my eyes back to the page and read some more.

My indignation at finding my name and business address published in a third-rate novel turned to something altogether more disconcerting when Conway proceeded to describe the contents of my office, down to the brown leather cap that had been hanging on the coat rack when I moved in and has remained there unperturbed ever since. I looked up from the book with the eerie sensation that I was being watched. I peered around me, didn't see anything out of the ordinary, then lowered my eyes back to the page. I reread the description of my office, telling myself that it had to be a coincidence. I read on. Then, in the middle of page three, I read the following passage:

```
The man was built like a linebacker. He clasped
King's outstretched hand in his iron grip. 'Lester
Griswold,' he scowled. King offered him a seat and
a glass of bourbon. Griswold took both. 'We buried
my brother Max yesterday,' he said. 'Car accident.'
He took a drink, swallowing hard. 'So they say.'
```

I pulled my handkerchief from my back pocket and wiped the chilly sweat from my upper lip and quickly skimmed ahead. There I was in Prospect Park, tailing Tiffany Griswold on her rendezvous with the airline pilot. There I was, being harassed by Hicks and Stiles at Sam's Joint while trying to sip my Old Grand-Dad in peace. There I was, being beaten to a pulp by Lester Griswold's muscle for getting too close to the truth.

I turned back to the beginning of the book and read the opening scene again, as if maybe I hadn't read it right the first time. Nothing had changed.

I turned to the copyright page. The novel had been published twelve years ago. I couldn't remember the exact year of the Griswold case, but it didn't seem that long ago.

I closed the book and sat there trying to think, but the sting of violation made it impossible to concentrate. My heart was thumping hard against my sternum. I got up and took the book with me back to the librarian, whose reproachful glare—she must have heard my expletive after all—made me feel like the class troublemaker.

"Do you have any more of this guy's novels?" I asked her. She glanced at the spine of the book, as if she had already forgotten who had written it.

"Did you search the card catalog?" she asked with perfect condescension.

"Yes," I said. "This was the only one listed."

"Then I'm afraid that's all we have."

"How about some kind of *Who's Who of American Authors*?"

She exited her bunker through the hinged partition and bade me without uttering a word to follow her. We walked a good distance to a wall of reference books where she pointed out three fat volumes. I found the entry on Baxter Conway: "The pseudonym of Walter Morris, a writer of crime fiction best known for his series of novels featuring the detective Eddie King."

My blood pressure rocketed as I scanned down the titles.

Guttersnipe
Blinded by the Sun
Due Diligence
Murder at the Crossroads
All but the Chorus
Blood City
Dying to Know
King's Ransom

I closed the book and stood before the shelf for some time, telling myself to keep calm.

I returned to my friend at the information desk and asked her how one went about getting a library card.

"Circulation," she mumbled without bothering to look up. "Second floor."

There I was informed by a pallid, bespectacled young man with a shaving nick on his right cheek that I needed to show proof of identification and address. I handed him my driver's license.

"And do you have a bank statement, utility bill, or a letter from your landlord?" he cheerfully asked.

"What for?"

"Proof of address."

"It's there on the license."

"I'm afraid I can't use your license."

"Why not?"

"It needs to be a current bill, a bank statement, or a letter from your landlord," he repeated. "Something with a recent date on it."

"I renewed my license two months ago. The date's right there."

"I'm sorry, but it's library policy."

"You accept the license as proof of identity but not proof of address? I'd say there's a contradiction there."

"No," he replied. "The photo verifies that you are who you say you are."

"All the photo verifies is that my face can be photographed. How do you know it's not a fake ID?"

"I can't imagine anyone going to all that trouble for a library card."

"Then you have a poor imagination."

"Insults do not improve your chances of obtaining a library card, sir."

I opened my wallet and removed a five dollar bill and placed it on the counter.

"Does that?"

He gave me a snide smile. "Are you for real?"

I left the library, novel in hand, promising myself I would return it when I was done.

5

OVER THE COURSE of the rest of the morning and afternoon, as I tailed and waited for Mrs. Fletcher, I read the entirety of that infuriating novel. Never in my life had I felt so violated. Someone, either Walter Morris, who unfortunately was not available for questioning, or a hired hand, had either copied or stolen my file on the Griswold case. There was no other way he could have acquired such precise information: the names and addresses of the key players, the exact sequence of events, from my first meeting with Lester Griswold to the shootout with the cops that ended his life, my various telephone exchanges with the police detectives, etc. Most troubling of all were the personal details: descriptions of me, my suits, my hat; descriptions of my apartment, including the name of the building and my apartment number; the make and model of my car; the places I frequent (Sam's Joint, the diner, the newsstand on Harcourt Street).

Back in the office, I went straight to the filing cabinet. To my surprise, the Griswold file was still there. I pulled it out and opened it. Everything, as far as I could tell, was there: the photographs, my daily notes, the affidavits, all the various and sundry documents Lester

Griswold had given me. As I went through the folder page by page, combing every document, every receipt, every scribbled note for correspondences with the novel, it quickly became evident that no one but me could have reconstructed the case from the file alone. Nothing was in order. The only papers with any dates on them were the affidavits and other official documents, which were few and far between, and there was no clear relationship between those documents and my notes, which I rarely bother to date. Nor were the notes as thorough as I had remembered them to be. Most of them were incomprehensible even to me. It would have been easier to assemble a jigsaw puzzle of a blizzard than produce a chronological narrative from that jumble of pages.

So how had this bastard done it? I sat thinking for a while then picked up the telephone receiver and unscrewed the cap on the mouthpiece and gave the wiring a thorough inspection. I did the same with the earpiece. I pulled out the drawers of the desk and examined every inch of them. I felt around inside the cavity of the desk. I looked under the chair, on the lamp, in the filing cabinet, around the window blinds. I climbed on top of the desk and had a look at the hub of the ceiling fan. The density of the dust up there was astonishing. If there was a bug in my office, it was beyond my powers of observation.

The publisher, according to the copyright page, was an outfit called Pegasus Editions. PO Box 24124. Minneapolis, Minnesota. I picked up the receiver and dialed directory assistance for Minnesota and asked for the number of Pegasus Editions, Minneapolis. The operator patched me through. A woman answered. I asked for someone in editorial. I got a guy named Daniel Geary, an assistant editor. He sounded young. I passed myself off as a West Coast journalist named Robert Justice doing an obituary on Walter Morris. He didn't know who Walter Morris was.

"Oh, my God," he said when I told him. "Baxter Conway is dead?"

I pretended to share his lament. He asked how, and I told him an apparent suicide. That shook young Mr. Geary up. I told him I was trying to get in touch with Conway's editor, the person he would have worked most closely with on his books.

"That would be Howard Stapleton," he told me, and without pausing for breath he went on about how much everyone in editorial loved Baxter Conway because his manuscripts always came in so polished. According to Mr. Geary, Howard Stapleton may have been Conway's editor, but he literally had had nothing to do when a new Baxter Conway manuscript landed on his desk but pass it on to the typesetters. Six commas, two hyphens, a misspelled "the," and an inexplicable blank line between two paragraphs—this was the sum total of all the editorial intervention that had ever been necessary over the course of the Eddie King series. Baxter Conway was legendary in Minneapolis editing circles. I asked Mr. Geary if I could speak with Mr. Stapleton. Mr. Geary informed me that Mr. Stapleton had already gone home for the day; it was past seven o'clock in Minneapolis. I asked Mr. Geary if Mr. Stapleton was the man whom Baxter Conway would have bounced his ideas off of. Mr. Geary was almost certain that Mr. Stapleton had never once been consulted by Baxter Conway on anything to do with the content of his novels, but if anyone in editorial had indeed fielded a rare request for input from Baxter Conway, it would most certainly have been Mr. Stapleton. Mr. Geary asked me if he could take a message for Mr. Stapleton. I told him that wasn't necessary, I would try again in the morning. We spoke a little about our respective climates then wished each other a good evening before hanging up.

I opened the drawer and pulled out the bottle and glass and poured myself a drink, every motion now accompanied by an annoying self-consciousness. I couldn't raise the glass to my lips without feeling that someone was standing behind me, observing my every action and jotting it down in a notebook.

At a quarter after five I opened the door and looked down the hall. Ramona was at the janitor's closet getting her supplies. I stepped back into the office, leaving the door open a few inches. When I heard her nearing, I opened the door as if I were about to step out on my way home.

"Oh, hey, Ramona," I casually greeted her from the doorway. "Keeping busy?"

"Yes, Mr. King."

I had long since given up on trying to get her to call me Eddie.

"Good, good."

I was pretty sure Ramona was older than me, though I never would have guessed it had she not mentioned once when we were chatting after a minor earthquake that she had been seven years old at the time of the San Gregorio quake. I always behaved as if we were old friends, when in truth I knew virtually nothing about her. The fact of the matter is that I had never been interested, never had any reason to inquire about her private life. Nor had she ever given me the impression that she had any desire to step out of the prescribed role of deferential Mexican cleaning woman, at least around me.

"Could you spare a few minutes?" I asked her.

"Yes, Mr. King?"

I gestured to my office. "Here, come on in."

Her sixth sense for the slightest atmospheric turbulence in the workplace far more acute than my own, she leaned her mop against the wall outside and warily stepped in. I closed the door behind her. I knew better than to suggest she have a seat. Strangely, I began to feel nervous myself.

I smiled. "I just wanted to say I appreciate the quality of your work."

No response.

I tried another tack. "Are you happy with what they pay you here?"

"Yes, Mr. King."

"If you're not, I could have a word with Mr. Schwartz."

"No, Mr. King."

She was standing with her arms straight down at her sides, diligently keeping eye contact.

"How long have you worked here?" I asked.

She thought for a moment.

"Twelve years."

"You must have started the same year I set up," I said. "How time flies."

Her expression did not change.

"Is there anything I can do to make your job easier?" I asked. "I know I'm not the cleanest person. Sometimes I leave the office in a mess, files strewn everywhere."

"No, Mr. King."

"You would tell me, wouldn't you? I know I'm a bit messy when it comes to my papers and stuff."

I watched her carefully, studying her eyes for the slightest flicker of fear or contrition, but I saw nothing more than eagerness to return to her mop.

"You would tell me, wouldn't you?" I persisted. "I'd hate to think you would be concerned about offending me."

"Oh no, Mr. King."

There was no way around her wariness of anyone remotely affiliated with the law. If she herself wasn't illegal, surely someone in her family or her neighbor's family was.

Seeing that this was going nowhere, I thanked her and said I'd see her around. She turned and left my office, shutting the door gently behind her.

I sat there for a while, thinking. I picked up the receiver and dialed Hicks's line in Homicide.

"Hicks," he answered.

"Eddie King is the name of his detective," I said.

"Who is this?"

"Eddie King."

"Yeah, what is it, King?"

"Morris wrote crime novels."

"Come again?"

"Walter Morris, a.k.a. Baxter Conway, wrote detective novels. Eddie King was the name of his detective."

I could almost hear the rusty gears of his mind starting to turn.

"Is that right?" he said with feigned nonchalance a few seconds later.

"He shares an office with me," I said. "Drives my car, even lives in my apartment."

"What the hell are you talking about, King?"

"You remember the Griswold case?"

"The party magician?"

"Yeah. Well, I've got a novel in my hand by Walter Morris, a.k.a. Baxter Conway, about a guy named Lester Griswold who kills his brother and tries to frame it on his wife. The name of the detective is Eddie King. You're in it too."

That perked him up.

"What do you mean I'm in it?"

"Read the novel," I said. "*Guttersnipe*. You'll have to find your own copy. They're all out at the library."

"Hold on. What do you mean I'm in it?"

"You and Stiles are the hardboiled homicide detectives always on King's ass. That part's pretty amusing, I must say."

The line went silent for a good ten seconds.

"Let me get this straight. You're telling me this guy wrote books based on your cases or something?"

"One at least," I said. "One too many. It's called the Eddie King series. Thirteen books. I don't know about the rest."

"I don't get it," he said. "How?"

"I don't know, but I intend to find out."

"What's it say about me?"

"I wouldn't want to spoil it for you."

"I've got a full-time job, King. A wife. Kids. A mortgage. I don't have time for books."

"He's got you on the Griswold shootout," I said.

"That's ancient history," he said, not very convincingly.

"Just read the book."

"Where am I supposed to get this damn thing?"

"Try a bookstore. It's a place where books are sold."

"Wise ass. Give me that other name again."

"What other name?"

"You said he had some other name."

"His pseudonym. Baxter Conway. That's the name he published under."

He asked me to spell it. I did, in NATO phonetic. I heard his pencil scratching a pad. Again there was a long silence. Then he said:

"What the hell is going on, King?"

"Could you be a little more specific?"

"What kind of game are you playing? What's with all these coincidences?"

"What coincidences?"

"Some guy dressed like you shows up at his house three weeks ago flashing his iron. Then this letter in Morris's lap with your name on it. Now it turns out he's written books about you, using your cases."

"I think you got the order wrong there."

"You're a bourbon drinker, aren't you?" An image of Hicks staring down at the empty bottle beside the seat cushion flashed across my mind's eye. "According to the coroner's report, Walter Morris was soused on bourbon. There was enough booze in his bladder to pickle a baboon."

"You don't have to be sober to put a gun to your head and pull the trigger."

"The empty bottle in his drawer was Old Grand-Dad," he said, as if making a profound revelation.

"So the man had good taste in bourbon."

"Just another coincidence, eh?"

"Call it what you like," I said. "It's hardly evidence that I had anything to do with his death. If I were you I'd be looking for the guy in the black suit and fedora."

"What do you think we're doing? You're the first one on our list."

"Who else is on it?"

"No one."

I set the novel down and shifted the receiver to my other ear.

"Something smells rotten on this one, King," Hicks said, "and you're downwind of it."

"That's a relief. You and Stiles keep to the upwind trail. What's the address of the Morris place?" I asked.

"I'd stay away from this one if I were you. You'll only dig yourself in deeper."

"Just give me the address."

Inexplicably, he did.

6

ACCORDING TO THE map, Lord Curzon Way was out on the northeastern edge of the county, in a subdevelopment called Sunset Acres. In an attempt to lend dignity and class to an otherwise soulless suburb, the planners had named all the streets after famous British military figures and explorers. I was soon lost in a maze of cul-de-sacs which even the likes of Shackleton, Cook, and Livingstone couldn't help me out of.

After an hour of nauseating U-turns, I finally happened upon the convergence of Oliver Cromwell Court, Horatio Nelson Lane, and Lord Curzon Way. I turned onto Lord Curzon to see the twin gables of a shingled mansard roof towering above the other houses in the distance, a strange architectural anachronism in that realm of beige stucco bungalows, xeroscaped lawns, and kidney-shaped swimming pools. The house numbers here were in the ten thousands. I was looking for humble 231. I pulled over and took another look at the map, scanning it for one of those prodigal blocks far removed from its lineage by some geological or political obstruction. As far as I could tell this was the only Lord Curzon Way in Sunset Acres.

I drove down to the cul-de-sac where the old house stood alone. Owing to what must have been a remarkable concurrence of preternatural longevity and unaccountable blindness on the part of Sunset Acres's developers, the house appeared to have been plucked straight from the Victorian era and replanted smack dab in a future of affordable housing for the commuting masses. It was a two-and-a-half-story tinderbox, grayish blue with white trim, the tall, dry grasses and weeds of the front yard patiently awaiting a carelessly stubbed cigarette butt. A raised, screened-in porch, relic of a swampier era, girded the front of the house. Peering with a mixture of perplexity and enchantment into that deep shade, I spied three patinaed copper numerals above the door. I cut the engine and sat for a while before getting out, pondering various scenarios to explain the anomalous address.

A powerful throb of déjà vu rolled through me as I stood before the house. I had been here before, standing on this very sidewalk, gazing at this very house. Everything was the same: the angle of the shadows of the porch posts against the horizontal slats of the front cladding, the ticking of the car engine as I dropped the keys into my front pocket, the wingbeats of a formation of Canada geese passing overhead. A thousand simultaneous impressions. It felt as if a warm wave were breaking over me, as if I were made of some porous substance and the energy of the wave was rolling through me, firing every synapse before returning to the sea of memory. All in the space of a second or two, leaving me with a wonderful feeling of levitation, as if I were full of fireflies, my soul buoyed on their silent wings.

The uncanny sense of familiarity didn't entirely leave me as I walked around the right side of the yard, mounted the porch by two creaking steps, and approached the front door. I pulled open the rotting screen and rapped twice. I waited. After a while something moved behind the gauzy curtain of one of the tall, arched windows to my right. I lowered my head self-consciously.

Footsteps approached the door.

"Who is it?" She didn't sound hospitable.

"My name is Eddie King. I'm a private detective."

And there we stood, for a good thirty seconds or more, in perfect silence, until at last a bolt clicked. The door opened about six inches to partially reveal a woman in a full-length black dress, collar and cuffs tightly buttoned. My indignation at being so ill used by her late husband softened at the sight of her face. She was in her mid-fifties, maybe early sixties, with features that I am inclined to say were of Irish origin. Whether or not that was on account of the forward perk of her ears, the pallor of her skin, or rather of some gamesome glint in her slate-blue eyes that I, rightly or wrongly, associate with that long-suffering race, I cannot say. Despite her evident annoyance at being summoned to the door by a stranger, it was a pleasant face to behold, the sort of face one feels fortunate to take a scolding from.

"Mrs. Morris?"

"Who are you?"

I smiled reflexively and removed my wallet from my inner jacket pocket and opened it to my detective's license, holding it up to the gap in the door, through which I could feel the chilly interior air against my fingertips.

"As I said, my name is Eddie King. I'm a private detective. Which is what I'd like to have a few words with you about, if I may be so bold to trouble you in your time of bereavement," this antiquated claptrap, no doubt inspired by the strange decorum of both herself and her house, issuing unbidden from my mouth.

Her cursory glance at my license didn't betray the surprise it merited. Not a single crease across her smooth, pale brow.

"I have nothing to say to you, whoever you are," she said. "Go away."

"I'm sorry about your husband," I replied, returning my wallet to my pocket. "I'm not here about his death. That's a police matter. I'm more interested in his books. If you could just spare five minutes of your time it would mean a great deal to me."

She stared at me, squinting against the glare of the naked world beyond. Then, inexplicably, she opened the door fully and said, apparently mocking me: "Get in here. You'll catch your death of cold." The fact that even in the shade of her porch the sweat was condensing on my upper lip underscored the absurdity of her injunction. I smiled, keen to show that I could roll with her punches. But as she stood aside, waiting for me to enter, it became apparent that she was in earnest. Sensing my hesitation, she grabbed my wrist and tugged me into the house. I acquiesced, not quite sure what to make of her ludicrous remark, so sharp on the heels of her obstinacy.

Releasing my wrist beyond the threshold, she bade me follow her into the gloom. I removed my hat. It took a few moments for my eyes to adjust, my momentary blindness only magnifying the sudden chill, which the crackling flames of a good-sized fire in the hearth off to the right seemed to be doing little to alleviate. The dank, musty smell took me back to the basement library of my grade school and the mythical mouse whose droppings at the foot of the shelves seemed as magical to me as Jack's beanstalk seeds. Apart from the fire, which radiated as little light as it did warmth, the only source of illumination in the room was the sunlight seeping through the front windows, which, owing to the tempering effect of both the broad porch and the gauze curtains, seemed rather to deepen the shadows than brighten the objects that cast them.

Gradually these objects acquired sufficient solidity for me to identify them: an assemblage of musty sofas, chairs, settees, and ottomans befitting the age of the house; various end and side and parlor tables in dark wood; a massive, tripartite china cabinet, its stowed wares dully flickering behind the panes; a Victrola with a blackened bronze horn; and a collection of lamps, vases, pots, figurines, bottles, lustres, clocks, mirrors, and other assorted bric-a-brac lorded over by a revolting glass chandelier hanging lifelessly from a vaguely apprehensible ceiling.

She gestured towards a high-backed sofa in the middle of the room, taking for herself the colorless velvet wingback chair opposite and facing the hearth. Even amidst all that antiquated clutter, the sofa stood out as a genuine eccentricity. Framed in ornate walnut, the three soaring arcs of the back were nearly as tall as me, making me feel like a child lost in Wonderland as I sank into the threadbare cushions of yellowish green velvet. I set my hat beside me. When we were both seated she folded her hands in her lap and, prefacing her question with a placatory smile, said:

"So, Mr. King, if that indeed is your real name."

"I'm sure you must think I'm some deranged fan of your husband's novels, but I assure you that isn't the case."

We stared at each other for a while.

"What, pray tell," she said, "*is* the case?"

"How familiar are you with the content of your husband's novels, Mrs. Morris?"

"I can't say I . . ." She stopped mid-sentence and stared blankly into the fire. I waited for her to continue. Her neck throbbed with a hard swallow. She sighed deeply and shut her eyes. When she opened them a few moments later they were shiny with restrained tears. I looked away. We sat that way for another minute or so, unable to look each other in the eye, enveloped in perfect silence save the periodic twitches and crackles of the fire. At last she inhaled sharply and, forcing a smile of politeness, said:

"Would you like a cup of tea?"

"Yes, please." I don't, as a habit, drink tea.

She excused herself and left the room through a swinging door far away in the shadowy distance. While she was absent, I got up and walked over to the fireplace and took a look at the framed photographs standing on the mantle. By all appearances they were original daguerreotypes. A man with a handlebar moustache. A woman in a tight collar with pinned-up hair. To modern eyes all men and women in such prehistoric portraits look the same—wax figures of themselves, the highlights and shadows of personality reduced to their essence: Father, Mother. Another picture showed the same man and woman together with a blurry boy in a sailor's suit. I don't know if it was the influence of the widow's surge of grief or something intrinsic to the tone and texture of that old photographic technique, but the picture of the child moved me nearly to tears.

In time she returned carrying an enameled tin tea tray bearing a complete tea service in blue and white china. She set it gently on the coffee table.

"Walter's great great grandparents," she said, noticing me turning away from the photographs. "They were from Poland."

"Who's the boy?" I asked.

"Walter's grandfather."

I took a closer look, but the child had not been able to hold still for the photographer, and his face was nothing but a ghostly blur.

I returned to the sofa. She finished pouring the tea and settled with her cup and saucer back into her chair. I took a lump of sugar from the bowl and, dropping it into my cup, gave it a stir with the tiny silver spoon, which chimed enchantingly against the wafer-thin bone.

"You have a lovely home," I remarked.

"It was Walter's family's home," she said. "His great great grandfather built it. There was nothing here in those days but fields and trees. It's remarkable that it survived."

"And the developers?"

"They're waiting for me to croak." She managed a little self-deprecatory smile.

We sat for a while sipping our tea in strangely agreeable silence. When I sensed an opportune moment I asked her again:

"How familiar are you with the stories of your husband's novels?"

"Quite," she said with evident pride.

After her earlier prevarication, the succinctness of her reply surprised me.

"Do you mind my asking where he got his ideas from?"

She sighed, as if it were the millionth time she had been asked this question. "Where does any writer get his ideas? From his life, imagination, newspapers, books. Everything." She stared into the fire and said, dreamily, "He was the farthest thing from a tough guy you could imagine. Couldn't kill a fly. I mean that. He'd waste an afternoon trying to get a fly out of the kitchen."

I cleared my throat.

"Mrs. Morris, twelve years ago a man named Max Griswold, a party magician who called himself Titus Andronicus, was killed in a car accident. No other cars were involved. It appeared to be a clear-cut case of drunk driving, but his brother Lester suspected foul play. Getting nowhere with the police, Lester hired me to follow up on a hunch of his that Max's wife was having an affair with an airline pilot, and that either she, acting independently, or both of them had conspired to have Max murdered. Over the course of my investigation, I discovered that Tiffany Griswold was indeed having an affair with the pilot. I also discovered that previous to this affair she had had an affair with Lester, the brother. In the end, it turned out that Lester was the one who had orchestrated his brother's death and tried to frame it on his sister-in-law. His motive for killing his brother was lifelong hatred and envy, and for framing his sister-in-law, seething jealousy over her dumping him for the pilot. All in all they were an unwholesome lot. Lester Griswold met his death in a gun battle with the police. Does any of that sound familiar, Mrs. Morris?"

She studied me warily, as if not quite sure I was mentally stable, then, to my astonishment, she burst into a cackle, after which she said: "You can't be serious!"

"I'm dead serious."

She laughed again, lightly patting her knees with the palms of her hands as she rocked a little forwards and back.

"It's the plot of *Guttersnipe*," I said.

"Yes," she said, still laughing, "it is."

When at last she stopped laughing, she leveled her gaze at me and said:

"I must say, you are amusing, if nothing else. Even if what you say is true, that your name is Eddie King, that you're a private detective, and that somehow my husband based the novel on this case that you worked on . . ."

"You have to agree it's pretty suspicious."

"Are you suggesting that my husband stole his ideas from you?"

"Steal is perhaps too strong a word," I said, "but you have to agree that this isn't just a coincidence. Everyone in that book is a real person. Hicks and Stiles, the police detectives handling your case, they're in the novel too. If you're as familiar with his books as you say you are, then that couldn't have escaped your notice."

"I'm afraid I must now kindly ask you to leave."

I reached for my hat and placed it on my head. I stood up. "Thank you for the tea."

She followed me to the door. Before stepping out, I turned and said:

"Did your husband have any enemies?"

"I thought you were only interested in his books."

"Force of habit."

"Walter was a writer," she said. "Writers sit in locked rooms all day making up stories. He scarcely had any friends, let alone enemies."

I nodded and adjusted my hat. "Were you here when that man came brandishing his gun?"

"Yes."

"Did you happen to see him?"

"No," she said. "I was in the kitchen."

"How long ago was this?"

"Three weeks ago."

"Did your husband mention what he looked like, what kind of car he was driving, anything that might help identify this person?"

"I've already told the police everything I know about that."

I thanked her for her time and opened the screen door.

As I was walking away, she said:

"He was dressed like Walter's detective."

I turned around.

"Excuse me?"

She repeated herself.

"Could you be a little more specific?"

"He was dressed like you," she said. It was less a statement than a broadside from the safety of the doorway.

I thanked her again for her time and, reiterating my condolences, made my way across and off the porch. She closed the door behind me. I lingered in the yard for a moment, soaking up the welcome blast of heat and sunlight.

7

I SPENT THAT evening rereading *Guttersnipe*. The outrage was addictive.
I read until about one a.m. then turned off the lamp. Half an hour later
my mind was still churning over that strange woman in that strange
house. It was as if she hadn't set foot outside for so long that she had no
idea what season it was. Even allowing for the disorientation of grief,
there was something very peculiar about her. I could still feel her cold
grip on my wrist as she tugged me inside, an urgency which upon
reflection seemed less predicated on the temperature than on prying
neighbors. I couldn't shake the images of that dark, cold, oppressively
antiquated living room, the fire blazing away in the hearth, my own
mannered fingers tweezing the dainty handle of the china teacup. That
full-throated cackle of hers after I had laid out the Griswold case kept
echoing through my brain, its pitch and volume somehow incompatible
with a husband fresh dead.

I turned the lamp back on and got up and dressed. I grabbed my coat
and hat and left the building. Gone were the days when the freeway at
that time of morning was a man's private speedway. Nowadays the twin

rivers of cars never ceased, never diminished, no matter the time, gushing like corpuscles through the city's arteries, red in one direction, white in the other. I joined the pulse at the dark and empty coliseum. Half an hour later I exited at Sir Francis Drake. The roar of the freeway receding behind me, I rolled down my window and eased my foot off the accelerator.

At the mouth of Curzon's cul-de-sac I pulled over and cut the engine. All the houses up the block were bathed in the spectral aura of mercury vapor streetlights. All, that is, but the Morris house, which stood shrouded in total darkness, as if the developers, powerless to wipe the house off the map, had settled for depriving it of illumination. I sat for a while looking at that incongruous silhouette, its twin gables piercing the dim yellow belly of the sky. I opened the glove box and grabbed my flashlight.

It was as quiet as the grave out there. Silently I trod the sidewalk, marveling at the persistence of the heat. If anything, the air under the suffocating blanket of suburban night felt hotter than it had during the day. Halfway up the block the chorus of crickets, spooked by my arrival, resumed their shimmering pulsations, the bravest first, then, as if shamed by example, the remaining ten million or so. In the front yards, children's bicycles lay oblivious to the concept of theft. The cars in the driveways, most of which had been absent during the day, rested equally confident in their distance from vice, their shapeless heft speaking of smooth rides to subterranean parking garages.

When I reached the cinderblock wall separating the Morris property from the house to the right of it, I availed myself of its shadow to venture down the strip of dead grass and weeds along the side of the house.

The back yard was an irregularly-shaped clearing in what otherwise appeared to be a vast expanse of native woodland, the grasses ceding ground to dense black masses of deciduous trees. I paused at the corner of the house, amazed by the noises emanating from the darkness—frogs croaking, owls hooting, the yowling of feral cats, all in delightful syncopation with the choir of crickets. More uncanny yet, sparks appeared to be rising from the grass, swirling around before being extinguished. Only when one flitted past my head did I realize that the erratic yellow-green flickers were fireflies. It was my first encounter with these magical insects. Some abnormal pressure system must have driven them from their native domain. I stood watching them for a long time, mesmerized by their silent pulsations.

I found the ladder, as I knew I would, on the ground against the side of a shed at the back of the yard. Before returning to the porch, I stood enchanted for several more minutes, gazing into the darkness of the throbbing woods, the soft breaths of cooler air tempting me to venture into its darkest recesses, to lie in the damp mulch and sleep off the dregs of the world's longest hangover. It seemed as though I were on the edge of some primeval forest, untouched by man, so dark and cool and wild were its earthy aromas. No doubt this was all a trick of night. I knew that if I ventured out there I would only find a wall, beyond which would be the back neighbor's swimming pool.

I carried the ladder, an old wooden thing with rusty catches, back through the prickly grass and weeds. Leaning it against the roof of the porch, I tested my weight on the first few rungs before climbing up. The well-baked shingles crackled underfoot like charred embers. I crept as lightly as possible to the nearest window and peered through it with the edge of an eye. The reflections of the streetlights on the glass made it difficult to make out much of anything inside, though it seemed unlikely that an old woman, believing her husband to have been murdered a few nights ago, would be sleeping in a room without the curtains drawn.

Squatting before the window, I placed the flat of my palms against the pane and pressed upwards. The frame jerked up about six inches then jammed with an awful squeal. I ducked below the sill and waited, listening for half a minute. Then squatting again I got both hands under the frame and worked it up with short, controlled thrusts to a gap of about two feet. Still hearing nothing save the crickets, I pulled the flashlight from my pocket, rose up, swiveled the head and aimed it in.

By all appearances—a wall of books, a desk and office chair, a floor lamp beside an armchair—it was the study. The door was closed. I trained the beam onto the floor near the window and, seeing no obstacles, turned off the flashlight and climbed in.

The armchair was a blocky thing with stumpy wooden legs, upholstered in olive-green velour. The piebald lay of the nap, alternately flat and bristled, in broad, straight-edged swathes, indicated a recent steam-cleaning. But even by the weak light of my flashlight I could see the discoloration of the bloodstain. The brunt of the scrubbing had been done on the right half (from the sitter's vantage), suggesting he had been left-handed. I turned the flashlight towards the wall to my left. No sign of a bullet hole. I turned it back to the chair.

Standing before that dreadful thing, lit only by the merciless beam of my flashlight, I imagined with perfect clarity the moment Walter Morris put the barrel to his head. Perhaps it was the lingering ache in my own temples that made me see it with such nauseating precision. I felt the adrenaline that must have been coursing through his veins as the cold circle of steel pressed against his skull. I felt the mist of clammy sweat oozing from his pores. I felt, without knowing the particulars of its origins, the black despair and longing for death that, after a long and seemingly productive life, had delivered him to his final moment. His eyes were open, staring straight through me, through everything, clear to the end of the universe. He mumbled a farewell to his wife, begged her forgiveness. Then, closing his eyes, he pulled the trigger.

The floor was hardwood, weathered oak boards laid out in stairstep parquet. Judging from the scuffing near the chair, the legs had habitually rested a few inches back from its current position. I knelt down and looked under the chair. Nothing. I lifted the cushion, examining the underside, which judging by the sag and the general wear of the fabric appeared to have spent more time facing up than down. I set it aside and felt around in the gaps, retrieving a ball-point pen, a popsicle stick, a quarter, two nickels, and a penny. I pocketed the quarter and returned the rest along with the cushion.

The desk was a big gray metal thing, like something from a government office. On it stood a green glass banker's lamp, a typewriter, two stacked metal paper trays with some papers in them, a blue felt writing blotter, a mason jar of assorted pens and pencils, and a small wind-up clock presently reading 2:16. I pulled the papers from the top tray and leafed through them. There were about fifteen pages, covered in the black scrawl of a lefty. I skimmed through it, looking for anything familiar, but it didn't appear to be Conway stuff.

I went through the middle drawer first. Among the usual miscellany, I found a clump of Silly Putty, flattened to about a quarter of an inch, in a roughly oval shape a few inches wide and slightly longer. On one side it appeared to have been pressed to a newspaper, for in addition to half a dozen truncated lines of backwards text, it carried the faint impression of the bottom of a photograph in which not much was discernible beyond a man's shoe and a bit of his pants cuff. On the left edge were a few thin vertical bands, perhaps a ventilation grate on the wall of a building. A host of strange feelings and recollections swept through me as I stared down at that rubbery time capsule resting on my open palm. I saw my old bedroom in the house on Baltimore Drive, where I spent many a lonely afternoon reading and rereading my comic books, yearning for the day when I would be big enough to go out and fight the bad guys myself. I saw that grimy gray carpet, the white cinderblock walls, the little bed with the tubular metal frame painted a pinkish color (my mother had painted it in the back yard from a can of house paint). That room was my bunker, my place of refuge from the battles of my mother and father. Holed up in there against the outer bombardment, I vanquished villains with a single stroke of my broadsword. I dispatched them with pistols, rifles, ray guns. I blew them up with hand grenades and atomic bombs. Sometimes I beat them to oblivion with my bare fists. Not all my fantasies were of death and destruction. I liked to draw and color as well, or take impressions from my comic books with copious wads of Silly Putty, transferring the captured pictures and words onto the pages of a notebook that I reserved especially for that operation, in this way creating from those used-up pages entirely new sequences and stories of my own invention, however faint they might have been upon arrival in their new home.

What was a grown man doing with a clump of Silly Putty in his desk drawer? I inspected the impression more closely but was unable to determine the context from the snatch of text, or if there was any correlation between the picture and the words. The text, backwards on the Putty, read as follows:

<blockquote>
time. They rely on several privat

a vital link between the agency

f which is Ruth Brenner. A sin

"a difference in people's liv

fact that she herself gre

t. Jerome's, bu
</blockquote>

By all appearances it was just a random impression, perhaps a momentary indulgence in nostalgia. I put the Silly Putty in my coat pocket.

I was about to inspect the bookshelves when a loud creak broke the silence. I flicked off the flashlight and froze. A gently rising patter of slippered footsteps sounded from the other side of the wall, growing louder as they neared. A few centuries later they reached their apex of clarity and volume, held steady for another aeon, then gradually receded to something approaching their original softness. I heard the click of a light switch, the footsteps changing timbre, the clatter and latch of a loose door handle. Then nothing save the crickets chiming through the open window, until, somewhere near the end of time, a toilet flushed. The faint drone of the running water grew abruptly louder as the slippers passed the door again. The floorboard creaked. Eventually the toilet did stop running, though the pipes somewhere else in the house went on making a moaning racket for several more minutes before grinding to a shuddering halt.

I stood motionless in the dark for a long time afterwards. Then, turning the flashlight back on, I got on my hands and knees and looked around the floor under the desk. I shined the flashlight over every beam. I stood up and aimed it through a variety of possible bullet trajectories.

The bookshelves occupied most of the right-hand wall. Plenty of pages there for a bullet to hide between. He was a surprisingly well-read man, considering the crap he wrote. In addition to a 26-volume encyclopedia and a series, twice as broad, called *Great Books of the Western World*, the shelves contained a wide range of titles, too numerous to catalog here. I found his own books, that is Baxter Conway's, occupying two shelves at waist level, two or three copies of each title, some in hardback with dust jackets, most of them paperbacks with lurid covers of scantily clad women sprawled out on sofas against the backdrop of a city.

Emblazoned in bold white capitals across the entire top third of every cover was my name, ten times larger than the humble "Baxter Conway" relegated to the bottom.

I pulled out ten of the paperbacks and stuffed them into every available pocket. I gave the room another quick look then turned off the flashlight, parted the curtains, and climbed out the window, carefully closing it behind me.

8

I BEGAN WITH *Due Diligence*, the third book in the series (I was missing *Blinded by the Sun* and *Fair Market Murder*, the second and ninth installments.) It was the Buckler case. Beautiful young Nancy Buckler had asked me to investigate a series of unusual anonymous gifts that had been received by her father, Red Buckler, half of Buckler and Steine, Wholesale Furriers. This was about ten years ago. One gift, a dead cat with a mysterious note in a silver locket around its neck, ended up giving Red Buckler a heart attack, which ultimately killed him. After that Arnold Steine (and his sultry wife Leila, who made more than one pass at me) began receiving anonymous gifts as well. My suspects were Leila's nudist son, Robin, who was Nancy Buckler's boyfriend, and a host of servants. The gifts included some poisoned egg salad, a petrified starfish, a burned book, and a bundle of soiled diapers, all accompanied by cryptic and ominous notes, which seemed to reference a mysterious and violent incident in the past of both Buckler and Steine. I worked out the significance of the gifts and the link that connected the notes and arranged a dramatic surprise that trapped the criminal.

It wasn't my intention to read the entire novel, but I soon found myself sucked into it, reading it word for word. As with *Guttersnipe*, I read in a state of enthralled revulsion, unable to tear my eyes away. It was as much my outrage at the brazen theft as disbelief at how mercilessly he had butchered reality that made me see it through to the bitter end. When at last I looked up from the book, my apartment was flooded with morning sunlight.

Over the course of the next five days, largely while waiting for Mrs. Fletcher to emerge from places like Thrifty Nickel and Bargain Town, I read every one of those novels cover to cover. Despite already knowing the solutions to the crimes, I devoured them to the very last page, desperate to know how it would all get resolved. On the one hand I was revolted to see my cases, my name, my life put to the service of such gimcrackery. On the other hand, it was with a kind of perverse fascination that I watched that cardboard Eddie King moving through that cardboard city, tangling with vicious villains, cracking wise with cornball cops, lusting in shorthand after tacky tarts and trollops. It was a world in which one man stoically patched the cracks in the dam, single-handedly holding back the flood of mankind's inherent vice. All these outrageous events, the corpses piling up, the blackmailing, the scores of encounters with shady characters, the brawls, the drunken moping, the steamy romances—this veritable maelstrom of activity was miraculously crammed into the space of three seemingly endless days and nights. No case of mine has ever been wrapped up in less than eight weeks.

The facts were there, sure, but the characters bore almost no resemblance to their real life counterparts. A perfunctory attempt at physical description, riddled with clichés like everything else in the novels, was the extent of Morris's efforts to faithfully portray the lives of the people whose names he had pilfered. He wasn't at all interested in what might have driven these individuals to do what they had done: the miserable childhoods, the abusive fathers, the endless series of bad breaks. In his hands they were just bad people, through and through.

His rendition of me was the hardest to swallow. In his hands Eddie King was more an absence than a presence. Less a man than a mood, a brooding, wounded cynicism, what little there was of him I found utterly preposterous. He never seemed to sleep. His diet consisted of nothing but steaks and fries. He drank about a gallon of bourbon a day and never suffered any ill effects. He was either impervious or oblivious to all the gorgeous women all but begging him to sleep with them. He could kill a man in one scene and get his shoes shined in the next. He was a man of deep (I would say pathological) principle. God knows how he paid his rent. By my calculations he couldn't have made more than three hundred dollars over the course of the entire series.

In short, Morris's Eddie King was nothing like me. He had steel-gray eyes (mine are brown), bristly black hair (brown again, thinning at the top), an aquiline nose (mine is almost African in width). He kept massaging his right earlobe with his thumb and middle finger, which to the best of my knowledge I have never done in my life. Most ridiculous of all, he had "the body of a linebacker—shoulders as wide as a dump truck, a chest like a bank vault." I am five foot six and weigh a hundred and fifty-five pounds. The one thing about me Morris did get right, which made me think he must have been near enough to hear me at least once, was my "velvety voice," to which the occasional good luck I have had with women must be attributed.

I wasn't the only character given short shrift. Everyone in those novels seemed to have been plucked straight from the rack of stock characters. Men in scarlet-lapelled smoking jackets with hawklike faces and piercing black eyes. Solid men with square, rugged features the color of raw beef.

Queers with slender, well-manicured hands and faintly contemptu-
ous smiles. All those male glowerings and female gigglings, all those
thoughtfully bitten underlips, all those wide and dewy and innocent
eyes. The quiet sobbing, deep-drawn breaths, shudderings at recollections. The dialogues, of course, were all invented, in the most stilted
language imaginable, littered with out-dated slang, wooden deliveries,
long-winded expositions, language that, apart from the likes of Hicks
and Stiles, I have never heard any real human being speak.

Still, I must give credit where it is due. Baxter Conway could tell a
ripping yarn. He knew how to take the inchoate grist of reality and mill
it into something that gave the reader an illusion of coherence, however
insubstantial it might have been. What he lost in detail and veracity he
gained in headlong momentum. Once you started one of those books
you couldn't put it down until it was finished. In my more generous
moods I was intrigued by how Morris had transformed those strange,
almost incomprehensible events into something else entirely, with its
own peculiar kind of life. But mostly I was left with the indignant feeling that this wasn't the way things were at all.

As the initial stab of violation began to recede, replaced by a more
sober hunger for knowledge and justice, I tried to read more objectively,
with an eye towards ferreting out the traitor(s). At first it seemed impossible to imagine a single individual possessing such thorough knowledge
not only of all my cases but of my physical movements around the city,
the details of my office and my apartment, etc. But upon closer inspection I realized that this at times almost terrifying omniscience was in fact
an illusion. Only in *Guttersnipe* had Morris made any attempt at all to
describe the contours and textures of my world. Having already sketched
out a few details in that first novel, he must have seen no further need
to do it again. Just as his readers filled in the gaps from their own

imaginations, I had been filling them in from my own experience. I began to reconsider the possibility that he had acted alone, that he actually had written the novels solely from my files and whatever he could glean from the newspapers.

At various points during my reading marathon, I pulled the relevant case files from the filing cabinet and went through them again, again trying to reconstruct the events, but, as with *Guttersnipe*, my memories of the cases seemed to have been all but obliterated by the novel in question, replaced by a rag-bag of contrivance and cliché.

9

I WAS IN the middle of *King's Ransom*, the eighth book, the day Mrs. Fletcher decided to slum it. She was driving south on 16th Street when instead of turning left on Naples Boulevard and continuing on to the coast road and home as usual, she drove on another two blocks then turned right onto Buchanan Street, which took her directly into the Silage.

If the Silage is the city's heart of darkness, Buchanan is its clotted aorta. The storied purveyors of cutlets and tenderloins may have long since vanished, but the six-block stretch between Taft and Garfield Streets is still called Butcher's Row. If you need someone murdered on the cheap, a stroll down Buchanan offers no shortage of competition. It was no place for Heidi Fletcher to be showing off her pearl necklace.

The car alone was enough to set the urchins scurrying like rats in every direction, shouting the news down the alleys to big brothers and gang leaders that the Queen of England was piloting Fort Knox down Butcher's Row. I might have only been hired to follow her, to report back to her husband on the nature of her excursions, but the laws of conscience, drafted in a higher court than ours, demanded that I protect her, from her own stupidity if need be. I closed the distance to half a block, ready to intervene the moment the vultures descended.

Only when she finally got it into her head to get off of Buchanan did I begin to breathe a little easier. But no sooner had I relaxed, letting a full block drift back between us, than she turned into the underground parking garage between Hayes and Monroe, a two-dollar-a-day affair used by the small-time lawyers and bail bondsmen who populate west Bond Street, two blocks down. I pulled to the curb opposite the entrance and peered with what I can only assume was a dumbfounded expression into the darkness that had swallowed her. I waited. A few minutes later she walked out, on three-inch heels, in a stunning aqua-green, open-back silk dress. I shielded my face with my hat brim until the clacks of her heels had advanced some distance up the block, then I got out and crossed to the other side of the street.

If Morris were describing this he probably would have said something like, *She walked back to Buchanan and disappeared around the corner.* Factually correct but devoid of all sense of awe. It is probably safe to say that it had been more than a century since such a sight had been seen on this block of Pierce Street. Everything about her walking up that sidewalk was a negation of reality. The drab gray concrete, the iron grilles, the glaucous tubing of dead neon signs may as well have been dreary stock footage of the city in front of which this Technicolor dream goddess was gliding. Beneath the cascade of golden tresses her naked back was a virgin landscape fringed by the sharply slanted V of her dress, the valley of her lower back fluting gracefully up and fanning out into the gently palpitating ridges of her shoulder blades. Her ass was a miracle of nature, a formation of perfect rotundity, not so much enveloped by the vapory silk as of a piece with it, as the skin is to a pear. Fortunately the only people on the sidewalk at that moment were an old Chinese man and two middle-aged Filipinas. I can only assume that the hardship of their lives had blinded them to the uncanny, for though their downcast eyes did briefly lift, this heavenly apparition was clearly no match for the gravity of the daily grind.

I jogged the rest of the way to the corner and craned my head around it. A pair of predatory eyes had already locked on her. Faced with the improbability of what he was seeing, the guy froze slackjawed in his tracks for a three-count before recovering his senses.

"*Goddamn!*" he shouted. Another dozen pairs of eyes swiveled in their sockets. I stepped around the corner. This was enough to halt the advance. They didn't need to know the precise nature of my business with her to gather that she wasn't alone. Still, refusing to be cowed on their own turf, they let rip a volley of ungentlemanly expressions. Paying them no heed, either out of fear or willful deafness, Mrs. Fletcher likewise took no notice of their sudden change of heart. Had she been more observant she might have turned around, effectively ending my brief term of employment with her husband.

Instead she stepped over to the door of the Ambassador Hotel and pressed the buzzer. I turned to admire an imitation Rolex in the pawn shop window two shops down. I kept her in my peripheral vision until she was buzzed in, at which point I turned around and eyed the pack at my leisure. It eyed me back. I hung out there for a few minutes, enjoying the companionship of my revolver, then walked over and took a look through the window. A fat man with a toupee about as convincing as a dead crow was standing behind the reception counter reading the racing news. He was alone. I pressed the buzzer. He looked my way, folded his paper with a certain umbrage that suggested he had a good guess why I was there, and buzzed me in.

The lobby, for lack of a better word, had all the charm of a root canal. I approached the counter.

"The bird that just flew in here," I said. "She ever been here before?"

"That's privileged information, pal"

"Nothing in this pus hole is privileged." I took out my wallet and showed him my detective's license. He wasted a synapse or two on it.

"Private dick, eh? How's business?"

"Slow. How about we speed it up."

He stared at me for a good ten seconds. Things were going on behind his torpid eyes. Whether or not they deserved to be called thoughts was another matter.

"I don't know nothin about her."

"I'd be surprised if you did," I said. "Has she been here before?"

"Never seen her."

"What did she say to you?"

"Why should I tell you?"

I took a five from my wallet and set it on the counter.

"I'd appreciate it if you did."

He studied it for a few seconds then succumbed. His fingernails looked like something a cat had given up on.

"A man came in, about half an hour ago," he said. "Real cracker barrel."

"What did he look like?"

"How should I know?"

I put another five on the counter.

"Save your money, pal. I ain't any good at descriptions."

"What do you mean 'cracker barrel?'"

"Big cheese. Fat cat. Goose liver."

I let it go.

"So what about this guy?"

"He asked for a room."

"Is he still here?"

"Unless he climbed down the fire escape."

"What's his room number?"

"Slipped my mind."

I scanned the key rack for missing numbers. Too many to ponder.

"Give me a room," I said.

"How long?"

"Couple hours."

"Ten bucks."

I put fifteen on the counter. I could claim it as expenses. He turned and pulled a key from the rack and handed it to me.

"You oughta be comfortable in that one."

"Treat yourself to a manicure," I said.

Before heading up the stairs I went back out and around the corner to my car, opened the trunk and retrieved my kit. Back in the hotel I climbed the fetid stairwell to the third floor.

If the lobby was screaming for a dentist, the third floor corridor was a serious sinus infection. A chorus of snoring, wheezing, sputtering, and hacking behind closed doors accompanied me down the snot green passage. I paused at the door of 312 and listened. Hearing nothing, I carried on to 313, unlocked the door, and went in.

The room was furnished with a single bed, a chest of drawers, a wooden chair, and the stale air of loneliness. I closed the door and stood beside it for a moment, arrested by a vision of my retirement. There I was, sad old bag of bones, prostrate on the bed, watching day by day the mold spores colonize the ceiling, pondering not the great questions of life and death, for I had long since lost the stomach for mysteries, but whether or not I should bestir myself to make the journey down the hall for a shower or lie there in my own stench for another day or two.

I walked across the room to the window. It wasn't a view you would find in a travel brochure, but the sight of sunshine on brick and iron was enough to scour my mind of such morbid thoughts.

The bed was next to the wall shared with 312. I opened my kit and removed the stethoscope. I placed the bell against my chest and listened to my heartbeat, a ritual of mine whenever I don the scope. The sound of my old friend knocking around in there always intrigues me. At that moment it was hammering away as loud as coupling boxcars, the adrenaline surge from tailing Mrs. Fletcher down Buchanan apparently still oiling the works. I stretched out on the bed and pressed the bell against the wall. All quiet save the termites. So it remained for the next few minutes.

The movement began with a single plaintive squeak of bedsprings. Then two distinct pairs of shoes, one light and crisp, the other heavy and dull, moving in different directions across the floor. A wooden chair creaked to accommodate someone's weight. The man cleared his throat, conjuring a vague impression of ill-humored stoutness, an image which I retained for the duration of our brief aural acquaintance. A series of shufflings and stirrings followed, not unlike the fidgets of an audience before the start of an opera: the padded thuds of unshod feet, the creaking of the chair, the deafening clank of a belt buckle striking the floor. Then silence, from which there eventually arose a low, monotonous rumble, rolling out a phrase about five words long, their clipped edges rendering them unintelligible. In reply the bedsprings lightly chirped.

Over the next few minutes, a recurring pattern developed: the man murmuring something in his burnished baritone, the woman (who I couldn't help but envision, absent all visual proof, as Mrs. Fletcher) replying with contented mewling. Her voice, however muffled and unnaturally amplified in my ears, had the sweetest tone, like the tolling of a village bell on a lazy summer's day, barely perceived from a distant field. A tranquil voice, softly fluting some half-forgotten melody.

Suddenly the chair squawked like a startled goose. Graceless feet thumped the floor. A groan of mild exertion accompanied two bony knocks to the floorboards. Then came a long stretch of concentrated silence, a good five minutes at least, culminating in a distinctly feminine insuck of breath.

After a languorous fermata, the movement proper began with a trotting andante of squeaking bedsprings. The man tended to vocalize in heavyhearted, downward-curving phrases, often made up of alternating semitones and fifths—a zigzagging pattern that lent his delivery a doom-drunk, Wagnerian heft. At times he threw himself into the role with infectious, almost loony enthusiasm, occasionally plucking off higher notes, though on the whole he seemed to be applying the sustaining pedal to his voice, limiting his register to a haze of resonating tones with all the dynamic range of a lowing buffalo. Even Mrs. Fletcher was grounded in the same colorless key for perilously long periods. The problem, in my opinion, was less with the performers than the score, which despite countless attempts at innovation over the millennia has proven remarkably resistant to change. No doubt the conductor was also partly to blame, wielding his baton, by the sound of it, as though it were a blackjack.

With a few soft, shuddering strains, the man proclaimed that heaven was within his grasp. Mrs. Fletcher belted out seventeen high E's. Finally, fraught B-flat minor gave way to a simpler, starker A minor, on which the rhapsody ended. A stupendous ending, the feeling of resolution immense, all the more so for what the wall and the stethoscope had left to my imagination. A touching coda followed, an adaggio rephrasing of the finale, which gave a tender coloring to the preceding frenzy.

I pulled the earpieces from my ears and lay there until I could no longer feel the beating of my heart.

10

THEY WEREN'T THE sort for long goodbyes. No farewells, my lovely. In fact they said nothing at all. I heard the man's footsteps in the hallway. Hers didn't follow. The door closed. I gave him ten paces.

He was of medium build, well-dressed from what I could see of the back of him. This guy was no cracker barrel. He reeked of money. The tailoring of his greenish brown twist tweed suit gave his otherwise unimpressive bearing a sense of grace and power. The trouser legs swished and swayed just so as he ambled contentedly down the corridor, his maroon cap-toes glinting even in that murky light. I might have chosen a derby or a homburg if I were the one in the wool, but the slight leftward cant of his sable gray fedora gave a certain rakishness, wholly appropriate in the present context, to his air. As if to drive the point home, he took a coin, a quarter I believe, from his right trouser pocket and flipped it into the air and deftly caught it in his open palm, returning it to his pocket without so much as a hitch in his stride.

Poor Mr. Fletcher. I didn't relish being the messenger on this one.

He turned the corner to the stairwell and trotted down, too fast for me to get anything more than a fleeting glimpse of his left cheek. At the stairwell I leaned over and looked down only to see the top of his hat and shoulders receding before passing out of sight. I quietly followed him to the second floor then paused and listened before descending the last flight.

"Take her easy," the hotelier said.

"Much obliged." A gentle, almost timid voice, surprising after what I had heard across the wall.

Hearing the door buzzer and a surge of street noise, I finished my descent.

"That the guy?" I asked, making my way to the counter.

He made a little circular motion with his head, almost Hindu in subtlety, which I took to mean yes. I went to the window. He was already out of sight. I opened the door and looked out. He was walking down the sidewalk to the left, the way Mrs. Fletcher and I had come. Up and down the block, heads were slowly raising in expectation of the second half of that afternoon's double feature. I needed to get a look at the guy's face, and soon. Any minute now Mrs. Fletcher would be coming out of the hotel, and I would need to be in position.

He rounded the corner. I hurried after him. A few paces after taking the corner myself I put a cigarette in my mouth—I always keep a few in my inside jacket pocket for such occasions—and called out to him.

"Hey, buddy," I said. He was about ten feet in front of me. As he turned I opened my mouth to ask him for a light. The words never made it out.

The look on my face must have pleased him immensely, for that smug grin kept resurfacing during the course of the following conversation.

"Cute," I said. "I suppose this is your idea of amusement."

Positively beaming, Mr. Fletcher walked up to me. "Don't be sore, King. You did well." He patted me on the shoulder.

74

I wanted to slug him. I pulled the cigarette from my lips, crushed it in my hand, and dropped it to the ground.

"I don't like being a stooge."

"You've got it all wrong."

"So educate me."

"Not here. Let's go somewhere we can talk."

"This is as good a place as any."

He glanced around us, slightly nervous.

"Look, King, it's not what it looks like. I needed to test you."

"Don't flatter yourself. I don't go in for the spoiled princess type."

"I'm not referring to my wife."

"Whatever it is, I'm not interested. Find yourself some other aphrodisiac."

I walked off.

"Mr. King," he persisted, taking a few steps along with me. "This is an offer you can't refuse."

"Watch me."

I crossed the street and got in my car. As I pulled out I glanced in the sideview mirror. He was still standing there, a pathetic little figure in my mirror.

Back in the office I dialed my old friend Rob Justice. He and I went way back to my First National Bank days, where we were both security guards. He had since moved on to plusher carpeting. He was now working for the Kelsey Group, the biggest detective outfit in town. Halfway through the number my finger paused, stilled by a sudden suspicion. I replaced the receiver. Rob? No, it couldn't be. He did know a lot about my cases, as he was one of my few reliable sources of good information, freely sharing the Kelsey files with me in exchange for a bottle of gin or a couple of tickets to the ballpark now and then. Of course he knew where I lived, what kind of car I drove, where my office was. We had spent more than a few nights getting swacked in my apartment. He himself was in the novels, his red beard and hulking physique likened to a "Dakota bear." But that didn't necessarily absolve him from suspicion.

No, I thought. No way in hell.

I picked up the receiver again and dialed his number. His secretary answered on the third ring.

"Hey, Eddie," she said in her Midwestern twang. "What's cooking?"

Even Leslie, a woman I had never met and knew virtually nothing about despite having talked to her an untold number of times over the years, was no longer immune from suspicion.

"Could I have a quick word with Rob, if he's not too busy?"

"Sure thang." She patched me through.

"Hey, bud," he said half a minute later. "Long time no hear."

"I've had a weird week."

"Your whole life is a weird week."

"This one could be the weirdest yet."

I would be lying if I said that part of me wasn't listening very carefully to his response as I told him all about Walter Morris and the Eddie King detective novels. But that maniacal laugh of his, which erupted before I had even finished the story, effectively cleared him of all suspicion.

"You're shittin me," he roared.

"I wish I were."

"How have we never heard of these things?"

"Do you read detective novels?"

"No, but I know enough people who do," he said. "Are these bestsellers or what?"

"No. Not that I know of. They're published by some outfit in Minnesota."

"Twelve years, man. It's unbelievable. I've got to read one. Who are your suspects?"

"I was thinking the cleaning lady. She's got a set of keys to the office. But it's a lot more than just the files."

"It's not like you have a ton of friends."

"Thanks. I can always count on your honesty. I actually called about something else. I was wondering if you had anything on a guy named Gordon Fletcher. His card says he's the founder, president, and CEO of Fletcher Enterprises. Big money. A mansion in Palladian Hills. He's got a child bride named Heidi who looks like something out of the Ziegfeld Follies. He fed me a line about her two-timing him, had me tail her to every damn thrift store in the city. Today I follow her to a fleabag hotel in the Silage, only to discover that her mid-day rendezvous is Fletcher himself. He claims he was testing me for some other job."

"It's you, man," Rob laughed. "You're a freak magnet."

I gave him the address in Palladian Hills. He told me he would see what he could dig up.

I sat for some time in silent contemplation, then I opened the desk drawer and pulled out the bottle and the glass and poured myself a drink. Mid-sip, the telephone rang. It rang again. I let it ring six more times before I answered it. I had a sneaking suspicion it was Mr. Fletcher.

"Hey, Ed," Rob said. "I got some info on your guy Fletcher."

"Already?"

"That's what they pay me the big bucks for. Fletcher Enterprises is a conglomerate, everything from agribusiness to global investment services. He's the CEO and majority stock holder. He's fifty-six years old, born in Cedar Rapids, Iowa. Got his start selling orthopedic shoes door to door. He's on the boards of various other corporations. He owns a good chunk of the city, his most prominent property being the Cooper

Building. The list of civic bodies and clubs he's a member of is too long for me to bother reading out to you, but one of the more interesting ones is the House of Proteus. Around the time Nicanor Stigmatias was juicing the railroad barons for the deeds to Shepherd Hill he, Stigmatias, established a local chapter of an old boys' club called the House of Proteus, one of these secret societies like the Masons. It dates back to nineteenth century Germany, where it was a trade guild for North Sea shipbuilders, but the members claim it goes all the way back to ancient Greece. You don't join it. You're chosen. Once you're in, there's no way out other than death. All the members are assigned a Greek name that they only use when they're together. They're big on the gods. They believe that the ancient Greek gods are alive and well and still working their mischief on us. No one knows where their lodge is, or if they even have one. They're rumored to have a wild bacchanalian orgy once a year, out in the woods somewhere, but of course no one outside the circle has ever seen it."

"How the hell do you know all this?"

"Wikipedia."

I took a drink. It went down hard. We spoke for a few more minutes about the uncertain future of our profession, then I thanked him and hung up.

That evening, back at home, I finished *King's Ransom* and started *Drop Dead Date*. Halfway through it Eddie King picks up a hooker and takes her back to his place. The scene is no more than a punctuation mark at the end of the chapter, a bit of mood music before the plot takes over again on the next page. All of a sudden my head jerked up as if from a dream. My blood turned to acid as the face of my betrayer resolved in the air between me and the opposite wall.

11

SAM'S JOINT WAS tucked away down the dead end of Curtis Street, the one-block alley between the back of the warehouses south of the canal and the fenced-in no man's land around the freeway on- and off-ramps. It was an easy six block walk from my apartment. This proved handy on nights when I needed a good soaking.

I got there around one thirty, half an hour before closing time. I always felt when I walked through the door of Sam's Joint that I was right where I belonged. It was a dim and dirty little place, frequented by dim and dirty little people. Dozens of framed photographs of Sam in his glory days (arms raised in sweaty victory, smiling and shaking hands with the legends, gloves up, head tucked, eyes brimming with confidence) decorated the peeling plaster and wood-paneled walls.

It was a quiet night, five or six men at the tables, three at the bar, each man softly luminous in the darkness, as if lit by some internal source. Nothing was playing on the jukebox. The lamp above the pool table shone coldly on the barren baize.

"Mr. King!" Sam affectionately hailed me, as he always did, as I made my way to the bar.

Sam had been in his late sixties, so it seemed, for the past two decades or so. Halfway to his mouth his nose veered left and dead-ended in a fat pink bulb capped by the rind of a thousand glancing blows. His eyebrows were a crinkled parchment of scars. He talked from the back left corner of his mouth, with a voice that sounded like a street brawl between a bullfrog and a meat grinder. The world for Sam was a million-round match between the big man and the little guy, and though he knew the fight was fixed, he never stopped believing that if only the little guy could muster up the guts he could knock the big man out of the ring. He got his news from the trashiest papers and believed every word of it. Every cop was on the make, every politician a stooge, every foreigner a leech on the system. In short he was a proud, honest, beaten old man. He was the last person I would have thought capable of selling me out. But who knows what a man will do when he's against the ropes?

I stepped up to the bar and parked myself on a stool. I set my hat on the bar.

"Still fighting the good fight?" Sam asked, as he always did, and set to pouring me a generous glass of Old Grand-Dad.

"I wish," I replied and took a big swallow.

Two of the men at the bar I knew. The third I had never seen before. He was passed out, his face dissolving into the woodgrain.

"Hey, Sophocles."

That was Jack, the typesetter at the *Evening Herald*. He was two stools down, a sheet or two to the wind. He raised his empty glass to me.

"Socrates, Jack," I said. "Socrates."

Next to him was Fred, who only seemed to work when the census rolled around. Jack and Fred tried to snare me into their diatribe against the government. I drank my drink and grunted and nodded as necessary. My thoughts were elsewhere. Even as they spidered through my mind it seemed as though they were not my own but the tailings of so-called wisdom mined from time immemorial. Could it be, I wondered, that my mind was as riddled with clichés as Walter Morris's novels?

"Boys," Sam said, pointing to the passed-out drunk at the end of the bar. "That there is the greenest green there is."

We all looked at the drunk. Sam launched into the story of this man, John, who had just lost his wife to his best friend. John's sad fate—it could be distilled from Sam's account of the story that John had told him six whiskey sours ago—was to lose all that mattered to him to his best friend. In short he had spent his entire life envying the man, at first in secret, later openly. Somehow this had never endangered the friendship, had in fact strengthened it, for both men believed that God—they were religious if not spiritual men—had assigned them their respective roles for a reason. John accepted his envy the way a man born blind accepts his dark but noisy world, less as an encumbrance than an invitation to exploit his other faculties. In John's case he poured all that was good in himself into being a good husband. He was a wife's dream: sensitive, caring, liberal with money. In regards to marriage, and marriage alone, he was envious of no man. Naturally, this was the one thing his bachelor buddy envied in him. It was only a matter of time before this unnatural balance between the two friends was upset, and all of the envy restored to the man to whom it properly belonged. It seemed John's wife found him painfully boring and could not resist the effortless charisma of her husband's best friend, whom she had spent many a night and day condemning as arrogant and childish. The story ended at the only place it could, with John discovering his wife and his best friend in his own bed earlier that afternoon.

What troubled me about this story, more than the poor bastard's misery, was the fact that Sam was telling it at all. It wasn't like him to gossip about his customers, especially when they were right there in front of him, however unconscious. It was out of character.

After Sam's story, Jack and Fred said they had to hit the road, leaving only Sam and I and the drunk in the bar.

"Kick that bum out for me, will ya," Sam said a few minutes later. "He's down for the count."

I got up from the stool and went over and shook the guy. He almost got an eye open. I caught him by the underarms and yanked him to his feet. He wasn't too interested in helping me out. I draped him over my right shoulder. As I neared the door the chronic plantar fasciitis in my right foot flared up, a stabbing pain right up the middle of my sole. I winced through it and carried on out the door and slumped him unceremoniously against the wall. "Sonofabitch," I muttered to the pain, lifting my foot and swiveling it around in the brisk night air. I could see my podiatrist shaking his head. He kept insisting that I take some time off. Easy for him to say.

Probably in anticipation of his present state, the man had put his wallet in his front right trouser pocket. I pulled it out. It had a picture of a kid in it. I took a look at his license, removed two of the three one-dollar bills, returned the wallet to his pocket and hoisted him back over my shoulder. I limped with him down to the corner and stood there busting my back for ten minutes before a cab came along. I slid the drunk into the back seat and gave the address to the driver. He made a stink about it. I gave him another two bucks on top of the drunk's and told him to dump him in the yard.

High above the warehouses the concrete underbelly of the freeway curved out into open space. Not a single star was visible in the sky above it. At this hour the freeway traffic was light downtown, the occasional sound of a car or rig passing overhead as quiet as midnight surf. But for the occasional taxi or squad car, the surface streets were dead, not a soul but me out there on the sidewalk's cheerlessly sparkling mica. The silence down here at night was altogether different from the blunt silence of suburbia. This silence was as sharp as Occam's razor. Suddenly a strange weightless sensation came over, as if the soles of my shoes weren't quite touching the ground. I looked down. My feet were firmly on the ground. I wondered if I wasn't coming down with something. I hadn't been quite right since the binge.

Just as I was about to turn and go back into the bar to have it out with Sam, a city squad car pulled up beside me. The passenger's window rolled down. It was Hicks.

"Well well, if it isn't Mr. King," he said. He was chewing bubblegum. Stiles seemed to be rubbing off on him. Even from ten feet away I could smell the artificial sweetener mingled with his cop breath (coffee, bile) as he smiled and moved his wad of gum around from one cheek to the other.

"What now?" I said.

He glanced across to Stiles then back at me. "We need to have us a little talk."

"What about?"

"Get in."

"What's the charge?"

"No charge. Yet."

"Then if you don't mind," I said, "I'll be on my way."

"Get in. We're going for a ride."

I looked around, figured I was in no shape to run, with nowhere to run to, so I opened the door and got in. Stiles eyed me in the rearview mirror as he slowly pulled out onto the street.

"Why'd you do it, King?" Hicks said without turning around, the muscles of his jaw expanding and contracting as he chewed his gum. Stiles was chewing his own wad. Between both of them, the car reeked. Not only of all those cop smells, but of the even viler smell of murderers and rapists.

"This is getting old," I said.

Hicks shook his head. He was disappointed in me. He turned on the overhead light. A moment later he held up a paperback copy of *Guttersnipe*.

"I didn't think you guys could read," I said.

Hicks put on a pair of black plastic drugstore reading glasses. The touch of erudition they lent him only exaggerated his sadism. He opened the novel and flipped aggressively through it until he came to the scene he was looking for. The pages were marked up with a yellow highlighter. He cleared his throat and, still facing forward, began reading aloud:

"'Hicks was on the take, padding his nest with whatever he could skim off the top of the sludge pool . . . It was his old nemesis, Randy Hicks. Appropriate name, Eddie said to himself. Three hicks from the sticks rolled into one . . .'"

Hicks turned a few pages. "'Hicks was a certain kind of mean cop who would sooner run over a limping dog than wait for it to cross the street . . . He had a reputation for an itchy trigger finger, especially in the Silage . . .'" He turned more pages. "'His waist size was higher than his IQ . . . Hicks was the one man on the squad who could be depended on to breathe down Eddie's neck. Stiles was his lapdog . . .'"

He lowered his glasses to the end of his nose and turned around and stared at me.

"I told you it wasn't exactly flattering," I said.

"That's not the best part," he said. He pushed the glasses back up his nose and returned his attention to the book. He flipped through some more pages until he came to the one he was seeking. He read:

"'It was Spooks Flannagan. And behind him was Detective-Lieutenant Randy Hicks, with a briefcase full of money . . . Hicks fired three times into the Mex's back. The Mex fell to the ground and lay there drowning in his own blood. Hicks walked up to him. "That's the last time you cross that border, greaser," he growled and fired the killing shot into the back of the Mex's head.'"

Hicks lowered the book, removed the glasses, and remained facing forward as he spoke. We had finally made it to the end of the block. Stiles took a lazy right and we continued coasting west down 3rd Street.

"You, me, and Stiles," Hicks said. "We were the only ones there that night."

"You think I like it any more than you do?" I said. "Those are my cases. I'm on every page."

"You're a sick and twisted individual," Stiles remarked.

"What are you worried about?" I said. "It's a novel. Not exactly admissible evidence. If you really want to cover your ass, get proactive: sue the publisher for libel."

"There isn't any Baxter Conway, is there?" Hicks said.

"Of course there isn't, Einstein. That's the pseudonym. Walter Morris is the writer. Was, at least. I told you all that myself."

"Yeah, pretty convenient," Stiles said. "Save it for the jury, King. You'll be writing the next one from prison."

It took a few seconds for that to sink in. I laughed.

"What?!" I laughed again. "You think *I* wrote this garbage?!"

No reply. I looked back and forth between the backs of both of their heads. "You have to be joking."

They weren't.

We coasted along in silence for a while, turning right again when we reached the end of the block. We continued coasting north on Jefferson.

"We got a call a couple days back from the Morris widow," Hicks said. "Said some nutcase calling himself Eddie King, wearing a black suit and black fedora, paid her a visit, asking all kinds of questions. Spooked her half out of her wits."

"That old bird, spooked? She's living in a haunted house."

"I told you to stay out of it."

"What do you expect? I'm trying to find out how this guy ripped off my cases. That's something you and Stiles might be interested in, isn't it?"

"That's not what she said. She said you were snooping around while she was out of the room, asking all about her family, about the house, like you were casing the joint or something. That same night she thought she heard a prowler. She got up and made some racket, hoping to scare him off. The next morning she went into the study and noticed that some of her husband's books were missing. You wouldn't know anything about that, would you?"

"First I murder the guy, then I go back and steal his books? This is getting better by the minute"

We turned east onto 4th.

"If you really think he was murdered," I said, "maybe you should lay off me and read the rest of his books. There's enough dirt on every big cheese in the city to have them all fried."

"I'm not warning you again, King," Hicks warned me. "The next time I hear you're anywhere near that woman I'll haul your ass in for sexual harassment."

I yelped with laughter. "Now it's sexual harassment! Hell, you might as well throw treason in there while you're at it."

I looked out the window. We were stopped. We were back in front of Sam's Joint.

"We're not done with you, King," Stiles said, eyeing me in the mirror. "Not by a long stretch."

Hicks got out and opened the back door. I stepped out. He put his hand on my shoulder paternally and looked me in the eye.

"There's blood in the streets," he said. "It's up to your knees."

There was a new odor coming off of him, one I hadn't detected before. The sour stink of fear. He got back in the car, and they drove off. I stood there on the sidewalk for a while, gazing at the receding tail-lights of the squad car. It turned right on 3rd and disappeared.

Sam was counting the night's take when I stepped through the door.

"I was about to lock you out," he said.

"I'd never leave without my hat."

His eyes zeroed in on my limp, the predatory gaze of the old boxer casing his opponent's body for the slightest sign of weakness.

"Foot bothering you again?"

"That bastard was heavier than he looked."

"Why don't you see my bone guy?"

"I've got someone."

I sat down on the stool in front of him and took *Drop Dead Date* out of my back pocket and pretended to take up where I had left off. Sam glanced at the cover without breaking his rhythm.

"You ever read this guy?" I asked casually, knowing full well that Sam didn't read anything thicker than the morning *Metro*.

He shook his head. I waited for him to finish counting. I turned to the page I had marked, read a little to myself, and chuckled.

"Here, listen to this," I said and started reading aloud. "'Her name was Rita. Only it wasn't a her. Under that dress she was a strapping dark Filipino by the name of Rudolph Pacpaco. But Eddie King didn't know that. He thought he was taking home the Queen of Siam. Some nights in this lonely city a man doesn't care if the thing beside him in bed is a woman or not, so long as it's warm and doesn't break the bank.'"

I glanced up and studied Sam's face. If he was feeling any contrition, he certainly wasn't showing it.

"Sound familiar?" I asked.

"What?"

"Ring any bells?"

"Does what ring any bells?"

"The broad, Rita."

"I thought it was a story."

"It is."

"I'm not following you."

"Rita, the broad I told you about."

He squinted a little.

"Not that one who . . . ?"

"The same."

He smiled. "I'll be damned. Someone put him in a book?"

I held the cover up for him. He squinted at it, perplexed, for a few seconds.

"You wrote this?" he asked.

"No, Sam, I didn't write it."

"That's your name there, ain't it?"

"The other guy's the writer."

He studied the cover again.

"You know him?"

"He's dead."

Sam nodded.

"Can't say as I knew him. You want me to ask around?"

"You're not following me, Sam. Don't you remember when I told you about this broad?"

"Sure I remember. I'd never seen you so busted up over a broad. What, you think she bumped him off?"

"Sam, listen to me. You're the only one I told. Get it?"

He looked confused.

"Spit it out, man," he said. "Stop pulling your punches."

"Who did you talk to?"

"Your private life is your business, Eddie. Believe me, I've heard plenty crazier stories than that. What would I tell anyone about it for?"

"I don't know. For a laugh."

"I wouldn't do that."

"You just did," I said. "That story about the drunk."

"You know that ain't the same."

"Why not?"

"I don't even know the guy."

We stared at each other for a while.

"You swear you didn't tell anyone?" I said. "Not even your wife?"

"Are you kidding?"

I could see he was hurt, his dignity wounded, the old fighting spirit coming out as he thwacked the bar with his towel.

"You're the only one I told," I said again.

"So what? There's plenty other ways people find out stuff. Maybe someone saw you with her. Maybe the guy blabbed about it. Scoring with a private dick."

I smiled.

"Look, Sam. How long have I been coming here?

He shook his head.

"A good fifteen years, I'd say," I said. "I've always considered you a friend, someone I could trust."

"Glad to hear it."

"I've talked about a lot of my cases with you, haven't I?"

"Some damn peculiar ones at that."

"Remember that little problem you had with your liquor license?"

His brow tightened. "That's a low blow, Eddie."

"I'd like to think that if you had something to tell me you would."

"I don't have a goddamn clue what you're talking about."

"Don't lie to me, Sam. You talked to that writer."

He straightened up, his old ribs and shoulders tightening with indignation.

"No one calls me a liar."

"I've told you everything, Sam. Everything. You could have written those books yourself from all the stories I've told you."

"You're on Queer Street, Eddie. Start from the beginning and tell me what's eating you. I don't like seeing you this way."

"I want to know who the hell betrayed me."

"What happened?"

"Haven't you been listening to anything I've said? This half-ass writer got to someone close to me. He stole my cases and passed them off as novels. He made a living off of me. Now the cops think I bumped him off."

Sam picked up the book and looked at it a little more carefully. He read the back cover. He opened it and read a few paragraphs. He set the book back down, frowning.

"Wasn't me, Eddie. You know me better than that."

I picked up the book and skimmed through it until I found the scene at Sam's Joint. There wasn't nearly as much description as I remembered there being. I showed it to Sam. He read it and grinned.

"Imagine that," he said. "My joint in a novel." He read a little more. "What's he say about me?"

"Nothing, in this book. It's one of the other books where he introduces you."

"What's he say?"

"It's all hardboiled nonsense."

"Bring it in next time."

"Yeah, I'll do that."

I put on my hat and stood up.

"Forget about it," he said, as I made my way to the door. "The guy's dead. Throw in the towel."

I waved goodnight with the back of my hand and stepped out.

12

THE NEXT AFTERNOON I drove back out to Sunset Acres to have another chat with the Morris widow.

"I figured you'd be back," she said, as one does to a dogged bill collector. Without further comment she stepped aside. Her dress, if no longer black, was as Quakerish as before. A knitted cream afghan hung loosely from her shoulders.

The living room, like the widow herself, had a less funereal aspect than it had on my first visit. For one thing, the curtains were open, the strong afternoon sunshine dispelling much of the Victorian gloom. It was still oddly chilly, but the outlandish fire was no longer blazing in the hearth.

"Did you find the rest of the novels?" she asked, leading me back to that crazy couch.

"Yes," I set my hat beside me, avoiding her eyes for a spell.

She adjusted her dress and shawl as she took her seat and turned her attentive chin my way.

"So?" she said. "Mr. King, isn't it?"

I ignored the sarcasm.

"You have nothing to fear from me, Mrs. Morris," I said. "I'm a nice guy, really. But I have to ask you again, do you have any idea where your husband got the material for his books? The plots. The stories. The names of the characters."

"I don't know why you persist in asking me that question."

"Because every one of them is based on one of my cases."

She indulged me with half a smile.

"You want proof?" I said, exasperation stealing into my voice. "I can bring my files here and we can go through every one of them side by side with the novels."

Her smile broadened ever so slightly. There was something intriguing about her face which I hadn't noticed, at least consciously, the first time. I sensed a sly intelligence about it, as if she were practiced at withholding herself from the moment in order to form a clearer picture of it at her leisure. Whether this was something in her eyes, her mouth, or perhaps not issuing from her face at all but rather from the totality of her body language, I couldn't say. Coupled with this, definitely emanating from her slate-blue eyes, was what struck me as a great capacity for tenderness. These conflicting impressions, along with the knowledge that she had called the police on me, left me off-balance, not sure whether I was being coldly appraised, empathized with, or both simultaneously.

"What exactly do you want from me?" she asked.

"Did Mr. Morris keep the rough drafts of his novels? Any notebooks? Research notes? Interviews? Anything at all related to his process?"

"Yes."

"I don't suppose you would allow me to have a look at them."

She gave it some thought before saying no.

"Look," I said. "I have no intention of taking legal action, if that's what you're worried about. I just want to know who it was, who his inside person was. I'm sure you can appreciate that. Someone was still helping him as late as last year, or the year before, whenever he was writing *King's Gambit*. For all I know this person might go and find some other writer to sell or give my confidential records to. I can't have that going on. My clients trust me, pay me, to be discreet. If they wanted their private affairs made public they would have gone to the police. Some of these people I've had to associate with, sometimes my own clients, are not nice people. If it turns out that any of them has already found out that all his dirty laundry has been aired in a novel, well, I don't know any other way of putting it—some of these men are killers. Frankly I'm surprised it hasn't . . ." I stopped myself short.

She turned from me and gazed abstractly into the empty hearth, gently rubbing the knuckles of her left hand with the fingers of her right, as if lost in some old memory. I leaned forward, bracing my elbows on my knees. I studied the floor. She turned her face to me. I sat back.

"He was so happy," she said quietly, as if to herself. "He was finally working on the book he had been dreaming about all his life." She smiled a little. "His masterpiece. That's how we always referred to it. It was all in his head, he said. A beautiful novel. Something he could be proud of, that he could put his own name to. He could quit hiding behind Baxter Conway."

She went quiet again, and my attention was drawn to the sound of a clock ticking somewhere in the room, some heavy old grandfather judging by the deep timbre of the tocks. Strangely, when I was only half listening to it it seemed to be slowing down, and yet when I focused on the silence between the ticks and the tocks it was the usual interval.

"What do you mean, 'hiding'?" I asked her.

"It's not easy to bare your soul to the public, Mr. King. But that's exactly what great art has to do. Walter wanted his own name on a book he could be proud of."

"How far along was he on it?"

"It's not that simple. You have to understand that he had to work out everything in his head before committing anything to paper. That was the way he worked, even on the King novels."

"I thought you said he was finally working on this masterpiece."

"Yes," she said. "In his head."

"So how was this different? If it was still just in his head?"

"It was different."

"How?"

"It just was," she said. "Walter was a very sensitive man. You wouldn't get that impression from the Eddie King novels, but he was. He could go into raptures over a piece of music, or the beauty of a sunset, or even the smell of a broiling steak. He was an artist at heart. A romantic. Words always fell short of what he was actually feeling."

Again she turned her eyes towards the empty hearth, and I saw such sadness in them that I couldn't help feeling cruel for coming here a second time when she clearly had more important things on her mind than plagiarism. I placed my hand on my hat, resolved to put this business out of my mind until I had given the woman some time to grieve. I was about to say as much when, still staring into the hearth and speaking with a touch of irony in her voice, she preempted me.

"It was never Walter's ambition to be a detective writer." Then, turning to me with an apparent need to unburden herself: "It started as an innocent challenge. We were on vacation in Mexico, in the hotel room one night. I had picked up a cheap mystery to read. He read a few pages of it and scoffed at how poorly written it was, saying he could write ten times better than that. I said it wasn't as easy as he thought, making up those plots. He accepted the challenge and wrote the novel in about six months. That was *Guttersnipe*. He submitted it to some publishers under

Baxter Conway, not wanting his own name associated with such low-brow entertainment, and one of them, to his astonishment, accepted it. Sales were good enough to get him thinking he could quit his job and take up writing full time. He was so unhappy at the office. Writing gave him a feeling of liberation, of starting over. He wrote the next two novels very quickly. They also did well, establishing the series as a viable enterprise. He was finally able to quit his job. He knew then that it was all or nothing. He had to make it work."

I removed my hand from my hat.

"Things were going well until *All but the Chorus*, the fifth book," she said. "That was when he began to fear he might never break free from Eddie King."

Every time she said my name in reference to that character, I felt strangely hollow, as if the air had been sucked out of my lungs, stripped of one of the oxygen molecules and pumped back in.

"We had become dependent on the income from the books," she went on. "He wrote a literary novel, but he couldn't get it published. So he returned to Eddie King. He was so miserable working out those plots. He couldn't stand that part. To him it was all so contrived, so unrealistic. Once he had solved the puzzle, he was fine, but until then he was impossible. A real ogre. Every year it got a little worse, the dread of starting another Eddie King novel. Every time he finished a book he sank into a deep depression. It could last for weeks, sometimes months. The dream of the masterpiece only grew stronger with each passing year."

"What makes you think he was really working on this masterpiece this time?" I asked.

"Because he told me," she said. "About three weeks ago he came to me one morning and said, 'I've got it. I've got the novel.' You should have seen his eyes, Eddie."

That caught me off guard, the sweet, almost yearning tone of familiarity in her voice, the acknowledgment at last of my own reality.

She went on, oblivious to my reaction. "It was as though he had glimpsed El Dorado. He always got excited when he had finally worked out the puzzle of one of the King novels, but this was different. He looked like a man who had come home after a long exile. At last he was free of Eddie King. I begged him to tell me what it was about, but he said he wasn't ready. He needed to keep it to himself until he had it all worked out and was well underway. He was always superstitious about talking about a novel before he had it under control. Maybe superstitious isn't the right word. He didn't want any input, however well-meaning. It had to be his own baby."

"So that's why you told the police you thought he'd been murdered?" I said. "When they asked you about the note?"

"What?" She turned and gave me the strangest look, as if she couldn't fathom who I was or how I had come to be there on her sofa.

"When the police asked you about the typewritten note," I repeated. "What did you tell them?"

Her senses gradually returned.

"I told them I didn't know what it meant," she said. "I still don't."

"But you knew Eddie King was the name of his detective and you didn't tell the police."

"It never crossed my mind that they wouldn't know," she said. "The pride of an author's wife, I suppose."

A long silence followed, neither of us looking at each other but certainly mindful of the space between us. When I sensed her growing impatient with our interview, I asked her if she still believed her husband had been murdered.

"Yes," she replied without hesitation.

I gave her conviction due pause, then said:

"There's no real delicate way to put this, Mrs. Morris. Isn't it more probable that Walter killed himself? You told me yourself he had no enemies."

"And you, Mr. King, said that some of these men you associate with are killers."

Finally sensing an opening, I said, "Then you admit the correlation between the novels and actual facts?"

"I never disputed it. It's your accusation that Walter stole from you that I don't accept." She looked at her watch, a delicate silver thing on her left wrist. "It's after six. I must be starting dinner."

I reached for my hat.

"Walter was very punctilious in his habits," she explained. "I could set the clock by him. Every day at noon precisely the door to his study would open and down he would come to have his lunch. The same with dinner. He had to eat at exactly six o'clock. I'm more spontaneous, or used to be at any rate. If you live with someone long enough, you can't help but acquire their habits."

I was about to stand up and wish her a good evening when, out of the blue, she said, "Would you care to join me?"

I pretended to give it some consideration.

"Thank you, but I should be on my way."

If the crestfallen look on her face was any indication, she wasn't simply asking out of politeness.

"I wish you would stay." She reached out and gave my hand an affectionate squeeze. "It has done me a world of good talking to you." She looked into my eyes and smiled. "You can have a look at the rough drafts while I prepare dinner."

That was a proposition I couldn't refuse.

13

TWO MASSIVE ACORN finials, or perhaps they were timeworn artichokes, marked the entrance to the dark stairwell at the back of the living room. I followed her up, each stair protesting our steps as we ascended, hers a little less vociferously than mine.

We emerged to a spacious hallway, roomy enough for an ornate waiting chair with a beveled mirror in its high back, a tall umbrella stand with ingenious tin drip trays in its base, various tables and whatnots cluttered with the requisite porcelain and glass bric-a-brac. Sunlight was seeping from several scattered doorways and from a window at the far end of the hall. I immediately felt the intrusion of my presence in this intimate space, coupled with the desire to absorb every detail of it: the scents of private life embedded in the crimson and emerald convolutions of the carpet, in the stained oak doorframes, the aged ivory and vine wallpaper. A pair of men's slippers, dark brown suede, open-heeled, lay poignantly empty one atop the other on the bare wood margin of the floor.

As we passed one of the little tables I noticed a framed studio photograph of Mrs. Morris and a man whom I assumed was Walter Morris. It was the first image of him I had seen, since none of the novels carried his picture on the back cover. He looked vaguely familiar, as men with no distinguishing features do. He was bald back to his crown, with a round face that suggested he had been a good thirty or forty pounds overweight at the time the photograph was taken, at least ten years ago judging by the changes Mrs. Morris's face and hair had undergone in the interim. The thick, black-framed glasses he was wearing gave him the air of an accountant or an engineer. From his contented, almost smug expression, I surmised that he considered himself lucky to be wed to the woman beside him.

Mrs. Morris opened a closet door halfway down the hall and removed a wooden rod about three feet long with a small hook screwed to the end of it. Raising the rod to the ceiling, she hooked a latch there and pulled on it. Down dropped a hatchdoor, revealing an aluminum ladder resting at the edge of the opening to the attic. She handed me the rod and asked me to pull down the ladder. It telescoped steeply down to the floor.

"You go on," she said. "There's a string overhead."

I started up the ladder.

"They're in boxes to your left, I think," she said when I was halfway up. "I'd suggest you bring some of them down and look at them in the study. It's too cold up there, and the light's bad."

At the top of the ladder I groped around for the string and, finding it, ignited a bare bulb above me. You could have played a match of doubles tennis in that attic, barring lobs. The longer walls sloped to a point overhead, low enough that I had to stoop as I neared them. At either end, small dormer windows did little more than blind me with searing squares of sunlight. Naturally it was chock full of clutter, everything gray with dust.

"Oh, while I'm thinking of it," Mrs. Morris called up, "could you do me a favor while you're up there and fetch me down my sewing machine?"

This little favor turned out to be a half-hour saga that left me with an aching back and a sweat-soaked shirt. I thought I was looking for a compact electric model until she yelled up something about a tabletop. It was, of course, an ancient treadle machine, cast iron and solid oak. She meant me to earn the privilege of looking through her husband's rough drafts. I groaned at the sight of it, wary of doing anything to aggravate my foot. It must have weighed seventy-five pounds. The width of the cabinet and the depth of the bulky drawers rendered it nearly impossible for one man to pick up, let alone carry down a ladder at an eighty-degree slant. But in my experience whenever you find yourself lacking the necessary tool, look hard enough and you'll always find a suitable substitute near at hand. In this case it turned out to be a plank of plywood siding and a heavy-duty extension cord.

"Oh, I'm so thrilled," Mrs. Morris exclaimed as I carefully slid the machine down the plank. "I've been wanting this down for years. It was my mother's."

When it had safely touched bottom, she stepped forward to stabilize it. I pulled the plank back up and made my way down the ladder to untie the extension cord.

"Where do you want it?"

I followed her down the hall to her bedroom, wheeling the squeaky old contraption behind her. Two things stood out from that quick glimpse: the canopy bed and the birdcage. The bed was a queen-sized Rococo affair of solid mahogany, with voluted pillars and an elaborate japanned cornice from which dove-colored curtains with a lining of green silk hung in elegant festoons, presently drawn back to the headboard, against which a mountain of brocaded pillows was piled. I couldn't help but think that sleeping in a bed like that would drive any heterosexual man to suicide. The birdcage, in keeping with the baroque or Victorian or whatever period, if any, that everything in the house seemed to belong to, was a tall, bronze, domed wire affair about three feet high, resting on a small marble-topped table that wouldn't have gone amiss in the back corner of a Parisian cafe. Inside the cage were two strawberry finches who chirped sweetly at the sight of their mistress.

I rolled the sewing machine against a wall out of the way. Before heading back down the stairs to make dinner, Mrs. Morris showed me to the study, where I pretended to be seeing it for the first time.

Back in the attic, I turned my attention to the manuscript boxes. The name of each novel was written in black marker on one side of each box. Brimming with nervous anticipation, I pulled the boxes of the last four novels and carried them one at a time down the ladder to the study and set myself up at the desk.

I began with *King's Gambit*, the last novel. That was the Shannard case, still fresh in my memory. Howard Shannard, son of millionaire Diedrich Shannard, had come to me about two years ago with a request that I investigate what his father had been up to during a recent bout of amnesia. The trail led to what seemed to be a love triangle with Howard's stepmother, the beautiful young Sally from the wrong side of the free-way. A series of small and unusual crimes, seemingly committed by the father during his amnesiac blackouts, revealed a bizarre pattern. But it was only after the murder of one Shannard and the suicide of another that I solved the true mystery and brought the crime home to the criminal.

The box consisted of a typed manuscript with editorial commentary in red pencil on nearly every page: spelling corrections, questions about motivation and probability, word choice suggestions, etc. Flawless manuscripts? I thought. Also in the box were five 80-page, unlined notebooks, every page covered in tiny, black, left-handed cursive. Apparently the man was incapable of writing a straight line. The farther from the top of the page, the steeper the downward slope of his lines, which, upon reaching the bottom, culminated in an empty triangle in the lower left-hand corner. The text itself was virtually impossible to read. Not because his handwriting was particularly illegible but because scarcely a single complete sentence was to be found anywhere on the page. Rather, he seemed to have developed a kind of private shorthand. It wasn't only repetitive words and names that he abbreviated or dispensed with altogether, but entire passages, which he replaced with "desc." or "dia." or "fight," which presumably he intended to fill in at some later stage. When he did attempt to write a scene in its entirety, it was hopelessly littered with a single nonsense word—"flogo"—which appeared to serve as a placeholder for words he didn't know or couldn't remember. At first I thought it was some kind of invented police acronym or crime-world jargon, though I had no recollection of coming across it in the published novels. It soon became apparent what its true function was. An excerpt from one of the *King's Gambit* notebooks:

> K stepped up counter askd flogo flogo. Flogo, jammed w/ dust
> and flogo. Desc. What's your order, Mac? She wearing flogo
> flogo, w/ flogo flogo flogo. Broad hips, painted fingernails,
> blonde. Beach deserted. Nice day, K said, flogo flogo . . .

I read two or three pages of this gibberish, trying without success to locate myself either somewhere in the finished novel, in the events that inspired it, or both. Not only did I have to battle against the tiny, slanted, left-handed scrawl, the missing words, the abbreviations, and the sea of flogos, but I was soon snared in a bewildering web of revisions—lines radiating in every direction, connecting crossed-out words or groups of words to whatever white space he could find on the page, wherein was set down, often vertically, some equally unintelligible phrase full of flogos, apparently meant to replace the flogo-encumbered original.

I soon gave up any hope of deciphering this secret code. I perused the manuscripts and notebooks of the other three novels, but it was the same hopeless tangle of nonsense as *King's Gambit*. I searched the boxes for supplementary materials—newspaper clippings, copies of my files, notes from interviews, outlines, etc.—to no avail, then went back up to the attic and retrieved more boxes.

I was pleased to discover that the hieroglyphics diminished as I worked my way back in time, so that by the time I reached the *Guttersnipe* notebooks it was possible to read entire pages of proper English, entirely flogo-free. In the end this too proved about as illuminating as a window against a brick wall.

I did find among the manuscript boxes a box of publishing-related correspondence. There I found letters from Howard Stapleton. I skimmed through as much as I could bear, but there was little of interest to me: contracts, royalty payments, tax-related issues, publication schedules, etc. The only thing that gave me pause was the yearly sales figures. At the peak of his popularity (*Blood City*, the sixth installment), Conway was selling over 50,000 copies in a single year. The sales of the last two books (*Fair Market Murder* and *King's Gambit*) were dismal in comparison (12,300 and 8,900 respectively). Most of the books were in the thirty thousand range. So how was it possible, given the sheer quantity of these novels out there in the world, that I had never heard of them, that no one

I knew had ever heard of them, and that apparently no one else depicted in the books had ever heard of them?

One possible answer resided in the box of fan mail. All of his fans seemed to be from small-town middle-America and foreign backwaters: places like Hagarville, Arkansas, Voda, Kansas, and Germfask, Michigan. Even one from Athlone, Ireland. There wasn't a single letter from a real city. All the fans in these letters expressed in one form or another their love of the Eddie King novels. One recurring theme was their appreciation for how true to life his stories and characters always seemed! Most of their admiration was reserved for Eddie King himself, whom many of them spoke of as if he were a real person, some going so far as to say he had changed their lives.

Morris's longest running correspondent appeared to be a fan named Kathy Jerrell, from Roswell, New Mexico. There were over fifty letters from her, spanning a ten-year period. Clearly they had struck up a long-distance friendship, one in which each of them felt comfortable enough to disclose the trifles of their private lives. She was the wife of a Presbyterian preacher. At the time of her first letter, in response to *Guttersnipe*, she had had one boy, named Benjamin, and over the course of the correspondence she had had five more children, boys and girls alike. She wrote of her day-to-day life as a housewife and mother, her special obligations as the wife of a man of God, the struggles she faced raising her kids in a sinful world, her own periodic bouts of religious doubt, the family vacations, her love of crime stories, especially Conway's novels. She always looked forward to the next installment of Eddie King's urban adventures. She wanted to know what it was like living in a big city, what he had done before he was a writer, where he got his ideas from. Unfortunately, nothing in her subsequent letters hinted at his answers. At some point in their correspondence he must have given her his real name because most of her letters were addressed "Dear Walter." Most of them were insufferable. Dull, sycophantic, naive beyond belief.

I did find something interesting in one of her earlier letters, however. She had just finished reading *Due Diligence* (the third book) and was so excited that she had to write to Walter at once, babies crying be damned, to tell him how much she had loved it. The interesting bit was in the penultimate paragraph. I quote it in its entirety:

Sorry to hear you've been blue. I understand. It happens to the best of us. Sometimes God doesn't seem to be listening, huh? We do the best we can, I guess. You did what you needed to. I know it must seem hard right now, but once you face it you'll be grateful. You'll regret it if you don't. I think it would be good for you to meet him. Tell him everything. It'll be such a weight off your chest. That's my ten cents.

I reread the letter several times, each time more convinced that there was no other interpretation to the paragraph. It was the first damning piece of evidence I had found. I folded it back up, slid it into its envelope, and put it in my jacket pocket.

Just then Mrs. Morris called me down to dinner.

14

SHE HAD SET out two places at the table in the dining room—bone china plates, a full complement of silver cutlery, linen napkins, wine and water glasses. The scent at this proximity of whatever she had made was overwhelming. Mingled with the aromas of pungent herbs, it seemed the richest, savouriest, juiciest meat I had ever smelled.

Presently she backed through the swinging door to the kitchen holding a heavy silver platter upon which, as she turned to set it on the table, was revealed a magnificent golden brown fowl.

"Turkey?" I ventured.

"Goose," was her reply as she placed the tines of the roasting fork and the blade of a bone-handled carving knife against the edge of the platter. "Now go into the kitchen and wash up."

The kitchen, about twice the size of my apartment, was in a cruder state than the rest of the house. The floor, judging by the furrows in its wide gray planks, must have been the original. The capacious cupboards, cabinets and drawers bore the plain, sturdy aspect of an era before nail guns and power saws. An open door revealed a well-stocked pantry bigger than my kitchen. But the *pièce de résistance* was a massive old cast iron stove, six cookers broad, with bulging doors, ornate knobs and fancy scrollwork, its fat stovepipe ascending through two in-built shelves to the ceiling and beyond. The only modern appliance in evidence was the refrigerator, and that stumpy white relic with its buckle-style handle hardly qualified as state of the art.

While I was washing my hands, Mrs. Morris returned from the dining room to dish up the accompaniments.

"Quite a spread," I remarked. An arsenal of culinary matériel, still hot from battle, lay strewn across the counters and work tables.

"Here, take this," she handed me a tureen of steaming gravy.

I carried it out to the table and set it beside the goose. She appeared a few moments later with a serving bowl of mushrooms in cream and a wicker basket of coarse brown bread thickly sliced.

She directed me to the end seat as she set down the dishes and relocated the tureen to the other side of the goose. Another trip to the kitchen produced a dish of something I couldn't identify and a beautiful etched decanter containing a golden liquid.

I pulled her chair out for her. Settling in with a sigh of pleasant fatigue, she turned to me and said: "Now, would you be so kind as to carve the goose, Mr. King."

I had to smile, not so much at one of the oddest strings of words to have entered my ears in recent times as her assumption that a) I was perfectly at ease performing this quintessentially paternal ritual, b) that I possessed the requisite skills, and c) that I actually considered it my God-given right as a man to carve the bird.

"I can't guarantee the results," I warned her, taking the fork and knife into my hands.

To my pleasant surprise I did a magnificent job, slicing into the juicy breast with smooth, controlled precision, stopping short of the bottom of the bird, and, with a single, deft lateral incision, cutting across the common termini of the slices so the smooth sheets of tender white breast cascaded over the back of the fork like so many pages of an open book fanning in a gentle breeze, down to the steaming bed of baked carrots and potatoes. It was as though I had done it a million times, when in fact I couldn't recall a single instance in my life when I had been called upon to carve the bird, be it one of the turkeys of the holiday season or the more prosaic Sunday broiler.

I transferred two slices onto Mrs. Morris's plate and served myself an equal portion before taking my seat.

"I wasn't expecting anything so lavish."

"Oh, I just cobbled a few things together."

As I was dishing up some carrots and potatoes, Mrs. Morris filled first my glass then her own with the golden liquid and raised her glass in toast.

"To the success of your investigation," she said. I chuckled. She did have a sense of humor, however dry.

Our glasses touched with an exquisite chime that somehow went on ringing in my ears long after it had ceased. I took a sip. "Nice. What is it?"

"Cowslip wine," she said. "It was one of Walter's hobbies."

I gave the remark an appropriate moment of silence, then I dished up some of the mystery dish (rhubarb, as it turned out) and grabbed a slice of warm bread. I cut a piece of the goosemeat and forked it into my mouth. Where do I begin? The moment it made contact with my tongue and the inner lining of my cheeks, two jets of saliva shot from my submandibular glands with what can only be described as ejaculatory force.

Simultaneously my nostrils flared, sucking in the powerful, gamy aroma wafting up from my plate, and I experienced a kind of visionary burst of connectedness with the bird whose life force was now passing into me. As I chewed its warm meat I sensed the cycle of its migrations, the seasonal sojourns to the wellsprings of life, the serenity of instinctual flight measured only by the throbs of numberless wingbeats, the changing contours and colors of the planet below. How I knew this had been a wild goose and not some anemic farm-raised bird, I couldn't say apart from the story being told by the savour of its flesh. It was a shame that in the end I had to swallow it.

"This is hands-down the most delicious thing I have ever tasted," I said when at last my mouth was empty.

"I sincerely doubt that."

"No, word of honor. I would never lie about such a thing."

"Well I'm glad you like it."

"*Like* it?" I exclaimed. "This isn't on the same scale as 'like.' I don't know what the word to describe it is . . . I *flogo* it."

It just slipped out. It must have been my giddiness over the turkey. I apologized, only realizing after I had said it that it might be construed as insensitive. Mrs. Morris smiled graciously but otherwise made no comment.

I quickly finished off my modest portion of goose and helped myself to three more slices. Soon I was carving off a fresh sheaf. I dished up more carrots and potatoes, dipping the serving spoon into the juice pooled in the platter and drizzling it over my plate. I ate like there was no tomorrow. Even as I felt my stomach tightening, my breath growing harder to catch, I carried on, under the gracious but firm encouragement of Mrs. Morris, who couldn't conceal her delight at seeing a strapping man at her table engorging himself in raptures on her cooking. The goose, she said, had been shot by Walter last autumn at Crystal Lake. Everything else—the potatoes, the carrots, the rhubarb, even the cowslips for the wine—had been grown in the back garden.

"Tell me about the case you're working on," she said when I paused to catch my breath.

"Business is slow at the moment," I replied, then proceeded to tell her about some of the peculiarities of my former client and his wife: the long confession about his jealousies, their mansion in Palladian Hills coupled with her penchant for thrift stores, her driving the Sphinx with the top down through the Silage, their midday rendezvous at the sleazy Ambassador Hotel. While I spoke she gazed straight ahead, looking at nothing in particular, as if the better to imagine the scenes.

Before I knew it I had polished off half the decanter of the wine and was feeling a pleasant buzz. She went back into the kitchen and returned with a full decanter.

"So, was she cheating on him?" she asked, setting the decanter on the table and taking her seat.

"If not, she should have been."

"Why do you say that?"

"She's a good twenty-five years younger than him," I said.

"That's not an immediate disqualification for fidelity."

"Neither of them struck me as the sort who married for love."

"Why would such a man hire you to track his wife?" she asked. "No offense to your skills, but a man with those kinds of resources."

"As I said, it was all some kind of game. I told him where he could stuff his other job."

She smiled.

"What?"

"Oh, I'm just amused by how much like Eddie King you actually are."

That went straight to the top of my list of most memorable insults.

She took a sip of her wine and elaborated. "Please don't take offense," she said, "but I lived with Eddie King for so many years that I feel like I know you. In some ways he was as much my creation as he was Walter's."

I set my fork down and gave her my full attention.

"Is that right?"

"I was the one who typed up the manuscripts from his notebooks."

"The notebooks in the attic?"

"Yes."

"How is that possible?" I said. "Half of it wasn't even written. All those missing passages, the abbreviations, the flogos. Surely he filled in the gaps before he gave it to you."

"Yes and no," she replied. "Over the years we developed a system whereby I would recycle passages from the previous novels, changing a word here and there to match the context. As I'm sure you know, mass market murder mysteries are not exactly Tolstoy. Once you have a character and a formula, the only thing that really changes from novel to novel is the plot. It got to the point where I knew precisely which passage in which novel to go to to get what I needed. I could get everything from the first three novels."

"But all those flogos," I said, still incredulous. "It was left to you to replace them?"

"Trust me, it was much easier than it sounds. All I did was steal from what Walter had already written. The only time I had to draw on my own knowledge was with the descriptions of women. Walter was hopeless on that score. He didn't know a cloche from a broach. He came to this realization while he was writing *Guttersnipe*. He would rack his brain for hours trying to come up with the right terms to make a woman come to life on the page. The results were awful. They were nothing but pin-up girls. Finally I asked him to let me have a shot at one of his dames. He immediately saw the difference. After that he always left a blank spot on the page when he introduced a female character. That was the beginning of our collaboration. With each successive novel he left more and more for me to fill in. That left him free to devote his time and energy to the plots."

He didn't need much time for that, I felt like saying, but I held my tongue, fascinated by all that she was telling me. I was still trying to decide how old she was. During our first interview I would have sworn she was in her mid- to late-fifties. Now, under the warm glow of the chandelier, she could have passed for mid-forties, not too much older than myself.

"Tell me something about yourself," she said after taking a few sips of her wine.

"Not much to tell."

"Where are you from? Who are your parents? Where did you grow up? How did you end up becoming a private detective? Ironically enough, you're the first real detective I've ever met."

I took a sip of wine, reviewed my life history, and settled on the abbreviated version: "I was born here. Lived here my entire life. My parents are Gerald and Stella King, divorced. My mother has emphysema, and I haven't seen my father in five years. I became a private detective after getting fired from every other job I've ever had. That's the real Eddie King."

"Modesty does not become you," she said amiably.

At that moment I suddenly came over very tired. All that goosefat and cowslip wine was tranquilizing my brain, putting me in a soporific stupor. I pushed my chair back a little and set my soiled serviette on my plate.

"I should be going," I said. "I haven't eaten like that since childhood Thanksgivings."

"Won't you have some warm gingerbread?" she asked very sweetly.

"I really couldn't," I insisted. "I can hardly breathe, I'm so stuffed."

I stood up. "It was a wonderful meal. I'm afraid I've devoured half of your goose."

She stood up in turn. "You're in no condition to drive after all that wine."

"I regularly drive under the influence of much stronger spirits."

"Yes, I suppose you do," she said with what if I wasn't mistaken was a gleam of admiration in her eyes. She then looked down at her plate with a forlorn expression. "Well, if you must."

She came around the table and gently set her hand on my forearm. I was touched by the gesture.

"Before you go, Eddie," she said, "could I prevail upon you to do me a small favor? I hate to ask you, but . . ." She paused.

"Yes?"

"It's my feet," she said. "I've got a touch of rheumatism. Not at all bad, but on these chilly nights they can really ache."

"What would you like me to do?"

"There's some cream in the upstairs bathroom."

Surveying the remains of our repast, I appreciated anew the truism that nothing in life is free.

The bathroom, like the rest of the house, was not of this century. The tub was an old enameled cast iron thing with claw and ball feet, boxed in at the front with a matching hood a good eight feet tall. The shower rose was big enough to douse a small family. It made the old iron cistern mounted high above the crapper look positively modern. I couldn't resist relieving my bladder, if only for the chance to tug on the udder-shaped ivory pull, an indulgence I regretted when the pipes launched into a familiar groan. In the drawer of an antique shaving stand, along with a couple of straight razors and a well-worn strop, was the tube of Molten Snow.

Back downstairs, having relocated to the living room, Mrs. Morris was reclining on her customary chair, her bare, blue-veined feet propped on the ottoman in front of her. I handed her the cream.

"That's very kind of you," she said. "If you could just rub a little of it into them I would be most grateful."

I couldn't think of a nice way to decline.

"How should I . . . ?"

"Whatever suits you."

"How about . . . ," I gestured towards the ottoman. There was a certain grace and agility in the way she lifted her feet and drew them back to accommodate me, shins and knees together, feet extended, that spoke of an athletic youth. I kneeled on the floor before the ottoman.

Taking the tube back from her, I squeezed a generous dollop of the dense white cream onto my fingers and, starting with her left foot, began rubbing it in. Her feet were long, narrow and bony. It felt strange having them in my hands. I was surprised by the shapeliness of her ankles, which had I not known approximately how old the rest of her was I would have sworn weren't a day over thirty. As I worked the cream into both feet, which were cold at the outset but soon warmed with my rubbing, Mrs. Morris sighed with relief and thanked me. A great serenity came over me as I sat there working the cream into her feet, a gentle radiance in my brain, the reward for a small charitable act. It settled into my temples and stayed there glowing softly as I took the liberty, confident that she wouldn't protest, of massaging the cream into her soft soles. The pockets of tension here and there soon succumbed to the ministrations of my thumbs, and the lengthening of her breaths suggested that the effect was not confined to her feet.

"You're very kind, Eddie."

"Does this stuff really work?" I had to ask.

"Oh yes. It does me a world of good."

"I have a little foot trouble myself."

"Do you?" Her head raised in genuine concern. "You're welcome to take that tube. I have plenty."

"Thanks. I'm all right."

"I insist." She pulled her feet off of the ottoman and sat up. "Take your shoes and socks off. I'm going to rub a little into your feet."

"I'm fine, thanks."

"Don't be contrary."

"Really, I'm fine."

"I'm not asking you," she said sternly. "Now take your shoes and socks off."

Seeing no alternative, I obeyed.

"You'll feel like a new man after this," she said, squeezing some of the cream into her hands and getting to work on my right foot, which was presently propped on the ottoman, though I remained standing. It was cold at first, the strange chilly bite of camphor and eucalyptus oil. As she rubbed the cream into my foot, the sensation gradually shifted to one of stinging heat, as when the refrigerated chile pepper you've blithely bitten into turns out to be much hotter than you anticipated. Why I wasn't feeling it on my hands was a mystery to me.

"You live downtown, don't you?" she asked after a while.

"Yes, the Regal Arms, as you would know from the novels."

"I wouldn't have made that assumption," she said. "I suppose you enjoy living in the thick of it."

"It has its moments."

She rubbed my foot for a while in silence. It really did feel nice. Much nicer than Dr. Auerbach's clinical hands.

"Give me your other foot," she said. I switched feet, and she went to work on the left.

"How much do you pay, if you don't mind my asking?"

I told her. She gasped at the number.

"For a studio apartment? That's highway robbery."

I hadn't mentioned that I lived in a studio apartment.

"It's standard for the location."

"It's outrageous," she said. "I can't believe you pay it."

"Not much choice."

Her proposition, which I sensed coming before it arrived, was this: I could move in with her, live rent-free in exchange for helping her out now and then with things she couldn't manage herself. Mostly, she said, it would give her some peace of mind having a man about the place, particularly a man of my qualifications. That, to her, was worth more than I could know. "You like my cooking. I like your company," she said. "It seems we might be able to help each other." I pretended to give it some thought, then replied:

"As tempting as it is, I'm afraid that wouldn't work for me. My work is in the city."

"Everyone on this street works in the city," she said. "They seem to manage."

"Mine isn't a normal job. I keep all kinds of crazy hours."

"I wouldn't be any bother to you. You could come and go as you pleased. Think of the money you could save."

"Saving money has never been my ambition."

"Don't you want anything of your own?"

"Like what?"

"A house. A family. A nest egg for your old age."

I smiled.

I thanked her again for her hospitality, put on my shoes, and wished her a goodnight at the door. Crossing the yard, it felt like I was walking on air.

15

THERE IS NO stillness like Sunday morning in the heart of the city. The workers gone, the streets empty, the buildings locked up. Even the pigeons seem to have deserted the ledges. It's always on a Sunday that I succumb to the dream of a family.

I lingered in bed long after waking up, watching as a disinterested bystander might the passing traffic of my mind, which was fairly dense that morning, a couple of bad pile-ups at vital intersections. I considered my options. Rather I closed my eyes again, hoping to drift back to sleep. Somewhere in the building a baby was crying. It must have been several floors down, or up, for it was as faint as the bleat of a goat in a distant valley.

Half an hour later I was still in bed, the sun shining in my face. Get up, I told myself. Rise and meet the day with alacrity. It's a nice day. You should get out there and enjoy it. Take a drive up the coast. The windows open, sea breeze whipping through your left sleeve. Clear the mind. Stop in some little seaside town for a bite to eat, flirt with the waitress. Drive on. Stop for gas. Drive some more. Turn around and drive back. It was all so vivid that there seemed no point in going through with it.

I considered other options. A museum? Too quiet. The zoo? Too many kids. The beach? Too hot. Mental and spiritual paralysis stole over me as one after another I entertained and rejected every species of diversion that flitted through my mind.

A movie!

What was playing? I would have to go out and get a paper. At last, having a concrete objective, however inconsequential, the paralysis lifted and hope returned that I would find a pleasant way to spend the day.

I got up and took a shower. I chose my tan suit, on the grounds that, tonally speaking, it was the lightest of the three. Another point in its favor was the relative infrequency with which I wore it, which by some quirk of perception rendered it thinner, less impenetrable than the others. The darkness, the density of the navy blue and the black suit, the warp and weft of whose fibers were steeped in all my experiences of man's inhumanity to man, encased me in a kind of armor. In my dark suits, I knew I could take anything the nasty world dished out to me with no more than a wisecrack to buffer the pain. It was for that very reason that I rarely wore the tan suit on the job. Despite its superior fit, it had proven incompatible with the demands of my profession. I didn't feel quite myself in it, which was precisely what this odd morning called for.

I put on the slacks and a freshly laundered shirt. It was amazing how light I felt in it, almost buoyant. I didn't bother putting on the jacket to go down for the paper.

Sundays were Arturo's day off. As much as I liked Arturo, there was a certain pleasure in being truly alone in an elevator, free to pick your nose or fart or whistle without the slightest concern of raising an eyebrow or a flattering comment from the operator.

On the way down, the elevator stopped on the second floor. The door opened to reveal an Irish setter sitting alertly before it. The dog and I exchanged looks. "Hello there," I said. The dog swiveled its head left and peered expectantly down the hall. I pressed the hold button and leaned out. No one there. "Coming?" I asked. The inner ridges of the dog's brows rose eloquently. I released the button. "Suit yourself."

As I opened the door of the building and stepped out onto the silent, empty street, a fresh wave of anxiety rolled through me. It was going to be another miserable, lonely Sunday, I knew it, like all the Sundays before and all the Sundays to come. Already the heat was rising from the blindingly bright sidewalk. Up and down the block the parking meters stood like cops at the funeral of a fallen comrade. Absent all the traffic and parked cars the street seemed as wide and desolate as an abandoned airfield.

I made my way down the block to the newsstand at the corner. Halfway there I could see that it was closed, but I carried on nonetheless, obliged to allow my disappointment the satisfaction of a close-up. Nothing on the bolted shutters indicated why Witold wasn't there today. He was always there, even on Christmas day. I stood for a moment, thinking about where else I might get the paper, but the feeling of the sun on my cheeks and hands suddenly made sitting in some dark, musty movie theater seem neurotic. I returned to the apartment, having if nothing else on this fruitless errand eliminated one of the possibilities.

Back inside, I reconsidered the beach. The advantage there was the women, sometimes gorgeous ones, as well as the philosophical profundities one is given to in the presence of the sea. The disadvantages were the sand, the heat, the difficulty of getting comfortable in anything but a fully supine position, which I refuse to assume in public. I considered other options. I made a cup of coffee and sat drinking it at the kitchenette table, reading and rereading every scrap of text on the label of the empty ketchup bottle. Half an hour later I made an executive decision.

It was roasting inside the car. I rolled down the windows and gave it a few minutes to air before getting in. I decided to take the longer route and drive through the park. The plan had been to enter at Talbot Avenue, but as I neared the junction I was reminded by all the barriers there that they closed it off to traffic every Sunday for the cyclists and skaters and family strollers, so I carried on down the south side of the park and turned in at 19th.

Out in the fields, families and friends and lovers were kicking and throwing balls, playing frisbee, sitting on blankets. Dogs were sprinting joyfully. Smoke was rising from portable barbecues. It was a heavenly scene, everything drenched in Sunday sunshine, the cleanest, brightest sunshine there is. It made me miserable. The cars were parked bumper to bumper down both sides of the road, men and women and children walking along beside them. Progress was slow, as every other car was cruising for somewhere to park. I began to lose my patience. I had envisioned coasting unimpeded all the way through the park to the beach, the cool breeze rushing around me. Instead I was crawling at a snail's pace, stopping and starting every fifteen feet, the sun cooking me through the windshield. Predictably, I began to yearn for the speed and solitude of the coast road.

The traffic gradually thinned as I got beyond the family fields and into the dense eucalyptus and cypress groves at the western end of the park. Passing the duck pond, I thought of Mrs. Fletcher. I saw her beautiful backside strutting up Pierce Street. I heard her beautiful voice across the wall. I took my foot off the pedal and glided down the grade deeper into the dappled chill of the eucalypti, emerging at last to the resplendent sunshine of the coast road, the beach, the blue-gray ocean.

The beach was packed. Lingering at the stop sign, I entertained the possibility one last time of taking a right and carrying on up the coast and out of the city, far from the madding crowds. An impatient honk behind me settled the issue. I crossed the road and started looking for parking. The first lot yielded nothing. I crossed into the second and continued my search.

Stuck in a line of cars, I found myself studying a surfer in a wet suit who was strapping his board to the roof of his Roadmaster. Something about his feet caught my eye. The fact that they were bare on the hot asphalt may have had something to do with it, but not everything. No, it was their perfection that captivated me. They were the color of stained oak, the tendons as taut as telephone wires, honed from years of balancing the rest of him against the might of the waves, the coppery brown on top giving way to golden sandstone at the sides, all the more riveting against the black of his wet suit, which stopped just above his ankles. His feet spoke of an unshakeable belief in the sovereignty of the sea.

The line advanced. I drifted past him like a shark cruising for prey. Finally after fifteen minutes of driving in rectangles around the lot someone began to back out a few cars ahead of me, and I closed in for the kill.

I parked and sat there for a while, relishing the end of the ordeal. With the engine off, I could hear the roar of the ocean behind the squeals of children.

I grabbed one of the Conway novels, several of which were still in the glove box, got out and hiked up the scrubby embankment to behold the immense tapestry of pinkish white flesh, dashes of bold-colored beach towels, striped umbrellas, sand, sand, sand, stretching in a shallow curve for miles to the north and south, sliced off by the scimitar of the Pacific. I stood there for a moment seeking out an unoccupied and sufficiently spacious patch of sand.

I walked down to my chosen spot, careful with my steps to avoid getting sand in my shoes, and plopped myself down. If not for the cool breeze coming off the water, it would have been too hot to sit there fully clothed. I sat upright, my hands behind me in the hot sand, legs outstretched in front, watching the people. Fat, pale men in disgusting shorts, with hairy backs, parading their offensive bulk for all to see. Big, lumpy women with massive, saggy udders, saddlebag thighs, in bikinis. Frenetic kids running every which way. A man in a white uniform came along selling pink cotton candy, barking his mantra as he trudged through the sand. Of course there were the requisite gorgeous people, men and women alike. In the end, they weren't as interesting to watch as the less aesthetically pleasing ones.

I did watch a splendid-looking guy and gal throwing a frisbee for a while. At one point, caught by a sudden updraft, the frisbee soared straight up. Up and up it went, to an amazing height, as the man and woman craned their necks to follow its trajectory. All forward momentum ceased as caught by the opposing air current it reversed course and accelerated back the way it had come, quickly overtaking the man's position and flying ever faster the wrong way down the beach and curving out over the water. The man turned and started running after it. The frisbee picked up speed as it banked down. Finally, fifty yards down the beach, it splashed into the shallows and was soon tumbled by a breaking wave. The man was sprinting now, determined to save it. The frisbee was sucked under for a few seconds then appeared scooting along the grit of the backwash before being pummeled anew.

Weary of bodies I stared at the breaking waves for so long that it seemed they were flowing backwards, that the source of their energy was the land, not the ocean, that they had traveled unimpeded across the continent only to break against the solid shelf of the sea. I studied the sand around me. The breeze was making off with the uppermost granules, while other grains were tumbling into craters and declivities, sliding down to come to rest sheltered from the wind. I closed my eyes and listened for a long time to the rhythmic susurrations of the surf, the wind, the squeals of children, barking dogs. I entertained the idea of taking off my shoes and going down and stepping into the water, but the thought of having to deal with wet, caked sand on my feet wasn't appealing.

My shoulders were starting to ache. In the end I gave in to it. I took off my jacket and spread it out behind me and scooted down enough to allow my head to rest on it. I took my hat off and set it over my face. The breeze kept threatening to make off with it. The smell of my head was strong in it, a fine, musky scent that helped send me off.

According to my watch I was only asleep for fifteen minutes, but when I lifted my hat from my face and looked around, everything had changed. The people who had been around me were no longer there. None of them were the same people who had been there before I drifted off. The sun had shifted position, however slightly, the shadows a few inches longer.

I sat up and pulled *Murder at the Crossroads* out of my back pocket and reread it for a while. Dotty Dupree had hired me to find her daughter Galatea (a.k.a. Galley). Galley was married to a small-time mobster named Joe Balantine, who, as it turned out, was also missing. A big-time mobster named Franky Gold subsequently offered me five grand to find Balantine. The investigation quickly acquired a body count. I kept bouncing from Galley to Gold and back again trying to tie together details that seemed as random as they were violent. The novel pretty much got all that right. The problem was Dotty. Here is how she is described in the book:

> She was tall. Thick blonde hair fell to her
> shoulders in metallic waves. Her eyes were a
> vivid blue, and when she turned their full force
> on King, it was like a physical impact. Her body
> was ripe, lush. Swelling breasts showed over the
> top of her gown. Her legs were long, sensuously
> shaped. Full rounded thighs swelled into high-
> set hips, converged into a narrow waist.

The real Dotty Dupree wasn't much over five feet tall, her jet black hair coiled in chin-length ringlets. She wore velvet cut-away jackets (green, burgundy, or buff), matching knee pants, and a ridiculous ruffled collar. She was addicted to lemon cough drops, always one clicking against her teeth, lolling around her tongue. She made no effort to conceal her tyrannical nature, ordering her employees about as if she owned them. Ironically, the almost comical disparity between her conception of herself and the dull little vessel she carried it around in stirred a strange lust in me, which thankfully I managed to keep at bay.

In that first angry reading of the novel, it had entirely escaped my notice how Dotty Dupree had been transformed from Little Lord Fauntleroy into a sparsely garmented *Playboy* centerfold. Upon reflection, I recalled similar transmogrifications in the other novels. While the male characters, apart from Eddie King himself, usually bore a passing resemblance to their real-life counterparts, the women were almost always complete fabrications. All the important ones were blonde-haired, blue-eyed bombshells.

If, as Mrs. Morris had contended, they actually were her own creations, why did all the women read like an adolescent boy's wet dream? Contrary to her claims, they were just as cliché as everything else in the books.

These were my thoughts when a ball landed near me, followed soon thereafter by a boy of six or seven in red swimming trunks. He picked up his ball and stood looking at me like I was something washed up by the waves.

"Aren't you hot?" he asked impertinently.

"No, I'm very comfortable."

"You look hot in that suit."

"It keeps the sun off me."

He frowned. Then smiled.

"Guess how many eggs I found."

I made a stab in the dark: "Six."

"How'd you know?"

"Lucky guess."

"Bobby McGruder found twelve."

"Is that right?"

It finally sank in when he told me about Bobby McGruder's basket full of chocolates. I looked out again at the multitudes, seeing them now through the gauzy filter of Easter.

"Nick!" a woman yelled, rightly concerned that her boy was talking to a shifty-looking stranger. He turned towards the voice. "Come here!" the woman hollered. Nick ran off, kicking sand over my shoes.

Suddenly I felt a soft jab of hunger. Gradually it spread, becoming indistinguishable from the ache of loneliness that I was beginning to believe was the non-negotiable price of freedom.

16

AS I WAS pulling out of the parking lot, an old familiar guilt emanating from beyond the hills to the east tugged at the steering wheel. No matter the arguments I lobbed against it, it refused to succumb to reason.

I took Seaview Drive through the western suburbs, got on 480-East at Lake Park, and stayed on it across the vast cubist canvas of the metropolis.

Twelve miles from Merino, in the verdant apron of the Espolon Hills, the freeway narrowed to two lanes. At the approach to the Calaveras Tunnel, a sign advised me to turn on my headlights. The air boomed, my wheels roared around me as I entered the muggy darkness of that bullet hole through the earth. Far ahead, a pair of tail-lights hovered beneath a disc of sunlight the size of a quarter. Fluorescent streaks shot past with hypnotic regularity. The farther I drove into the tunnel, the more distant seemed the light at the end of it, diminishing in inverse proportion to my progress towards it, the quarter, now a nickel, now a dime, receding still farther into the paradoxical distance. For a moment I had the nauseating sensation that I was driving in reverse. Only when the sunlight began to spill again onto the tunnel walls did time and space reunite with a sonic boom.

The car slammed into a wall of light and heat. Hot wind singed my nostrils as the road snaked through a herd of parched blonde hills. Soon the business parks appeared, clusters of human aquariums ringed with nameless streets and parking lots and saplings designed never to reach maturity. Car dealerships stretched for miles along the access roads either side of the freeway, a thousand sparkling suns rolling over rivers of flawless windshields. Discount outlets, big-box retailers, warehouse clubs, and super stores as vast as military bases battled it out in fonts of Jurassic proportions. The ocean, the city, my apartment, may as well have been on the other side of the world. I had passed through a rabbit hole into middle America.

The offramp at East Pleasant Valley Road was half a mile of nothingness culminating in a congregation of gas stations cum mini-markets cum car washes servicing a division of armor-plated pickups and Sport Utility Vehicles. After the roar of the road, the silence at that soulless traffic light was absolute.

On the corner of East Pleasant Valley and César Chávez, the steep red A-frame of Der Wienerschnitzel caught my eye, and without thinking twice I pulled in line behind a black Camaro. There were about four cars ahead of me leading into the drive-thru that cut through the middle of the building. The waitress, a short Mexican girl about nineteen years old, in her uniform of red shorts, yellow shirt and company cap, was standing at the window of the car in front of the Camaro. Her legs were tanned and athletic. I pulled out my wallet and checked my cash.

The line advanced. The waitress served the Camaro. Then it was my turn.

"*Willkommen zum Wienerschnitze*l," she said. "*Darf ich Ihre Bestellung aufnehmen?*"

"Excuse me?"

"Welcome to Der Wienerschnitzel, may I take your order?"

"Was that German?"

"Yes."

"They teach you that here?"

"No. I'm in my second year at City College."

"Studying German?"

"Actually my major's Mass Com, but I'm getting a minor in German."

I nodded, impressed.

"So what can I get you?"

"Give me a chili cheese dog and a coffee."

"We have a special today," she said. "Order any two classic dogs and you get a free medium soft drink of your choice."

I gave it some thought.

"Which are the classic dogs?" I asked, just to humor her.

"The mustard dog, the kraut dog, and the flogo dog."

I turned and looked at her face.

"Could you repeat that?"

"The mustard dog, the kraut—"

"No, the last one."

"The relish dog?"

"That's not what you said. You said the flogo dog."

"The *what* dog?"

"The flogo dog. That's what you said."

"There's no such thing as a flogo dog."

"Then why did you say it?"

"I didn't," she insisted. "I said relish dog."

"You distinctly said flogo. Relish sounds nothing like flogo. Maybe you lapsed into German."

"Would you like to speak to my manager?" she said, switching into customer-complaint mode.

"No. I would just like you to admit you said what you said."

She looked towards the building, as if for guidance. She turned back to me.

"Do you want the special or not?"

"No," I said, agitated. "Just give me what I ordered."

She wrote it down and without further comment walked on to the car behind me. I adjusted the mirror to get an angle on her. I watched her lips as she went through her spiel. I didn't see anything resembling "flogo," not that I have any special capacity as a lip reader. When she was done with that car, there being no others behind it, she returned to the building and went in through a door that was all but invisible until she opened it, no doubt to tell her co-workers to watch out for the guy in the hat.

The Camaro pulled forward. A few minutes later I was in the shade of the drive-thru, abreast of the service window, through which I could see the teenagers working away. A pimply white girl handed me my bag and told me the total.

"Listen," I said. "Do you guys have something called a flogo dog?"

"Excuse me?"

"A flogo dog."

"No, sir. Only what's on the menu."

"Anything that sounds like flogo?"

"What?"

"Anything that sounds like the word flogo."

"I didn't even know flogo was a word."

"It's not. Not an English one, at any rate."

She looked at me. "I can give you a take-home menu if you want."

I shrugged. She stepped over to a shelf and returned to the window with a sheet of paper, which she handed to me. I gave her the buck and she gave me my change.

I set the bag beside me on the seat and carried on through the building and back onto the street. Memory Lane, Pontoon Way, Kingfisher Street behind me, I came at last to Lemon Lane.

It was one of the older neighborhoods of Merino. Decay was its only charm. Faux Spanish villas with dead century plants in their front yards neighbored side-gabled bungalows with American flags planted in their porch pillars. Pickup trucks, pre-millennial sedans, the odd motorboat or two, their sunbleached canvas covers stiff with dust, sat roasting in oil-stained driveways.

Her house was some underpaid architect's idea of revenge on the firm: Tudor Revival-meets-Doublewide Trailer. Expanses of white stucco crisscrossed with fake, reddish brown half-timbering, false shutters and mock masonry veneers. As if that weren't bad enough, the base of the house was trimmed with mottled pink and white brick which looked like slabs of raw hamburger. And she had paid a hundred grand.

I pulled up to the curb and cut the engine. There I sat, thinking about the peculiar exchange at Der Wienerschnitzel. It put me off my hot dog. I grabbed the menu and combed it futilely for flogos. I removed the lid of the coffee and blew across it. I took a sip and stared out the window at the withered patchwork of crab grass and mowed-down dandelions, the faded Neighborhood Watch sign all but welcoming would-be burglars. High above the slanted roof—the television aerial filled me with strange dread—towered the back neighbor's date palm, the final touch in this smorgasbord of incongruity. It was hard to believe she had been here nearly twenty years. For me it would always be the new house.

I got out and made my way to the front door. The TV was on, its exuberance electrifying every molecule in the vicinity. I pressed the bell, the single meaty clunk of which sent Daisy into paroxysms of yipping. I heard her grunt as she labored out of her chair. Then came a bout of wheezy hacking. On cue the first wave of irritation surged through me.

She opened the door.

"I thought it might be you."

We hugged, her stringy, loose-skinned arms clutching me hard. "Happy Easter, Mom." Under her sleeveless muumuu she felt as frail as a baby bird. It was always a shock to see how much she had shrunk. My memory only seemed to retain full-length studio portraits of her. Her hair was uncombed, patches of dry white scalp showing between her natural gray and the store-bought black.

"Is that a new suit?" she asked.

"No."

Daisy, in defiance of her frenetically wagging tail, strafed me with suspicious snarls and yips. At the sight of my shoe lifting from the porch she raced back into the living room and did a few mad laps.

Mom shuffled back to her chair and sank into it like a scuba diver dropping into the sea. I took off my hat and jacket and settled in at her end of the couch. On the lamp table between us rested an assortment of items, each of which tugged my emotions in different directions. Her olive-green plastic inhaler. A pack of More Menthols and a yellow disposable lighter beside a full glass ashtray. Wadded-up tissues. A well-scuffed emery board. A paperback mystery with a pizza coupon sticking out of it. A blue-green tumbler containing an inch of cola beside a can of Diet RC. The TV remote.

She didn't turn it off. I didn't ask her to, not sure myself if I could take her without a chaser. On the screen a smiling blonde woman was extolling the virtues of a remarkable stain remover.

"Did you see that mess on Pleasant Valley?" she asked.

"What mess?"

"Where they've dug it all up. It's been that way for weeks. Rush hour, forget it. You're better off going clear down to Woolsey."

My eyes came to rest on my high school debating trophy, front and center on the mantle. For her it was a reminder of what might have been. With my voice and my good looks, she had had hopes. I could have been a lawyer, or an actor.

"Did you have something to eat?" Before I could answer she said, "You should've told me you were coming. I would've made you something."

She picked up her pack of cigarettes and shook one out and put it to her lips and lit up.

"Mom," I groaned.

"Don't start," she mumbled through the cigarette, which jerked up and down to the articulations of her lips.

"You can't be sitting there puffing away on Pirbuteral in one breath and a menthol cigarette in the other."

"What difference does it make?"

"It's your funeral."

"Damn right."

"Well, I hope you've saved up for it, because I'm sure as hell not shelling out for it."

The smiling blonde, whose name we soon learned was Leslie, was presently discoursing with a grinning imbecile with slicked-back hair and a mouth wide enough to park a frying pan in. Craig was his name.

"Nothing good on TV anymore," Mom complained. "All that reality shit. I hardly ever watch it anyway. The only thing good is Bob Kingsley. He had that Chinese chef on the other day, I forget his name—Ho something. You wouldn't believe some of the stuff that guy has lived through. Fourteen kids. He showed pictures of them. So sweet. His wife is an accountant, you know. CPA. Bob asked him why he moved around so much, and the Chinese guy said it was the school districts. Fourteen kids. Can you imagine? No sooner are they in a good school than the neighborhood goes to pot and they have to move on. The Chinese are big on education. That science fair they had, the top ten students, every one of them was Chinese. A couple of Indians, I think. Oh, I do like that Indian guy on *Life as Usual*."

She rambled on, but Craig had captured my attention with his demonstrations. We were treated to several clips from the "amazing" instructional video that came with the package when you ordered all three Atlas 9 products.

Mom shook the inhaler and squeezed two puffs into her mouth and sat concentrating on her held breath. She exhaled and set the inhaler back on the table.

She resumed smoking her cigarette. With every passing second the fibers of my nerves seemed to be unraveling from their neuronal twine. After a few puffs, she set the cigarette in a lip of the ashtray. From the imperceptibly advancing ember, a fluid stream of smoke rose in a vertical line. Two feet up it rippled into a run of fanned crimps before dispersing in the gusts of air-conditioning.

"I tried calling you the other day," she said.

"What for?"

"You got something in the mail."

"What was it?"

"A credit card offer or something."

"I've told you a million times, just throw that crap away. I don't know how they even got this address."

"The banks sell them."

"I never gave this address to any bank."

"Once it's out there, forget it. It goes viral."

Now it was time to apply the Atlas 9 Strong, the world's strongest oxygen-based stain remover.

"This country's gone to hell." She was off again. "All anyone cares about is getting rich. The government. They're all corrupt, the whole lot of them. They should all be taken out and shot. All the money they're taking from us. It's robbing the poor to feed the rich. Sooner or later they're going to say enough is enough, and that'll be the end of the whole damn thing. I'll be dead by then, thank God. I'd hate to see what's coming down the pike. I'll tell you what's coming. The Chinese. They're just waiting for their moment. You think when we start going down they're just going to sit there and watch? Hell no. Your father may be a bastard, but he's right about that. Biggest army in the world. When they decide to take over there won't be any stopping them. They'll swarm in and take over everything, round us up and put us to work in their factories. They won't touch the Mexicans. Too lazy. Oh, it's a disgrace the way these Mexicans treat their dogs, Eddie. You drive around town and it's nothing but stray dogs everywhere you look. They just let them run wild, let them starve. They don't give a damn. It makes me sick the way they treat their animals. This used to be a nice place to live. All down the block it's Mexicans now. Where the Parkers used to live, that's a Mexican family. Alice Schumacher's house, that's Mexican. Rich and Barbara moved to Castillo to get away from them. Mexicans moved in. I don't have anything against them, they just need to stay in their own part of town. They're driving down the property values. Mary Jo told me hers dropped sixteen thousand since the Mexicans started moving in. I'm afraid to get mine reappraised. I don't want to know. Forget it. They drive down the property so their cousins can move in next door."

It was time to spray on the Magic, with its pleasant citrus odor. Craig did so, and while he waited we were treated to another real life story, this one about dog urine on the upholstery of a guy named Ted's Corvette.

"You won't catch me giving my credit card number out to anyone anymore. I was watching *You Could Be Next* the other night, on that outfit the Quakers. Have you heard of them? They're these scam artists. They get your credit card number and address, and instead of stealing from you they order a bunch of crap in your name, have it sent to you, as if you ordered it yourself. They call it quaking. You got quaked. So all this shit you didn't even order starts landing on your doorstep. You're stuck having to deal with it, calling the companies, paying for the return shipping, calling the bank. On and on. One lady had stuff coming to her every day for a month: appliances, flowers, books, CDs, clothes. They even sent her an antique canopy bed. You name it. It about drove her batty trying to get to the bottom of it. Another lady they hit stopped trying to fight it and just ended up keeping it all. She said the time and money it would have cost her sorting it all out was worth more to her than the cost of the stuff. No way in hell you'll get me giving my credit card out on the internet."

"You don't even have a computer," I pointed out.

"And I don't want one either. It's nothing but porn on there anyway. I've seen it. They had a class at the center, trying to convince us how great the internet is. I asked them to look up Vitamin-B for me and up pops some naked woman with tits out to here . . ."

The ash of her cigarette, still burning on the edge of the ashtray, was nearing the end of its battle with gravity, which in my experience, at sea-level, with cigarettes thicker than hers, is about two and half inches in length when unmolested by air drafts, earthquakes, or sudden fluctuations in barometric pressure.

There's a newsreel of the demolition of the bell tower of a church that had the misfortune of ending up stranded in the dead zone between East and West Berlin when the wall was built. As sad West Berliners look on from rooftops, the GDR's pyrotechnicians detonate the charges, and the noble old steeple timbers over under the weight of history and collapses in a cloud of dust. Something of the poignancy of that silent demolition touched me as at last Mom's cigarette fractured at the fulcrum, and that long, slender column of ash collapsed into the wreckage of butts littering her ashtray.

"I need something to eat," I said. "I'm going faint."

"What do you want?"

"Anything." I got up. She got up with me. Daisy got up with her.

"I've got a nice canned ham. Do you want a ham sandwich?"

"Sure."

"What do you want on it?"

"Everything."

"Do you want mayonnaise and mustard?"

"Everything."

"Pickles?"

"Everything."

"Sweet or sour?"

"Just make it the way you like it," I said, making my way to the back door.

"It's your sandwich, not mine."

It was just as depressing outside. The right half of the yard was covered with fake red lava rocks, the black plastic underliner all chewed up at the edges, tough green weeds poking through here and there, others all shriveled up and brown. Briquettes of sunbaked dogshit everywhere. The rest of the yard bore witness to her failed vegetable garden. A few furrowed rows of dry dirt, in one of which lay a tennis ball bleached of all color, and some wild pink hollyhocks. Hundreds of dried and cracked seed cones littered the ground where the neighbor's juniper tree branched across the north wall.

I stood in the shade of the porch with all her artsy-crafty windchimes, half of them missing the chimes or hopelessly tangled in their own lines. A bee was flying in and out of the end of a tube of bamboo. Through the kitchen window came the sounds of her hacking as she worked on my sandwich. Daisy emerged from the rubber flap in the door. She went out and sniffed around her domain, raised her leg and peed against the dead rose bush near the south wall. From somewhere on the breezeless air came the scent of barbecued lamb. The date palm rustled softly.

"Your sandwich is ready, Eddie! Do you want it out there?"

"Yes."

"Do you want something to drink?"

"No."

"I've got iced tea, ginger ale, cranberry juice . . . water."

I found a rigid dishcloth and wiped as much of the dust and rust as I could from one of the old blue metal chairs, the only furniture she had retained from the old house. She came out with the sandwich and hovered around disturbing my peace. She had made it with a thick slab of processed cheese, dill pickles, a piece of wilted iceberg lettuce, and some kind of sweet sandwich spread. I was too hungry to dwell on the death of civilization that it bore testament to.

She shuffled out and picked the dead leaves from the rosebush and tossed them to the ground. Daisy sniffed them and moved on to better things. Mom came back and pulled up a chair and sat down in it next to me.

"How are your feet?" she asked, perhaps realizing in the process of making my sandwich that she had done nothing but rant since I had walked through the door.

"Fine," I said and took a bite. It was surprisingly good. "Someone wrote some novels about me," I casually mentioned.

"What?"

I pulled *Murder at the Crossroads* out of my pocket and held it towards her face so she could get a good look at the "Eddie King" on the cover. She looked confused.

"They're detective novels," I said. "I'm the main character. They're based on my real cases."

"Oh," she said. "That's nice."

I sat there eating my sandwich. She scratched her dry knees.

A few minutes later I said: "You remember that Mexican maid we had for a while?"

"Mexican maid?"

"Yes, a kind of short, plump woman with curly hair."

"We never had any Mexican maid."

"I'm sure we did. I have a distinct memory of her vacuuming with that old green box-vacuum, the one with my NFL stickers on it. I have another memory of me and her kid working on a jigsaw puzzle together."

"You must be remembering someone else's house. Do you think your father would have ever let me hire a maid, let alone a Mexican one?"

"I don't know."

"You're probably thinking of the Raffertys or something. They had a Mexican woman."

"No, that was Nieves. She was nothing like this woman. Maybe she only came a few times. Maybe she was a babysitter who did some cleaning while she was there."

The doorbell clunked.

"Do you want me to get it?" I asked.

"If you want. It's probably Mary Jo. She's supposed to be bringing me some pecans."

I got up and went to the door. It was a woman in her sixties with a brown-tinted perm.

"Oh, hi there." She clearly wasn't expecting a man. "Is Stella in?"

"Yeah. Around back. Come in."

"That's all right. I was just bringing around these pecans for her." She smiled at me. "You must be Eddie."

"Yes.

She handed me the bag.

"Happy Easter," she said.

"Happy Easter," I replied.

She told me to tell Mom that they had missed her at church. I assured her I would. I set the bag on the counter in the kitchen and stood at the window looking at Mom sitting there, perhaps regretting our inability to communicate, most likely thinking of nothing at all.

I stuck it out until five then told her I had to get going. She wanted me to stay for dinner. That would have killed me. I told her I had some unfinished business to attend to.

"On Easter Sunday?"

I kissed her forehead at the door and walked out to the car. I got in and pressed the ignition button and nothing happened. A glance at the dash confirmed my suspicion.

I walked down to the first house with a pickup parked in front of it and knocked on the door. A hirsute man answered, probably thinking that I was either a Jehovah's Witness or a Mormon. His belly was testing the tensile strength of a Miami Dolphins T-shirt. I thought I heard a football game on the TV, but it wasn't football season. I explained that I had left my headlights on coming through the tunnel. That seemed to gratify him. He came out and drove his pickup down to Mom's and pulled up to about a foot from the front bumper and popped his hood, leaving the engine running. I followed him back on foot. He got out and walked over to my car, jumper cables in hand.

"Hell of a car," he said. "What year is it?"

"'42."

"I'll be damned. You don't see many of these old tanks around anymore." He gazed admiringly at the grille, the fenders, the zinc trim. He walked over to the driver's window and bent down to have a look inside.

"They sure as hell don't make 'em like they used to," he said after a good long look.

I opened the hood and propped the rod in place. He came back around to the front and took a look at the engine.

"Flathead V-8?" he asked.

"L-head straight-6."

He nodded.

"What kind of mileage you get?"

"If it was any lower I'd need a tow truck to drive it."

"I'd hate to see your gas bill."

"You're helping to pay it."

He gave me a puzzled look.

"It's deductible," I said. "Business expenses."

"Oh? What's your business?"

"Insurance," I said, the quickest way to end that line of questioning. He nodded.

He hooked up the cables, first to my battery then to his. "I wouldn't think it'd be easy finding anywhere to fill 'er up."

"A couple of stations in the barrios still sell leaded. I keep a few spare cans in the trunk for emergencies."

He nodded. "Go ahead and give her a shot."

I got in and pressed the ignition. It turned over sluggishly a few times then caught. I revved it for a while then let it idle. He unhooked the cables. I could tell he wanted to go for a spin in it. I thanked him and said I would see him around.

Before pulling out, I glanced towards the house. Mom was standing in the window with the curtain drawn, looking abandoned.

17

MONDAY MORNING'S MAIL was full of surprises. The first was a letter from Mrs. Fletcher, postmarked a week ago at the Spring Valley PO. It was a masterpiece of concision: "King, Ditch the coat and hat. Heidi Fletcher." I was starting to like her. Her husband was next in the queue: an envelope containing a Fletcher Enterprises check for $150 for my week of service to him. The check was not accompanied by a letter of apology. Finally, a letter from the Bureau of Security and Investigative Services notifying me that my detective's license had expired thirty days ago and was now delinquent. I had mailed in the renewal form months ago. Just to be sure, I searched through a stack of papers on the filing cabinet, and there it was.

I checked my messages. Three from Mom: the first checking to make sure I had made it home all right, the second to make sure I had got the first, the third a follow-up to the second. Also one from Gordon Fletcher, asking when I would be in my office. He wanted to have a word with me.

After a few minutes of quiet meditation, I took my right earlobe between my thumb and middle finger and massaged it in a circular motion. I read the notes I had taken on the Fletcher case then tore the pages from the pad and wadded them up and chucked them into the garbage can. On second thought I retrieved them and ripped them up and returned them to the can.

It was unusually quiet in the building. Normally by this time of morning a veritable flamenco of high heels is clattering away above and below, accompanied by ringing telephones, mysterious hammering sounds, the murmur of male voices. Easter Monday, I surmised as I picked up the piece of Silly Putty and looked again at the shoe, the trouser cuff, the dim suggestion of a ventilation grate. I took my magnifying glass from the middle desk drawer and studied the image more closely. Part of the nostalgia it exuded, apart from the smell and texture of the putty itself, may have been due to the fact that the shoe and the trouser cuff seemed to belong to the 1970s: a bulbous toe and platform heel, flaring cuff. The text read like bad modern poetry:

> time. They rely on several privat
> a vital link between the agency
> f which is Ruth Brenner. A sin
> "a difference in people's liv
> fact that she herself gre
> t. Jerome's, bu

I studied it for a while, trying to convince myself that there was a deeper meaning to it, then I set it back on the desk and got up and went to the window. The blinds were down, the blades tilted open. Beneath the uppermost layer of dust, a cake of dark grime had taken root. It took some scraping with my fingernail to get through to the aluminum. There the mold spores had created tiny starbursts of rust where they had eaten through the coating. I grabbed the drawstring and yanked the blinds all the way up, flooding the office with merciless sunlight. Dust motes sparkled slowly down for the next several minutes. The city sprawled away to the west, dissolving in a thick band of smog, cars pulsing in and out of shadow, jet contrails scarring the sky. At that very moment someone was being murdered. Someone was screwing someone else's spouse. Someone was committing robbery, if not with a gun then with the click of a mouse. People were beating, defaming, blackmailing one another. There was no shortage of work out there. All one had to do was seek it.

I stood at the window for a while then went over and had a look at the case wall, where the Hardeman case, one of the most convoluted I had ever worked, was still mapped out. Walter Morris called it *King at Arms*.

Dozens of scraps of paper, newspaper clippings, time sequences, etc. were still taped to the wall, the blue ink faded to green. Layers of old scotch tape. Grimy handprints where I had leaned, the better to support my body while my brain worked the angles. My fingerprints so bold in places that they may as well have been inked on. Most of the Post-Its had long since fallen to the floor. There they lay to this day, curled and brittle as autumn leaves. Why hadn't Ramona ever swept them up?

The second client's chair, against this same wall, had been sat in maybe twice. It was a classy chair, in a Bauhaus sort of way: tubular stainless-steel frame, cushionless leather seat and back. I sat down in it. It wasn't especially comfortable, but it gave me a new perspective on the north wall. It was something of a revelation that the wall even existed, so rarely did it enter my consciousness. Of course I knew it was there. The filing cabinet was up against it, towards the back corner. But I had never given it any special attention. Not that in and of itself it merited any, being utterly bare. Rather it was the perspective it gave me on the office as a whole that suddenly commanded my attention, for at that moment it seemed nothing more than a plywood stage set, everything in it so many hollow props.

Back at my desk I opened the middle drawer. Pens. Pencils. Erasers. Scissors. A ruler. Paper clips. Business cards. Bullets. All peculiarly weightless in my hands. I pulled out my address book and went through it page by page. Some of the entries were so old that I hardly recognized my own handwriting. Annette. Barbara. Clarice. Names of women I had scored with and never called again. I turned the page. Dad. A whole page of addresses and phone numbers, the years penned in beside them. The last entry five years old. Tommy McClendon and Butch Porter. Names that filled me with revulsion for the jackass I had been in my twenties. All in all, a pathetic summation of my human relations over the past two decades.

I sat for some time in deep contemplation, then I opened the bottom right-hand drawer and pulled out the bottle and the glass and poured myself a drink. I emptied the first and poured myself a second. I moved the bottle aside and pulled the telephone over. I had just put the receiver to my ear when someone appeared at the door. I replaced the instrument and quickly returned the bottle and glass to the drawer. I feared it was Mr. Fletcher. I did not want to see that man. But as he neared the glass, his shadow resolved itself into the silhouette of a woman. A woman, by the evidence of her curves, straight out of a Baxter Conway novel.

The door opened and in stepped Mrs. Fletcher. She was in that gown, the one she had been wearing in the photograph, so tight to her curvaceous body that it seemed it would dissolve with one deep breath. It was a deep blue-green thing, shimmering like moonlight off the midnight sea, an evening gown, in broad daylight. It was a stunning vision, such a sight in my office. I was suddenly aware of the stink of myself filling it up. She closed the door.

"Good morning," I said. Nothing else came to mind.

"So this is a detective's office," she glanced around with an air of disappointment. She took a few steps forward.

"How can I help you, ma'am?"

"Aren't you going to offer me a drink?"

"Would you care for a drink?" I asked.

"Yes, please."

I pulled the bottle and two glasses out of the drawer and set them on the desk.

"I hope you like bourbon. It's all I've got."

"It'll do."

I poured the drinks and stood up and brought hers around and handed it to her. Her lips at that proximity were like two luscious, glossy red things native to some exotic clime that never once in the history of love poetry had been used to describe a woman's lips. She was looking at the case wall.

"Please, have a seat," I said, motioning towards the chair in front of my desk.

"I'd rather stand," she said. She turned and eyed me. "And you can stop playing dumb."

I smiled briefly. Perhaps I even blushed. I sat down behind my desk. It felt safer there.

"I got your letter," I said.

"Did you like it?"

"It had its moments." She didn't smile. "So," I said, "to what do I owe the honor of your visit?"

"Right to business, eh?" She ambled around, still checking out the place. She moved with a certain self-consciousness, perhaps a remnant of her days as a department store model, walking the runway with a thousand eyes on her, perhaps something she was born with, a studied intention in every step. She stopped about five feet in front of the desk and looked at me. It was hard work keeping my eyes on her face.

"Listen, Eddie, if you don't want to do this, just say the word and I'll be on my way."

"Do what?"

She took a drink, her eyes not straying from mine as she swallowed.

"I guess I was mistaken." She turned as if to leave.

"Hold on," I said. I got up and hurried across the room and opened the door and looked both directions down the hall.

"Where is he?" I asked.

"Who?"

"Your husband."

"At work, I suspect."

I closed the door and surreptitiously locked it. Her wrists, her neck, her ankles. Utterly sublime. She glided over to the window and leaned into it, as if to accentuate the silken elasticity of the fabric of her gown, the sunlight haloing her curves as she peered dreamily out at the city.

"Nice view," she said, as if challenging me to agree.

"Is this another test?" I asked.

"He didn't send me."

"Did you know I was there, on the other side of the wall?"

"If you must know, I thought it was mean, treating you that way."

"You didn't sound too heartbroken."

She turned around and placed her right hand on the crest of her hip bone and looked squarely at me.

"I came to tell you to get off this job."

"What job would that be?"

"The one my husband hired you to do."

"He hired me to follow you."

"Not that job. The real job."

"I seem to remember telling your husband where he could stick his real job."

"He doesn't take no for an answer."

"That's his problem," I said. "I'm not working for him, so you can stop worrying and get on with your bargain shopping."

She smiled.

"It's not me I'm worried about. It's you."

"Is that right? Why are you suddenly feeling so charitable towards me?"

"I don't want to see you get hurt."

That made me laugh.

"Look, lady, I can take care of myself. I've been in plenty of scrapes." I was starting to get annoyed with her. Her condescension. Her hokey femme fatale performance. What was her game?

"Consider yourself warned," she said, walking back towards the door.

"Why don't you quit yakking and show me your tits," I blurted out. How that managed to rocket out of my subconscious unhindered by even the most basic laws of decorum was beyond me. But now that it was out there, I had to roll with it.

She didn't bat an eye. She turned around. "You couldn't handle these, gumshoe."

I grinned. "Try me."

She sauntered over, hips sashaying side to side, staring me down all the while. She stopped just short of me, close enough that I could smell her perfume. It seemed familiar. A bit cheap, but certainly effective.

"Even if you had the money you wouldn't know how to put it where your mouth is."

"Come on, baby, I don't got all day."

"Let's see what you're packing," she said.

I chuckled. "Some wit."

"You want to see my tits, show me you can back it up."

"Fine," I said and unzipped my pants and pulled out my tackle.
She laughed.

I took it in stride. "The tits."

With a fabulous double-dip of her shoulders, first the right, then the left, she worked the straps down and unlatched the bra and bared her tits. I must say, they were magnificent. Full, ripe, bursting with youth. Beautiful taupe-colored nipples, slightly perky. I reached up to touch them.

"Ah-ah-ah," she said, wagging her finger. "You got your look. You really think that sad little toe between your legs is worthy of these?"

"It packs a punch where it counts."

She eyed me dubiously, then to my astonishment she reached forward with her right hand and grabbed it, pulling it, with me in tow, hard against her. I lowered my face to her tits and went lapping at them like a thirsty dog, slurping and sucking while she tugged me off. She had wicked, cold hands. Not ten seconds after I had achieved full erection I exploded in her fingers. It took all my strength to keep from collapsing to the floor.

"Jesus Christ, you idiot," she squawked, staring wide-eyed down at her fouled gown. "Do you know how much this cost?"

"A buck fifty," I panted, "at Bargain Town." I didn't give a damn if it was a million bucks. I was in heaven.

She scowled. "Don't just stand there. Give me a rag or something." She latched up her bra and yanked her straps back up while I pulled my handkerchief from my back pocket and wetted it with some of the bourbon. Only after she was attended to did I put myself back together.

"Consider yourself warned," she said, tossing my handkerchief at me and marching to the door and out. I stood there listening as her footsteps receded down the corridor. Then I went back to the desk, sat down, and picked up the phone.

18

AFTER ELEVEN RINGS the receptionist put me on hold, allowing me a rare opportunity to hear the original "Ain't No Sunshine" in its entirety. In editorial I got another receptionist who said she would transfer me to Mr. Stapleton. This time I got a stock market report. The Dow was up a hundred and thirty-six points in early trading on news of positive dialogues with the Chinese on a range of issues, including floating the renminbi. Mr. Stapleton's secretary interrupted the futures report to inform me that Mr. Stapleton was on the other line at the moment. Would I care to hold? I got the middle passage of Shostakovich's third opus, theme and variations in B-flat major.

At last I got a hello from a man.

"Howard Stapleton?" I asked.

"Speaking."

I hesitated, knowing how absurd it was going to sound.

"My name is Eddie King," I said. "I'm a private detective."

The line went quiet for a few seconds.

"Okay?" he said, rather dubiously.

"Listen, I know what it sounds like. I got your name from Walter Morris's files. I've been to see his wife."

He was listening a little more intently now. Still he made no response.

"Do you have a minute?"

"Do you mind telling me what this is about?" he said. "I'm quite busy at the moment."

"I just have a few questions."

That got a resigned nasal exhale.

"Did Mr. Morris ever discuss his process with you?" I asked. "What kind of research he did? How he went about gathering material for his stories? Anything of that nature?"

"Look. Whoever you are, I'm not about to discuss confidential matters about one of my writers with a complete stranger over the telephone. Now, if you don't mind . . ."

He left me no choice.

"Every one of Walter's books is based on one of my cases."

Again the line went quiet for several seconds. Only now the silence was filled with mental calibrations.

"You're a private detective, you say?"

"That's correct."

"Could you give me your license number and your business address and telephone number."

I gave it all to him.

"Let me get back to you," he said.

"I'd appreciate that."

He hung up.

I finished my drink and poured another. I hope that man has a strong heart, I thought as I got up and put on my hat and coat and made my way down the corridor to the elevator, because he's in for the shock of his life. His first thought would be *lawsuit*. And it wouldn't be me he would be worried about. As soon as he verified that I was on the level, his next call, or his ride up the elevator, would be to the boss, to warn him that there was legal trouble afoot with the Conway books. The publisher would telephone his lawyer, who would promptly mobilize his forces for battle. At some point in the next few days, if not sooner, my telephone would ring. On the other end would be an attorney representing Pegasus Editions, requesting an appointment to discuss my allegations. I would ask him to meet in my office, where I would lay my case files before him. Confronted with the preponderance of evidence, the lawyer would ask for some time to consult with his client . . .

This scenario unfolded in my mind as I pulled out of the lot and made my way across town in the general direction of Sunset Acres. Out on the freeway I got to wondering if I shouldn't hire a lawyer myself. Until then it hadn't occurred to me that I could stand to profit from this. If this wasn't intellectual property theft, what was? At the very least I could probably claim damages to my professional reputation. And I was the least of their worries, what with people like Randolph Terwilliger, Lefty Crane, and Bugsy Goldstein gracing the pages of the novels. In fact, it was looking more and more like grounds for class-action, though it was hard to imagine any of those people in the same room together, let alone on the same docket.

It was about a quarter after two when I pulled up to the Morris house.

"I've already made the tea," she said from within as I reached up to knock on the screen door.

"It's me, Mrs. Morris," I said. "Eddie King."

"Yes," she replied without hesitation. "Come in."

As usual, she was in the wingback chair, the tea service before her on the table.

"Were you expecting me?" I asked as I neared her chair.

"I thought you might stop by." The delicate lace collar of her parchment-colored dress was only slightly less evanescent than her smile. "Have a seat and tell me all about your weekend." She leaned forward and poured the teas.

"Never mind my weekend." I settled onto the couch, placing my hat beside me. "There's something I need to ask you. The women in the novels," I said, wrapping my fingers casually around my right knee. "You told me you were the one who described them."

"Yes."

"So why make them all gorgeous blue-eyed blondes? That's not realistic. Annabelle Blair, Lucy Rogelle, Sally Lyon—those broads are nothing like that. Mayme Montrose could give Bela Lagosi a run for his money."

"They're novels, Mr. King," she replied. "Works of fiction. Not investigative journalism. You don't seem to appreciate the distinction."

"I'm fully aware of the difference," I said. "But there's the niggling little fact that every one of those books is based on one of my cases. Those women are real people."

"A curious coincidence."

"He used my name, Mrs. Morris. That's no coincidence."

"Please, call me Imogen." She took a leisurely sip of tea and sat there with a smile of perfect contentment. She seemed to be enjoying herself. "How many cases do you typically work on in a year?" she asked.

"That's irrelevant."

"Walter published one book a year."

"One book that just happened, every time, to be one of my cases?"

"There's no copyright on reality, Mr. King," she stated amiably. "Or on a name."

"It's more than just a name," I pointed out. "It's my office address, my home address, my case files, my car. Everything."

She set her cup gently on the saucer and looked at me. We sat in silence for a while, appraising one another. Then I asked again:

"Why blue-eyed blondes?"

She took another sip of tea before answering.

"If you must know, she was Walter's fantasy. His eyes always riveted on women like that. So I gave it to him. A little gift, you could say. It helped keep the spark in our marriage."

As she said this her eyes misted over, and despite my frustrations with her, I couldn't help feeling guilty for pressing her so hard.

Apart from the ticking and tocking of the unseen clock, the silence was absolute. It really was peaceful in that house. So cool and quiet and spacious. It was hard to believe that anyone living there could have spent his days dreaming of murder and vice.

At length she asked again how my weekend had been. It took me a moment to recall anything about it at all. Then, with the image of the gravity-defying cigarette ash, it all came crashing back into my consciousness.

"I went to see my mom," I told her. "Big mistake. I don't know why I always give in to the guilt."

"She's your mother."

"That doesn't mean I have to like her."

"Don't say that," she said, seeming genuinely hurt that a man could talk about his mother this way. "Someday she won't be here and you'll wish she were."

"You can't have a meaningful conversation with her. You can't have a conversation at all. She doesn't shut up. It's just this endless stream of consciousness, most of it negative. She drives me mad."

"She loves you very much."

I shrugged doubtfully.

"Do you have any siblings?" she asked.

"No. Only child. All the pressure's on me."

"You're the center of her world."

"I don't want to be," I said. "It's a miserable one. She's got emphysema and smokes menthol cigarettes. She doesn't give a damn. She moved up here to be closer to me, thinking I'd be out there every Sunday for dinner, go to church with her. She never should have sold the old house. She had friends down there. Good memories. A community. She bought this awful thing out in Merino that cost twice as much. She got ripped off. Now she's all alone up here, miserable, angry at me for not driving out there every week to see her. She calls me expecting me to go out there and do stuff for her: fix her air-conditioner, do yardwork. I can't just drop everything I'm doing and drive all the way out there to rake leaves. The gas alone is twenty bucks. She can't accept that I have a life of my own. She's not interested. Never asks a single question. All the stuff I've seen, all my freaky cases, you'd think she'd be fascinated to hear about it. No. She'd rather watch *Days of Our Lives*."

Mrs. Morris was gazing at me with discomfiting empathy. I couldn't believe I had just said all that, to her, the woman whose husband had blatantly ripped me off.

"What about your father?" she asked.

"Dad?" An ironic little chortle bubbled up from my depths, and before I knew it I was off again. "He makes Mom look like Mother Theresa. Completely paranoid. I'm not talking your garden variety paranoia. I mean really and truly neurotic. Aliens trying to abduct him. The government has him under constant surveillance. The moon landing

162

was faked. Every conspiracy theory out there, he believes it. Too many drugs in his youth. He worked on offshore oil rigs. I don't know what it's like now but all they did in those days was smoke dope and drop acid. Three weeks he'd be out there, stranded on a platform in the ocean with a bunch of other guys. He'd be home for a week then out there again. It wrecked his brain. He's been trying to sue the CIA for the last twenty years."

She took a sip of her tea, a certain restrained pursing of her lips suggesting that perhaps I wasn't showing my father sufficient respect.

"Are you still in touch with him?" she asked, lowering her cup to her lap.

"I call him every now and then," I said, "just to see how he's doing. He's got all kinds of health problems: diabetes, gout, bad teeth. I haven't seen him in five years."

"That's awful," she frowned. "Is he getting help?"

"He's on disability," I said. "He's covered. He's got nurses. I can't deal with him. It's too painful seeing him like that. When I was a kid, I thought he was the coolest dad alive. He was funny. He was creative. He played guitar and made these crazy metal sculptures out of junk."

The next thing I knew, tears were rolling down her cheeks. What had I said? She lowered her head, making a valiant effort to preserve her dignity. The way she was holding her cup in her lap, as if to catch the falling tears, put a knot in my own gorge. I looked away.

"I'm sorry," she said when she had collected herself. The words were hardly out of her mouth before she broke down again, this time even worse. I couldn't just sit there doing nothing. I got up and went to her chair and kneeling beside it took her hand in mine and told her it was okay, she was going to be all right, to just go ahead and let it all out. She nodded and tried to give me a smile, which only brought on a fresh torrent of tears. It was hard to take. "You're very sweet," she said at one point, patting my head.

"Listen," I said when the worst of it was over and she seemed to be settling down again. "I've got a suggestion."

19

SHE GAVE ME the small bedroom at the end of the hallway upstairs. It was simply furnished with a single bed, a three-drawer unfinished deal dresser, a plain wooden chair, and a full-length mirror on the closet door.

I felt instantly at home as I hung my suits in the closet, arranged my socks and underwear in the drawers, set my grooming kit atop the dresser. Despite its size, the room felt very spacious thanks to the views through the windows. One overlooked the back yard in all its wild verdure. Even from the second story the giant old eucalyptus trees blocked out the world beyond, giving one the impression that the house stood alone in the woods. The other window faced the row of identical brown shingle rooftops with their aqua-blue air-conditioner boxes and red barbecue grills in eerily flawless back lawns.

The agreement we had come to wasn't exactly what she had envisioned. I told her I would stay out there with her for one week, at my basic security detail rate. I wouldn't take on any other cases. She would have one hundred percent of my attention. I acted as if I were making a sacrifice.

Ironically, I have never slept better than I did on that bed. The mere sight of the bedspread, a thin but surprisingly heavy white chenille embroidered in a dense honeycomb motif, smoothed and tucked to perfection each morning by Mrs. Morris, was enough to bring on a wonderful fairytale drowsiness. It was always deliciously cool to the touch, no matter how hot the day or night. I awoke invigorated every morning to the purling song of the strawberry finches, a haunting little minor refrain at the end of a two-note glissando, conjuring a strange, sweet feeling of loss. How was it possible, I thought, after all the beatings I had taken, all the abuses I had willingly put my body and soul to, all my brushes with death, that I was lying in this heavenly luminescence, feeling as fresh and pure as a newborn babe? If not for the tantalizing smells of a full cooked breakfast wafting in from under the door every morning, I might never have got up at all. I hadn't awoken with such an appetite since I was a teenager. I flung off the covers, put on my robe, and headed down the hall for my shower, where I worked those seven taps like the foreman of Hoover Dam. Mrs. Morris's soaps were all of the marbled seashell and peach pit variety, the sort you find at boutique bed and breakfasts in the wine country, perfumy and quick to lather away to nothing against a man's hairy hide.

After my shower it was down the stairs and into the kitchen to greet Mrs. Morris, who was usually busy preparing our breakfast. "Sleep well?" she would ask, cracking an egg on the edge of the skillet or slicing through a loaf of freshly baked bread. "Like the dead," I had the presence of mind not to say, though I came close on more than one occasion.

Leaving her to finish her work, I would proceed into the conservatory attached to the back of the house, where the *Herald* would be awaiting me on the glass-topped, wrought-iron table. Originally an herbarium, the conservatory was a magical space, a giant kaleidoscope of white cast-iron and glass, no two panes exactly alike in size or shape or degree of translucency. Some were as fogged with age as the storm-blasted panes of a seacliff cottage. Others were scalloped or fluted or otherwise molded for dazzling diffusions. Though none of the panes were colored per se, if you concentrated on any single one of them long enough you began to notice all the subtle complexions of the spectrum—tints of blue, shades of green, washes of yellow—only apparent in juxtaposition with the pane adjacent. Through this lattice of light the back yard was transformed into an impressionistic painting in dreamy green and gold.

It was in here that Mrs. Morris and I spent our leisurely mornings, drawing breakfast out for hours, talking about all sorts of interesting things. She was very well-read, effortlessly making references to Spinoza or Socrates or some other great thinker in the course of our conversations. She gravitated towards philosophical questions. Is man redeemable? Are we all truly capable of murder? What is the purpose, from an evolutionary perspective, of evil? Ironically, given my notorious cynicism, I was usually the one taking the more optimistic point of view.

Only after persistent prodding did I learn that she had gone to St Mary's College, where she had studied to be a schoolteacher—until she realized she wasn't fond of children. What she really liked was books.

"I was working as a librarian at the Sunset Acres Public Library when I met Walter," she told me one morning. "He came in nearly every week for books on a dizzying array of subjects: musicology, combustion physics, Greek mythology. I was always eager to see what this curious young man who never wore a hat despite his premature balding would check out next," she smiled. "More often than not we didn't have what he wanted and I would have to place an order for the book, ostensibly for the improvement of the holdings, but secretly because I found him intriguing. Without saying or doing anything in particular, he had a way of dominating the room. I would watch him standing at one of the shelves in the back corner, absorbed in some esoteric monograph, and it always seemed as though he was in the center of the library and that everyone was staring at him. But it was only me."

By her account, it was their shared love of books that eventually brought them together.

"One day I got up the courage to ask him what he did for a living, and to my surprise I learned that he managed the inventory of an import business. Considering his reading habits, and the hours he spent in the library, I had assumed he was in some intellectual line of work—a journalist or a lawyer. It only made him more alluring that his eclectic tastes had nothing to do with his job. After that, every time he came in he made a point of asking me what I was reading. Later he told me he started keeping a journal of our conversations, taking note of my reading preferences, extrapolating the hidden aspects of my personality from them."

My ears perked up at this.

"In the end he wooed me with a first edition of *Lady Chatterley's Lover*," she said with a mischievous grin. "We were married three months later." After the honeymoon she quit her job. "The expected thing to do in those days." She was also expected to begin having children, which, she said without any apparent regret, never came to pass.

To my queries about the house, she narrated the long history, starting with Walter's great great grandfather, a German-speaking Pole named Jozef Moroz, and ending with Walter himself. Walter had spent the first ten summers of his life out at the old house—the happiest days of his life, he would always say. For a city boy, it was magical spending entire days exploring the countryside, playing with the kids of the migrant laborers, learning to play the parlor piano. But once he reached puberty he lost all interest in country summers. The girls were in the city. Memories of the old house, of those idyllic summers with his grandmother and grandfather and great Aunt Zyta, always prevented him from buying a house of his own. No other house could survive the comparison.

Desperate to keep the house in the family, Walter eventually struck a deal with his aunt to buy it himself, allowing her to go on living in it for as long as she liked. She lasted a few more years before the upkeep became too much for her, and she moved to an apartment in the city. The house sat empty for four years before Walter moved in.

"Imagine my reaction when I first saw this place," Mrs. Morris marveled. "Some bachelor pad. The developers tried every tactic short of arson to drive us out, but somehow Walter always managed to fend off the vultures."

To my questions about her own family, Mrs. Morris's response was a matter-of-fact "All gone." She had had an older sister, but she had died some years ago. Nor did she seem to have any friends. I would have expected old family friends to be dropping by to check in on her, but not a single person came around, not even the neighbors. It seemed that she had so completely devoted herself to Walter that she had long since given up interacting with the world.

Although she spoke freely of Walter and their time together, Imogen (as she insisted on me calling her now that I was a guest in her home) steered clear of any mention of his death. It was obvious to me that she didn't really believe he had been murdered. The lack of any effort to seek justice was proof enough of that. Nor was she in the state of shock and debilitating grief that I have seen all too often in the survivors of violent crime. It wasn't that she didn't succumb to emotion now and then, swallowing her grief and turning away in silence until the wave had passed. I didn't doubt that in her own stoical way she was suffering. But on the whole, and I can't say exactly why, she struck me as someone who had been widowed for a long time, someone who had made peace with her loss long ago and was determined to get on with the business of living.

Rather than give me any insights into the man behind the books, her reminiscences only seemed to obscure Walter Morris further. I often found myself standing before the photograph in the hallway upstairs, trying to get a better sense of him. But the more I studied that dull, bureaucratic face, a face rendered familiar in its very forgetability, the more I wondered what exactly besides their shared love of books Imogen had ever seen in him. Apart from his study, there were very few traces of Walter's existence in the house, and those suggested that he had not been physically robust: the cushions for his lower back on both his dining room chair and the chair he used in the conservatory, his fleece-lined slippers, his nose-hair clippers, and other dainty male grooming apparati in the bathroom. If the punctuality of our meals, established by long habit, was any indication, Imogen had waited on him hand and foot, protecting him from the outside world so he could do nothing but write. The various old tools and work tables in the basement, which I periodically ventured into to retrieve more firewood, clearly pre-dated Walter's occupation of the house. The gun cabinet was down there, housing two Browning 20-gauge shotguns, a few boxes of shells, a hunting vest and cap, but frankly I found it hard to picture that plump, bespectacled man out in the woods with a shotgun in his hands.

Every now and then, drawn as ever by the solemn mystery of death, I would step into Walter's study, close the door, and stand there quietly contemplating a bullet ripping through his brains. Why me? I had to ask myself. Why, out of all the private detectives in the city, had he chosen me? Was it purely random, or was there some mysterious and ultimately unknowable link that bound us? Day after day, year after year, he sat at his desk for hours on end, pretending to be me. If what Imogen had said was true, that he had struggled for years to break free from the Eddie King novels, then couldn't a claim be made that his obsession with me had ultimately killed him? He couldn't see beyond me. His life was never going to be as exciting as mine. He would never be the one staring down the barrel, knowing that the only thing between him and the grave was the quickness of his wits. He would never be the one sifting through all the evidence to arrive at the one shining solution. In that sense, yes, I had killed him. I may not have pulled the trigger, but the hand of Eddie King was all over that gun. It was no mere coincidence that he had used a snubnose .38 and signed his suicide note, *Yours truly, Eddie King*. To my mind, that said it all. As sad as it was, I couldn't help feeling a little flattered. How many people can honestly say they kept a writer employed for more than a decade fantasizing about their life? The blood stain on the chair only made it all the more poignant. More than once I searched for the bullet, at one point pulling every single book from the shelves, but it was nowhere to be found.

"There's something I've been wondering about," Imogen said one of those sunny mornings over breakfast. "Please don't take offence."

"Don't worry," I assured her. "I have a thick skin."

"All those people who get killed in Walter's novels. By your account, it's all true."

I nodded. "I'm afraid so."

"Forgive the impropriety, but . . ."

"No, it's fine," I spared her the discomfort of having to spell it out. "Sometimes you're put in a situation where you have to use lethal force in self-defense."

She gazed out into the sunlight for a while, then turning her attention back to me, said:

"But something like six people are killed in *Blood City* alone."

"The Dawson case," I nodded. "Yeah, that was a bloody one. All those people had serious dirt on each other. None of them trusted each other. They were ruthless people who would stop at nothing to get what they wanted."

This provoked a broad smile from her, as if she were remembering some delicious private joke. I asked her what was so funny.

"Oh nothing."

"Come on."

She hesitated, then said: "That's the blurb on the back of the book."

"What is?"

"'They were ruthless people who would stop at nothing to get what they wanted.'"

"Is it?" I said, making light of it despite the annoying insinuation that somehow *I* was the cliché and not that claptrap on the back of the novel. That insidious stuff has a way of burrowing deep inside your brain and taking root there.

She grinned at my obvious annoyance. I took a long drink of my orange juice.

"What about that poor man who was killed with a golf club?" she asked.

"John Trabe," I said, nodding at the memory. "He had it coming."

She grimaced. "How do you deal with it?"

"After a while you just get numb to it," I explained. "It's like looking at a side of beef or something. The first two or three corpses you see, sure, it gets to you. But you get used to it, like anything else. You realize that all you're seeing is the body, not the person. The person is dead and gone. A lot of times the person was dead long before his body met its demise."

By the time I realized that this might be rather insensitive, it was already out. But if it pained her at all, she didn't show it. Leaning closer, she rested her fingers atop the table.

"So you believe we have a soul that goes on living after the body dies?"

"I don't know about that," I said. I've never been a fan of metaphysical speculation. "How can we know? Do you believe that?"

"Yes, I do," she said forthrightly.

Whether this was a lifelong conviction of hers or something born of Walter's death, I chose not to inquire. We usually lingered over breakfast well past ten o'clock, after which she would clean up the dishes then take to her sewing upstairs. I had no idea what she was making but I could hear the *whump-whump-whump* of the old treadle throughout the day as I lay in bed or sat out in the conservatory, rereading the novels.

It was a completely different experience reading them in the house where they had been written (if not conceived). For one thing, they were funnier. Perhaps I had been softened by all of Mrs. Morris's little ministrations, the way she always seemed to anticipate my every desire, reaching for the decanter a millisecond before it occurred to me that I could use another drop of orange juice, serving me the last piece of French toast just as my eyes were settling on it. Whatever the case, I hadn't really noticed before how witty Walter's Eddie was—much wittier than me. He, or perhaps I should say Walter, was a master of the devastating one-liner in the face of man's stupidity. What had struck me before as just plain ridiculous now seemed genuinely funny. Relaxing in a cozy home just like any other reader, away from the stresses of the job, I had to admit that the books were amusing. I could see how Midwesterners might get addicted to them. Even so, I never felt comfortable reading them in Mrs. Morris's presence. It looked too much like the baseball player who claims indifference to the sports writers, only to secretly devour every word they write about him.

Looking back on it, it strikes me as remarkable how the strange and decadent habits of others seem perfectly ordinary once they have become your own. While seldom as lavish as our goose repast, dinner was by any common measure always an extravagant affair. It was a rare evening that our main course wasn't some kind of wild fowl—guinea hen, quail, duck—all supposedly shot by Walter, whom she said had taken up hunting a few years back in an attempt to alleviate the aching sacroiliac of his sedentary life. The big industrial freezer in the cellar was full of plucked birds. Mrs. Morris clearly enjoyed pampering and indulging me, and who was I to refuse, seeing how happy it made her? "There you are, Eddie," she would sweetly say as she spooned the Brussels sprouts or beets onto my plate, and a warm wave of contentment would roll through me. And while her inner ear stayed perfectly tuned to my physical needs, she would effortlessly take up the conversation we had left unfinished at breakfast, the theme of which, unilluminated by the cleansing morning sunlight, usually acquired a more somber tone at dinner.

After dinner and all the cleanup it entailed, Mrs. Morris liked to spend the rest of her evening reading in front of the fire. Inspired by the holiday spirit that those dinners put me in, I took to building the fire for her while she worked away in the kitchen. A few strips of sloughed-off eucalyptus bark under one of the pine logs, already cut and stacked in the cellar (another one of Walter's physiotherapies,) were enough to kindle a cheering blaze. If from a purely calefactive perspective there wasn't any call for a fire, the interior of the house, particularly the living room, did seem drafty at times, not so much a physical chill as a certain spectral nip in the air, more a factor of the musty tawdriness of everything than of any chilling brushes with Walter's ghost.

Initially reluctant to impose upon her solitude, I soon gave in to her repeated entreaties to join her in the living room in the evening. And there she and I would sit, in perfect silence save the crackling fire, reading our respective books. She was working on a volume of Gerard Manley Hopkins poetry. I grabbed one of the volumes of the *Great Books of the Western World* series from Walter's study. Volume 54: *The Major Works of Sigmund Freud*. Interesting stuff. Some of it, at least.

Sometimes I would glance up from my book and marvel at how content we seemed in each other's silent company. Other times I was struck by how graceful she looked in the firelight, the soft orange glow smoothing away her wrinkles, rouging her pale cheeks, adding a touch of scarlet to her lips, much as she must have appeared to Walter when he first laid eyes on her. Then again, there were times when a flicker of awareness of how bizarre all this was would ignite my wine-soaked brain.

20

THERE IS ONLY so much tea and polite conversation a man can take, no matter how restorative. After six days of self-indulgence that felt like a month, I began to get bored. If I was to stay on with her, as she so earnestly implored when she handed me my pay, I would need to start doing some work. With the office rent due next week, and no other jobs in the pipeline, I figured I didn't have much choice.

Seeing firsthand what dire shape the house was in, I took it upon myself to attempt some basic upkeep. The first thing I tackled was the groaning pipes. After two days of sleuthing, I identified the culprit: a shot ballcock in the cold water tank. That the house even possessed a cold water tank in this day and age was a testament to how little touched by the hands of progress it was. Although the water came from the county mains, the pressure to distribute it came solely from the tank in the attic. When you flushed the toilet or ran the sink, particularly from the upstairs bathroom tap, the force of the influx of fresh water set the old ballcock vibrating against the aperture of the outlet, which when transmitted over the length of the pipes sounded something akin to a mid-octave A-flat on a French horn awash with saliva. To fix it I had to climb bodily into the tank, holding my flashlight between my teeth, and dismantle the old ballcock, a feat which, given the instability of my light source and the insufficiencies of the available tools, was no small accomplishment. Finding a replacement also called upon my investigative talents. After three hardware stores in two towns, I was eventually referred to Alfred Sawyer's salvage yard in Margaritaville, a forty-five minute drive into the blistering inland. The old man took one look at the ancient contraption encrusted with limescale and escorted me out through a labyrinth of the most amazing assortment of unclassifiable junk I had ever seen, into a tin shed where he rooted around in the drawers of an old dresser until he found a fairer twin of the offending item. The cost of the replacement: $2.50. He wouldn't take a penny more.

With that small victory behind me, I felt emboldened to tackle a bigger challenge: repainting the exterior of the house. Initially Imogen wasn't too keen on the idea, but escorting her outside and showing her the state of the wood where the sun had baked away the last paint job, I explained that if it wasn't repainted soon, the house was going to rot around her. When that didn't sufficiently alarm her, I pointed out that if she intended on selling the house in, say, the next five years or so, a new paint job could easily double the asking price. Any talk of selling the house was anathema to her, but after sleeping on it she deferred to my good judgement, on the condition that she pay me my standard per diem. I wouldn't hear of it, pointing out that I was eating better than I ever had, but she refused to back down, claiming that she had already prevailed far too much upon my generosity. Which, of course, was nonsense. I was there of my own free will, and I told her so.

It was our first argument. Immediately afterwards I felt the pleasant inner glow of filial belonging, something I hadn't felt in many years.

Whereas my arguments with Mom always had a sour, hopeless tinge to them, leaving me feeling edgy and deflated, this minor discord between Imogen and I had arisen out of genuine respect for one another, out of competing conceptions of honor. Having glimpsed in her eyes an intimidating determination to have her way, it was a pleasure to relent.

Nothing in detective work can compare with the visceral pleasures of scraping brittle paint from long-suffering wood: the crisp crackling sound it makes when the blade plows beneath it to unveil the naked grain, the flakes fluttering silently down, blanketing the ground like colored snow. At the end of the day, when you step back and see what you have accomplished, you can't help but feel a burst of pride. Hours passed in the blink of an eye. No sooner would I get out there on the ladder than Imogen would poke her head out the door and call me in for lunch, which, thankfully, was a lighter meal, usually consisting of a baguette on a plate of mixed cheeses, olives, and dried fruit. Where she produced this daily cornucopia from was a complete mystery to me, as she hadn't once ventured out of the house since I had arrived. After lunch I would nap for half an hour up in my room. (It turned out that I was sleeping in Walter's nap room, which he had used when he needed a break from 'writing.') I particularly relished those siestas, the feeling of the cool threadwork of that chenille bedspread against the soles of my hot, tired feet. Then it would be back out to scrape away the rest of the afternoon, daydreaming of nothing more than the gorgeous dinner that awaited me.

Miraculously, despite standing on a ladder all day, my feet felt better than they had in years. Whether it was the Molten Snow, which I was applying religiously twice a day, my improved diet, something homeopathic in cowslips, or simply the general atmosphere of leisure that brought about the change, I had no idea. Nor did I care. I was just happy to be free of that incessant ache. Pleasantly fatigued, I would call it a day around 5:30, go up for my second shower, then, freshly attired in my slacks and shirt—she lent me a pair of Walter's old overalls for my chores—it was back down the stairs and into the dining room to find the table set, the warm shards of chandelier light glinting in the silver, the wine already poured.

It wasn't until Friday afternoon of that second week, on the pretext of needing to get at the frames of the dormers, that I managed to climb back up to the attic and go through all the boxes again. I did find in two of them (*Blinded by the Sun* and *All but the Chorus*) some notes and outlines I had overlooked the first time. The notes were mostly in the form of questions and ruminations, with the occasional random image or phrase dashed off in the margin: "What if instead of finding the tarp in the hedges, K finds a scrap of it in the front flogo of Lucy's car?" "Perhaps they meet at the beach and proceed from there to the gambling den." "Why doesn't K just go directly to the source?" That sort of thing, written on the back side of the page in question. The outlines, on separate sheets of paper, were simple numbered lists of the key events of the novel. These were written in pencil, and it was clear where he had erased lines numerous times to shuffle things around, as if he were actually making it all up as he went along.

The lack of apparent evidence of a crime does not by any means negate its existence. Either Walter had not kept written records of his pilfered knowledge, which implied a prodigious memory, or he had prudently destroyed them as soon as they were incorporated into the novels, probably thinking (correctly) that sooner or later I was going to stumble onto one of his books and come looking for him.

I closed the boxes back up and stood before them for a while, considering my options. A faint scent, slightly sweet, slightly smoky, somewhere beneath the smell of dust and wood and musty cardboard, kept drifting in and out of my nose. It evoked a strange feeling of mild dread, but I couldn't quite place the source of it. It smelled a bit like barbecued meat, but that wasn't it, as there was a sharper edge to it, something singed. I walked over to the window at the front of the house and stood there for some time gazing out into the hazy suburban afternoon.

21

THE NEXT MORNING, around eleven o'clock, while I was up on the ladder scraping the north face of the house, an orange Chevy Nova with two white racing stripes running down the center pulled up in front of the driveway. A plastic Virgin Mary dangled from the rearview mirror. Out of the car stepped a squat, middle-aged Mexican woman who at first glance bore a striking resemblance to Ramona.

I watched her make her way up the driveway. I was waiting for the moment when at last this woman's unique facial features would overcome the distortions of my elevated perspective, revealing her in all her non-Ramonaness. That moment never came. The closer she got to the porch, the less probable it became that this woman could be anyone but Ramona.

"Ramona?" I said with what little remained of my faith in the innate goodness of mankind. I was still holding out the possibility that the woman would turn towards my voice with mild perplexity and politely correct my error.

She looked up. Two beats of silent bewilderment. "Mr. King?" More puzzled silence, then: "What are you doing up there?"

At that moment it seemed a truly profound question, requiring the whole of my mental faculties to produce a satisfactory response. In the end, "What are *you* doing here?" was all I could muster.

"I come here to clean and shop for Mrs. Morris."

At which point I climbed down the ladder and, lodging my scraper in the front pocket of my overalls, walked resolutely towards her.

"You clean *here*?" I said, astonished that she could be so guileless. "For Mrs. Morris?"

"Yes."

I stood there waiting for the guilt to start dawning across her face, but she betrayed nothing. I asked her a few more questions—How long had she worked for Mrs. Morris? Did she know that Mr. Morris had been a writer? Had she ever seen any of his books?—all of which she answered predictably, even having the presence of mind to ask a few herself.

"I better get inside," she said at last, stepping up onto the porch.

I snapped: "Let's cut the crap, Ramona." She turned back, a rosy blush spreading up her neck and into her cheeks. Of course she had to go on pretending she didn't know what I was talking about, her blush draining away to a nervous pallor, asking me if she had broken something in the office, if she had accidentally left the door unlocked, thinking she could just weasel out of the clutches of truth.

"Look," I said, exasperated with the charade. "Maybe you didn't realize the gravity of what you were doing. Maybe you just thought you were helping Mr. Morris with a few scraps of paper that no one ever looked at. I know Schwartz doesn't pay you much, and that Mr. Morris probably convinced you it was perfectly innocent, but that doesn't excuse what you did."

She was on the verge of tears now.

"Mr. King, I didn't do nothing."

"Whatever." He who argues with a fool is a fool, Mom always says— me apparently being Fool #1.

She gave me another few seconds of her best wounded look then said, with downcast eyes: "I have to go in now."

I scraped away the rest of the morning with the small satisfaction of knowing that at least I wasn't insane. Still, it is hard to feel proud when the solution walks right up to you and slaps you in the face. It takes all the pleasure out of being right.

"Did you say something to Ramona?" Imogen asked at lunch. "She was positively distraught."

"I did."

"What did you say?"

I popped an olive into my mouth and, allowing her a little time while I chewed it to appreciate the magnitude of what I was about to say, said: "Ramona is the cleaning lady at the Mandrake Building."

"Oh, for God's sake, Eddie," she tossed her napkin onto the table.

That wasn't the response I was expecting. I thought she would be at least a little relieved to have this nagging conundrum finally cleared up, if only for my sake.

"You don't have the slightest proof."

"She's been cleaning my office for twelve years," I said. "It's obvious. What more proof do you need?"

"You really are a heartless sonofabitch."

I may have smiled, but those words pained me more than any sucker punch ever had. She turned and left the dining room. I ate a few more bitter olives then returned to my scraping.

As the afternoon progressed and the sting of our spat gradually receded, I began to feel sorry I had ever brought it up. I hadn't given a moment's consideration to the effect my pronouncement might have on her.

"I shouldn't have gloated," I apologized at dinner. "It was inconsiderate of your feelings. You're right, I don't have any proof. It doesn't matter anymore anyway."

"Yes it does," she said sedately. "It changes everything."

I rolled out the platitudes in an effort to convince her that it was water under the bridge, that Walter still had to write the books, had to transform all those dry notes and documents into gripping plots, that all writers use research, etc., but as the days went by it became clear from the change in her demeanor that I had dealt her a blow in some ways more devastating than his death. I had trampled his integrity. On the surface she remained as cordial as ever, even behaving towards me with a kind of humbled respect which hadn't been there before. But a caustic undercurrent began to corrode our encounters. She began to make small, seemingly petty corrections to my table manners, telling me it wasn't polite to rest my left arm on the table, or that it was poor form to use my dessert spoon to stir my tea. My biggest infraction, it seemed, was talking with food in my mouth, which she could not abide, though it had never seemed to bother her before. It wasn't as though my mouth was crammed full of food. At most it was a few nibbles at the tail end of a substantial swallow, when I would shift the remainder to a cheek in order to keep the flow of conversation going. I thought I was being considerate, attentive. Apparently not. Or else it was all the paint flakes I kept tracking in. As if the house were as pristine as an operating theater, when in fact the whole place was as dusty as King Tut's tomb.

Sometimes there was no clear object to the tension. It was just there in the room, like cosmic background radiation, beyond conscious perception but nonetheless sensed. I would glance over at her, reading her book, and feel that my presence was disturbing her peace, which naturally troubled my own. Sometimes it was too much, and I had to get out, go for a drive.

"Where are you going?" she would ask, a little too proprietorially for my taste.

"Out. Do I have your permission?"

"Don't be a smartass."

On more than one occasion I went back to my apartment to check the mail and be alone in my own space again. For the first few minutes it felt nice. I would tell myself that I wasn't getting anywhere out there in that house with that old woman, that it was time to move on, to try to put this thing behind me and get back to reality. Then, after twenty minutes in the recliner, the loneliness would start coming on, a slowly expanding black hole behind my sternum. I would look around and wonder how in the hell I had lived in this place, all alone, for so many years. It was so small and barren, devoid of life. Another ten minutes was all I could take, then I was out the door, driving back to Sunset Acres.

One of those nights I stopped by the office to check my messages and the mail. Amongst the junk were two envelopes from Fletcher Enterprises, dated a week apart. I held them in my hand, recalling the feeling of Mrs. Fletcher's tits against my face. I opened them. In each was a check for $150. No letter, no note of explanation.

I carried them over to the desk and sat there with them for a while, and when it didn't add up there either, I telephoned Mr. Fletcher at his home. A man answered, the butler perhaps. I asked for Mr. Fletcher. He asked who was calling. I told him. A few minutes later, Fletcher came on the line.

"Good evening, Mr. King," he said.

"I'm holding two checks from your company for $150 each. Memo line: "Services Rendered." Signed by one Sheldon Rothblatt, Tres. What do you want me to do with them?"

"Whatever you like," he replied. "It's your pay."

"My pay for what?"

"Services rendered."

"You already paid me," I pointed out.

"That was for the first week."

"I thought I made it clear that our business was concluded."

"You did."

"So what is this?

"You've earned it."

I stared at the opposite wall for a few seconds.

"Did something I say give you the impression that I had any intention of continuing to work for you?"

Just then, I heard a woman's voice in the background. Whether or not it was Mrs. Fletcher's, I couldn't say. The mouthpiece was promptly muffled.

"I'm sorry, Mr. King," Fletcher said a few seconds later. "I have to take care of something at the moment. I'll give you a call tomorrow morning. We need to talk."

I hung up and stared at the checks, marveling at the gall of the man. I tossed them into the garbage can, locked up, and drove back out to Sunset Acres.

The next morning before breakfast, in a burst of gratitude for being on leave from people like Gordon Fletcher, I went out into the back yard and pulled a few stems of the irises and put them in a vase on the table. When Imogen came in and saw them she laid into me: "Don't tell me you pulled those up from the back yard."

"I thought you'd like them."

"You ass!" she stormed out to assess the damage. "If I wanted my flowers pulled up, I would have done it myself."

"Sorry" was all I could say to her departing back. It was a rather subdued breakfast, to say the least.

Enough was enough. After a few hours of scraping, I put the ladder away, went inside, changed into my navy blue suit and packed my few belongings. Before leaving I stood in the hallway for a moment, listening to the thumping of her treadle. I felt bad leaving like that, without even a goodbye, but I knew she would try to stop me if I said anything. I quietly made my way down the stairs and out the door.

22

IT WAS ABOUT eleven o'clock when I pulled into the garage under the Regal Arms. Arturo gave me a hearty handshake in the elevator, asking if I had been on vacation. "Sunset Acres," I replied. "I highly recommend the roast goose." We parted with another handshake at the fourth floor, and I made my way down the hall to my door. I unlocked it and stepped in. I reached up to take my hat off. The last thing I recall before waking up in a hospital bed was a swishing sound and a quick movement behind me.

It must have been around 1 p.m. when I came to, because the first thing I saw when I opened my eyes was a line of white sand streaming through an hourglass against a partly cloudy sky.

"Like sands through the hourglass," a familiar voice said, "so are the days of our lives."

I tried to sit up. Halfway there I got dizzy and vomited. Nothing substantial came up. A tube connected to a drip was hanging from my left arm. My right arm was free. With it I reached up and felt around my head. It was bandaged all the way around. I counted half a dozen points of pain. Pink abrasions encircled both wrists. I pulled back the sheet. My right knee was the size of a grapefruit. A bandage six inches long was showing blood on my left shin. I probed around my torso: sharp pain around the lower left ribs.

A blue curtain was drawn across the middle of the room, but I couldn't hear anything coming from the other side. The TV was mounted high on the facing wall. I saw no way to turn it off.

I've got to get out of here, I thought. Every passing second was costing me more than a weekend on the French Riviera. I was uninsured.

As the opening title sequence gave way to the first scene (zoom out from a crackling fire to see Roman and Marlena having breakfast in their ski chateau) it soon became apparent that the episode was either a rerun or was being piped in from the hospital's own video collection, because those hairstyles hadn't been seen on broadcast television, except in jest, in at least thirty years. That I remembered the names of these characters at all was a testament to how desperately bored I had been that week in the fall of 1983 when I stayed home from school to be with Mom after her hysterectomy. To this day she never misses an episode.

Suddenly I had an erection. It had nothing to do with the chemistry of the actors or the subtext of their lines. It was the studio lighting, the tacky sets, the bad acting, the synthesized mood music, the hairdos, and perhaps most of all the quality of the video itself—the soft, flat, metallic sheen of low-grade videotape. It may as well have been my old bootleg copy of *Insatiable*, which had given me so many hours of companionship during high school.

The first commercial break confirmed my suspicion. The ads looked positively quaint compared to today's frenetic editing and slick computer graphics. In the space of three minutes I was treated to nearly all the tropes of 80's daytime television advertising: stop-motion animated dancing sponges, droll basset hounds, aristocratic cats, long static shots of packages on tables, split-screen taste tests on unwitting consumers, cantankerous old women doing crazy things, arch British dandies, nerds, robots. It was heartbreaking.

I fell asleep before the end of the episode. When I awoke, Dr. Guhathakurta was standing at the foot of the bed, her dense jet-black hair framing a broad, round face, Bengali eyes, a long, smooth nose only bested in voluptuousness by her lower lip. She was far too young and beautiful to be a real doctor. Either I was still asleep or had slipped into *Another World*.

"How are you feeling?" she asked rather woodenly.

"I've been better."

She took a look at my charts and said, without looking up: "You've been out a long time." She then came around to the right side of the bed and asked my permission to look at my wounds. She raised the sheet and examined the dressings. Her ID badge swung freely from her soft brown neck faintly redolent of cardamom. Her first name was Chitralekha.

"Where am I?"

"Mercy Presbyterian," she answered, pulling the sheet back over me. Finally she turned her face to mine. "You're pretty lucky."

From her I believed it.

"How did I get here?"

"You were brought by ambulance this morning."

"Who brought me?"

"The police."

"Could you tell me their names?"

"You should get some rest," she said. "All your questions will be answered in time."

She seemed eager to be on her way.

"When do you think I can leave?"

"I would give it a few more days, see how you . . . What's wrong?"

I badly wanted to confess to her that I was uninsured, but the shame of it in the face of such beauty and self-assurance was too much.

"Nothing," I said vaguely and looked away.

Before she left I asked her if she could turn the TV off. She made a few obligatory glances around for a remote, but clearly she had more important things on her mind than my mental health.

During *Another World* there was a commercial for Flo-Go Systems, a local plumbing and air-conditioning company. I had never heard of it. It had probably long since gone bankrupt. It was a thirty-second spot, amateur in every regard, a man's voice asking a series of supposedly random people on the street: "Where do you go for the flow?" To which they exuberantly declare, "Flo-go!" while thrusting out a hand curled into an "O", as if launching an invisible javelin. Hearing that word, repeated over and over like that, depressed me.

Hollywood Squares cheered me up a little. That day it was Jimmie Walker, Joan Rivers, Florence Henderson, and Sandy Duncan, among the lesser luminaries. The only reason I could think of why the show's producers had ever conceived of sticking Florence Henderson (not exactly a renowned comedienne) in a giant tic-tac-toe grid was for the visual pun on the opening sequence of *The Brady Bunch*. Joan Rivers delivered the only decent joke. Host: "Jackie Gleason recently revealed that he firmly believes in them and has actually seen them on at least two occasions. What are they?" Joan Rivers: "His feet."

After *Hollywood Squares* I was treated to *Abbott and Costello in the Foreign Legion*. I nodded off on the boat to Algiers. By the time I awoke, the bumbling duo were being given their medals by the Commandant and honorably discharged. Next up was *Channel 4 News at Five O'Clock*, a real blast from the past: "Jurors in the Groucho Marx Estate trial have handed in a verdict that one lawyer says will never stand."

I should mention that in between all this entertainment a variety of nurses and nurse practitioners came and went, fiddled with the equipment, made notes, pretended to be interested in me. I did learn that I was alone in a shared room. I asked several times if I could turn the TV off. The answers ranged from: "I'll look into it" to "Why?" I ate a piece of freeze-dried chicken-fried steak, some frozen peas, a glob of instant mashed potatoes, and a cube of red Jell-O. I washed it all down with a half-pint of chocolate milk. I kept thinking that any minute now Imogen would step through the door with a care package, that somehow with that remarkable intuition of hers, she would have sensed that I was in trouble and made some calls and found out I was here. Every time a nurse walked by, my eyes turned to the door, only to be disappointed by a rushing white uniform.

Towards nightfall, the wan light of the fluorescent tubes flickering to life, the meal carts clanking and clattering in the hallway, the visitors leaving grateful for their good health, I decided to put the cost out of my mind for the time being. Apart from killing myself, there was absolutely nothing I could do about it.

23

IN THE MIDDLE of *The A-Team*, a good-looking kid in dark jeans and a white T-shirt entered the room. I figured he had come about the TV. He looked like someone who belonged on it. He was about twenty-five, with thick, curly black hair and the deliberately casual unshaven look of a men's cologne model, eyes the color of a Caribbean lagoon on whose untroubled waters, judging by his tan, he had been floating since he was born. He walked up to me as if he knew me.

"I'm Detective Gallo," he said in a voice nearly as rich as my own, pulling a wallet from his front left pants pocket and opening it to show me his shiny badge. He held it out long enough to convince me that my nose for cops was broken. He closed the badge case and returned it to his pocket.

"I guess you're not here about the remote," I said.

"Sorry?"

I tried to sit up a little but the rib had other ideas. I doubled the pillow under my head instead. "I'm afraid I don't have much to give you," I said.

"Talk to Arturo Sanchez at the Regal Arms. He's the doorman and elevator guy. I was with him right before they jacked me. That was just after eleven o'clock."

"Actually, I'm not handling the assault," he said, quite pleasantly. "Phibsboro PD took the call. It's their guys. I'm homicide, 66th Street Division. I'm on the Walter Morris case."

I took a few moments to digest this, after which I said:

"What happened to Hicks and Stiles?"

"They're not on the squad anymore," he replied with what underneath his obligatory posture of fraternal solidarity sounded distinctly like a hint of satisfaction.

"Oh," I said. "What happened?"

"I'm not at liberty to disclose." He crossed his arms in front of him, revealing the regular hours he put in at the gym. "The Morris case has been reassigned to me."

"Fancy that."

For a minute there the TV had completely vanished from my consciousness. Suddenly it was back, trying to sell me a dreamy glass of iced tea. I tried to block it out, but the kid's head was so positioned that I couldn't look at his face without also seeing what was going on on the screen.

"There appears to be a connection between your assault and the Morris case," he said.

He pulled his cell phone out of his right front pocket and brushed his fingertips across the screen.

Still looking at the phone, he said: "On the chalkboard in the classroom where you were discovered this morning was written the following: *I killed Walter Morris.*"

I worked on that sentence for about thirty seconds, turning it this way and that, trying to wring some sense out of it, before finally admitting defeat.

"Classroom?" I said.

He peered at me over the edge of his phone. "You were found unconscious in a classroom at Del Norte Elementary School in Phibsboro."

I stared at him for another half-minute or so.

"Are you sure you're in the right room?"

"You're Eddie King, aren't you?"

"Yes, but I wasn't in any classroom this morning. It was past eleven when they whacked me."

"That was yesterday," he said. "Phibsboro PD responded to a call at seven o'clock this morning. By all appearances you were in the school most of the night."

I stared dumbfounded at him for another large fraction of a minute. It took that long for the name of the school to sink in. I had gone there for third grade.

He looked at me over the edge of the phone. "It was written a hundred times, like a kid's penmanship exercise. I don't suppose you know anything about that?"

"About what?"

"I killed Walter Morris."

I began to wonder if I wasn't still dreaming. "You killed Walter Morris?"

He actually rolled his eyes. He turned his phone around and held it near my face so I could see a photograph of a chalkboard with *I killed Walter Morris* written a hundred times on it. He zoomed in.

"It's your handwriting," he said.

"That's a good one."

"We had it compared this morning to a statement of yours on file. The samples matched."

He slid his phone back into his pocket and gazed down at me with unsettling empathy.

"Can I get you anything?" he asked. "Something to drink?"

"A bourbon would be nice."

He smiled. This bastard was way too charming to be a cop.

"I just have a few questions, if you don't mind."

He then stepped over and grabbed the chair beneath the TV and in one seamless motion simultaneously slid it and turned it and plunked himself down in it just out of my reach.

"What was your relationship to Walter Morris?" he asked, leaning forward, forearms along his thighs, as if he were the host of a talk show and I its special guest.

"There wasn't any."

He sat back and looked at me thoughtfully.

"I understand that you're featured in his novels."

"You understand wrong."

He pulled his phone out again and brushed his fingertips over the surface. Again he turned it around so I could see it. This time it was a photograph of the front cover of *Blinded by the Sun*.

"Eddie King," he said. "That's you. Isn't it?"

"No, the bag of bruises you're talking to is Eddie King. That's just words on a page."

"Is it? Your office address. Your apartment address. Your case files. Are you telling me that none of that has anything to do with you?"

"No, I'm telling you that he was secretly copying my files for more than a decade. He was stealing from me."

He nodded, humoring me, and set his phone in his lap, where it had no intention of staying for long.

"And when did you learn of this?"

"The day after he died."

He studied me, nodding earnestly.

"You never knew of the existence of these novels before then?"

"No."

"How did you find out about them?"

"I went to the library."

"Why? Had someone told you something?"

"Your former colleagues were good enough to show me the suicide note while accusing me of murder. I got the name Baxter Conway from the obituary and went to the library to see what I could dig up on him. I like to know about the people I kill."

"And that's when you discovered that his novels were based on your cases?" he asked. I never thought I could miss Hicks and Stiles. As dumb as they were, at least they knew how to respond to biting wit.

"Yes."

"You had never met Walter Morris before this?"

"I never met him, period."

He sat for a moment, thinking, the manner of which was to look downward with a slight pout to his lips, gazing at his phone, that great repository of Everything.

He looked up: "Sorry to keep on about this, but what proof do you have that he was stealing from you?"

"Ramona Quintana," I said.

"And who is she?"

"A cleaning woman at the Mandrake Building. She's been there for twelve years. She also happens to be the Morris's maid."

He tapped the screen of his phone for ten seconds or so then returned his full attention to me.

"And what was her role?"

"She has the master key. Either she was giving him access after hours or taking the files out herself and copying them."

"What proof do you have?"

"Educated guess."

"So if, as you claim, Walter Morris was stealing his ideas from you, working from your files, what are you doing living with his widow?"

Now we were in business. He was of the cobra school: disarm your prey with an enchanting smile, then strike when they least expect it. I had underestimated him, which was precisely his intention.

"I'm not living with her," I said. Rather, those were the words I spoke, but they were no match for the guilty strain in my voice. His venom was already at work.

He stared at me for about five seconds: "I've just come from speaking with her. She claims you have been living there."

"I've been doing some work for her."

"So you're not living there?"

"I've been crashing there for the past few weeks," I said. "If that constitutes living there, so be it."

He scratched the back of his neck. There wasn't an itch within miles of it.

"Why have you been sleeping there, if I may ask?"

"Gas is expensive."

He stared at me.

"What kind of work are you doing for her?"

"Home improvement."

He did smile at that. Granted, it was only at the outer corner of his eyes, but a smile nonetheless. He was catching on.

"Is this one of your trades?" he asked.

"No. She hired me for security. I got bored, so I decided to do some repairs. You've seen the place."

He was quiet for a while, then, sitting back in his chair in a way that suggested we were old pals, he said:

"For some reason Chief Greeley has the impression that you're a good guy. He doesn't think you killed Walter Morris. He read Hicks's and Stiles's report. He believes it was suicide. There's no apparent motive." He paused, then said: "At least there wasn't until you started living with the Morris widow."

"I'm not living with her."

"He's giving you the benefit of the doubt. It's up to you to cash in on it. We can do it here or I can take you in. It's your choice."

I gave this some thought. From a purely economic standpoint it made more sense to finish my recuperation in jail. If nothing else, the television programming was bound to be current. The problem with jail isn't the cell, it's who you've got to share it with.

His existential itch had migrated to my right forearm. I scratched it and said: "I initially went out there just to ask her some questions. I wanted to know how my stuff had ended up in her husband's novels."

He sat up: "And what did she say?"

"Not much at first. I went back a few more times, trying to get some answers. She was reeling from his death. She was frightened. She didn't seem to have any family or friends. I indulged her until she began to trust me enough to let me look at the rough drafts. She was nervous, as you might expect of a woman who believed her husband had been murdered under her nose. She made an offer to employ me for a week for around-the-clock security. I accepted. I figured she knew more about her husband's novels than she was letting on, and I saw it as an opportunity to take a look around the place."

"What did you find?"

"Nothing. Until Ramona Quintana showed up for work one morning."

"When was this?"

"Last Thursday, I think."

"A week ago?"

"Yes."

He tapped the screen of his phone a few times.

"So even after you realized that Ms. Quintana may have been involved with Morris in copying your cases you stayed on out there with Mrs. Morris. Why?"

"I wanted to paint her house."

He stared at me blankly.

"Forgive me if I'm missing something here," he said, "but it just doesn't add up that a week after the only lead you've come up with you're still living out there with the widow of the man whom you claim was stealing your files for twelve years to write his books from. What am I missing?"

"Everything."

"What's that supposed to mean?"

"It means logic is overrated," I said. "Most of the time I don't know what the hell I'm looking for until I've found it."

He stared at me: "You know she has changed her story and now claims it was suicide after all."

"It was."

"What makes you so sure?"

"The guy was a writer. The gun was in his hand."

"So where's the bullet?"

"Ask Hicks and Stiles. They were the first responders. While you're at it, ask them where they were yesterday around eleven o'clock."

He sat back and studied me for a few moments.

"Are you suggesting that they had something to do with your assault?"

"No, I'm actually accusing them," I said. "When did they lose their jobs?"

"I'm not at liberty to discuss that."

"Well, look into it. The last time we spoke, in their squad car, Randy was reading to me from a well-thumbed copy of *Guttersnipe*. He was convinced that I had either written the novels myself or was Walter Morris's informant. Stiles made some threats. Hicks was particularly burned up about the depiction of him on the Jesús Rivera shooting."

"You were there that night."

"Yes."

"Who else?"

"No one, as far as I know."

He stared at me for a while, then looked down at his phone and did the finger-flutter across the screen.

"The whole squad is reading those books," he said, glancing up. "Everyone thinks you were either his collaborator or you wrote them yourself, that Walter Morris is as much a pseudonym as Baxter Conway."

"That's quite a sophisticated thought for a bunch of cops," I said.

He ignored that.

"What about this person who allegedly showed up at the Morris house a few weeks before his death?" he asked. "The man in the black suit and fedora."

"Exactly. What about him?"

"None of the neighbors have any recollection of anyone of that description in the area until you showed up. They all assumed I was asking about you."

"And I'm sure you made great efforts to disabuse them of that notion."

He twisted his neck to the right. It popped. He torqued it back to the left with a similar result.

"What other jobs are you working on?" he asked.

"None."

He stared at me. "You're not working for Fletcher Enterprises?"

I stared back.

"I was issued a warrant to search both your office and your apartment," he said. "There were two checks in your trash can from Fletcher Enterprises. Dated a week apart. I called and spoke to Gordon Fletcher. He claims you are working for him."

"Did you ask him what the job is, because I'd like to know myself."

"He's paying you, isn't he?"

"He's trying to."

"Are you claiming that you have never worked for him?"

"I tailed his wife for a week. When it turned out he was the Sancho I told him to get lost. He insisted he was just testing me for some other job. I told him I wasn't interested. What can I do if the man likes throwing his money in my trash can?"

He fiddled with his phone some more.

"There was a letter on your desk from someone named Kathy Jerrell, addressed to Walter Morris. I read it."

"Busy day. Did you read the part where she's encouraging him to come clean to me?"

"What makes you think she was talking about you? It could have been anyone. A family member, a friend he had a dispute with."

"His only family is a sister, and he didn't have any friends."

"Have you attempted to make contact with Kathy Jerrell?"

"No."

He tapped away at his phone.

"In Hicks's and Stiles's report they claim that your gun had been discharged within twenty-four hours of their questioning you."

"That's correct."

"Was it?"

"Apparently so."

He looked at me.

"Did you fire your gun?"

"I don't know."

"What do you mean you don't know? Either you fired it or you didn't."

"I have no recollection of firing my gun."

He stared at me for a while then lowered his eyes to his phone.

"Where were you between two and three o'clock on the afternoon of December 7th?"

"In my apartment."

"Were you alone?"

"No."

He raised his eyes.

"Who was with you?"

"A sad girl high on coke."

"What's her name?"

"Brandy. That afternoon, at least."

When he was finished fiddling with his phone he stood up and slid it into his front pocket. He artfully restored the chair to the wall and returned to my side.

He gave me a mildly pitying look. It was the same look I used to get from Doug Truax in sixth grade. Doug was a flawless boy and knew it. He occasionally took pity on me and picked me to be on his kickball team. I went to his house once and fell in love with his mother.

"If you want my advice," Detective Gallo said, "don't go back there."

He was out the door before I could think to ask him to please find someone to turn off the TV.

24

"OH, EDDIE," SHE gasped at the sight of my face as I made my way over and onto the porch. The next thing I knew her arms were wrapped around me. It was such a spontaneous overflow of emotion, I was startled. To be that missed, that concerned about, was a complete novelty for me. Tentatively at first, then wholeheartedly, I hugged her back. Until that moment I hadn't really begun to grasp what I had just been through. I still wasn't convinced it was over. Even lying drugged up in the hospital, force-fed daytime television, my nerves had been as tense as barbed wire. Somewhere in the back of my mind was the fear that whoever had done this to me might come back to finish the job. Only in Imogen's embrace did I finally begin to relax.

She stepped back and looked at me, her eyes shiny with restrained tears.

"What in God's name happened?" She pulled me inside and closed the door. "I was so worried."

I smiled apologetically. "Someone decided there were some gaps in my education."

209

Clutching my left elbow she tugged me into the living room. I limped along beside her over to the sofa. Once she was sure that I was relatively comfortable, she said: "I'll put on the tea."

"I could use something stronger."

"I would say so."

She went to the china cabinet and came back with the cut-glass brandy decanter and matching glasses. She set the glasses on the table and poured a couple of fingers of the spirit into each of them. I downed mine in one swallow, painkillers be damned.

"I was so worried," she said. She was perched on the edge of the seat cushion, her eyes riveted to my battered face. "Why did you go off like that without telling me?"

I hesitated, then said, a bit sheepishly: "I didn't want an argument."

"Oh, Eddie, you know I didn't mean it about the irises."

I poured myself another glass of brandy.

"It wasn't about the irises."

"What then?"

"I honestly don't remember." As I raised the glass to my lips I suddenly felt that there was no place in the world I would rather be at that moment than right where I was, on that musty old sofa, having a brandy with Imogen Morris. Despite everything, I felt ridiculously happy.

"Who did this to you?" she said with a serious lust for vengeance in her voice.

"I don't know. I can't remember anything. They blackjacked me as I stepped into my apartment, before I even had my hat off."

"Then what?"

It hadn't been my intention, but before I knew it I was telling her all about my stay in the hospital, including my insurance travails. She wanted to know everything. It wasn't enough to say that I had been tortured by 1980's television. She wanted details. Which shows? Why couldn't I turn off the TV? *Days of Our Lives*, *Hollywood Squares*. She got it all. When something wasn't clear she asked me to back up and explain it again, step by step.

"He was here," she said as I started to tell her about Detective Gallo. "He was asking a bunch of questions."

"I know," I said. I refrained from mentioning what he claimed had been written on the chalkboard. I didn't see the point of inflicting unnecessary guilt on her. But perhaps more than that, I wanted to keep that look in her eyes. She was gazing at me with such pride, such admiration, that I couldn't help feeling that despite doing nothing but getting whacked on the head I actually was some kind of a hero.

"All I wanted to know was if you were all right," she said, "and he wouldn't tell me anything, not even which hospital you were at. He wanted to know when you had first come here. Had Walter and I ever met you before? Was I sure that Walter had actually written his novels? Can you imagine? He was insinuating that *you* had written them, the most absurd thing I've ever heard. I assured him in no uncertain terms that my husband was the author of his novels, that I had typed every one of them myself from his notebooks. I told him that you had never even heard of the novels until recently. He had been around to the neighbors and found out that you were staying here, helping me with the house. He wanted to know what you were doing here. Had you coerced me? Had you blackmailed me? He even had the gall to suggest that you and I . . . I can't even repeat what he said. You'll be happy to know I told him all about Ramona. I told him that if he wanted to know the truth then go talk to Ramona Quintana."

"You didn't need to do that," I said.

"It's the truth, isn't it?"

I made no reply. Suddenly I came over very drowsy. The mixed cocktail was starting to do its work.

"You're safe now," she said.

She must have known what I was about to say, even before I did, because her face clouded over before the words had left my mouth.

"I won't hear of it," she said. "You're staying here tonight."

"Imogen . . ."

"Don't argue. I know you. You don't have a thing to eat in your apartment. You'll just go there and mope around and start drinking and wish you had stayed out here. Now, you're going to stay here tonight and have a proper dinner. That's all there is to it. We'll see how you feel tomorrow. If you insist on leaving, I won't stop you."

It was no use. I gave in, reiterating that it would only be this one night. Her evident relief was mixed with vexation that I could even conceive of leaving without staying for dinner. For a good ten seconds she couldn't look at me. Instead she looked down at her brandy glass, which she was holding in her lap.

"I'll go and get dinner started," she said to my drooping eyes. "You just stay there and rest."

That was fine by me. A few minutes after she had gone into the kitchen I nodded off. When I awoke, the table was set, wisps of steam rising from a platter of roasted quail. She called me over and I took my habitual seat, wiping the grogginess out of my swollen eyes.

"You know what kept me going when I was lying in that hospital bed," I said, knowing how much it would gratify her, as she ladled gravy onto my plate. "It was your dinners."

"Oh, please."

"No, I swear to God. I lay there reliving every second of them, every taste, every texture, every smell, telling myself that if I didn't make it at least I would go to my grave having tasted ambrosia."

"I don't believe a word of it."

I gorged until I was stuffed, if only to get the memories of that hospital food out of my mind. A heavy torpor stealing over me from the three glasses of wine, I tossed my napkin onto my plate, conceding defeat.

"I'd love to stay up and keep you company," I said, "but I can hardly keep my eyes open."

"Off to bed you go," she said.

She helped me up the stairs and down the hall. When we reached my door, instead of turning in she tugged me on towards her bedroom, saying, "You take my bed tonight."

"That's not necessary."

"Yes," she said. "It's more comfortable."

"I like my bed."

"I know you do, but you need more room."

I was too tired to argue.

"Where are you going to sleep?" I asked her.

"Just relax, Eddie," she said. "You've been through a terrible ordeal."

We carried on down the hall and into her bedroom.

"Do you need help undressing?" she asked before leaving.

"No. I can manage."

"Are you sure?"

"Yes."

She placed the cover over the bird cage and wished the strawberry finches and I a pleasant night.

It wasn't yet dark out, the gentle twilight bathing the room blue. I stood for a moment at the foot of the bed, soaking up all the feminine scents and textures. Then I took off my clothes, drew back the bedspread and climbed in. It was like falling through space in slow motion, so exquisitely soft were the mattress and sheets and pillows. I couldn't help but groan as I sank into them, painfully aware of how stiff I was in comparison. I lay there on my back for a long time, gazing up at the intricate woodwork of the canopy as the last of the evening blue faded to black.

In the morning, when I awoke, she was standing beside the bed, holding a silver tray with breakfast on it, smiling down at me as if she had been gazing at my sleeping face all night. Her hair was loose and still damp from her shower, which in contrast with the golden sunlight streaming around her made it look nearly black. The sweet song of the strawberry finches completed the heavenly vision.

"You had a nice, long sleep," she said. "Sit up."

I sat up and she set the tray across my lap. I felt like weeping at how lovely everything looked on it: two perfect eggs on a china plate, sunny-side up, just the way I liked them, the plump yolks as vivid as wet pumpkins in a snowfield, two pieces of toast sliced at the diagonal, thoughtfully wedged against the eggs, two ribbons of crispy bacon, a little glass butter dish with a silver knife resting beside it, a tall glass of orange juice, a cup of coffee with a creamer of steamed milk beside it, three sugar cubes on the brim of the saucer. But what really got to me was the little porcelain vase with one of her irises in it.

"What have I done to deserve this?" I asked.

"More than you can imagine," she said and turned and left the room.

I ate in a dreamy stupor, savoring every bite, turning it this way and that in my mouth before I swallowed. When she came back half an hour later I was reclining against the pillows, feeling like a king, gazing up at the canopy.

"You spoil me," I said.

"I haven't even begun." She took the tray from my lap and set it on the floor. She then unbuttoned her housecoat, beneath which she was naked, and let it fall to the floor.

For the first five seconds or so I didn't know what to make of it. I actually thought she must have only meant to remove a layer, using the opportunity of being in her room to change into something else, that she didn't realize she was naked under her housecoat. And yet, I couldn't turn my eyes away. Other than occasional inadvertent glimpses of Mom in a state of undress, I had never seen an older woman naked, and I had always assumed, regardless of how trim and elegant they might have appeared in their clothes, that beneath it all they were wrinkled, sagging bags of age-spotted flesh and varicose veins, repulsive to a man accustomed to the vanities of women half their age. I couldn't believe how smooth and supple and unblemished Imogen's blindingly white skin was. She was stunning. She may have been a little bony at the hips and shoulders, but her pubic hair was raven black against her milk-white belly. Her face alone betrayed her years, and those marks of wisdom and experience atop so ageless a body only made her all the more ravishing in my eyes.

It wasn't until she reached over and pulled back the covers and slid in beside me that it became apparent that she knew exactly what she was doing. Irrationally, I opened my mouth to apologize, but her lips were pressed to mine before I could utter a word. Something powerful rolled through me, starting at my toes and flowing directly up to my brain, which suddenly felt twice its normal size. She wrapped her arms around me. Another warm wave swept me, leaving me utterly paralyzed. I was afraid to look her in the eye, afraid that one knowing glance from her would reveal that she was only mocking me.

25

THE NEXT WEEK was nothing short of a honeymoon. Day and night, we were lost in a beautiful dream. We woke up, reached for each other when not already entwined, screwed like it was the end of the world, ate breakfast in bed, lounged around until one of us got horny again, went at it again, in some new position or in some other room, on some other piece of furniture, ate lunch, took a nap, and started all over again. At some point we stopped bothering to get dressed at all. It was our own private bacchanalian orgy, complete with pheasants and cowslip wine. We anointed the sofa, the divans, every ottoman and settee, the Persian carpets, even the dining table. Our crotches were sore and chafed, but nothing could keep us apart. Given the adolescent frenzy of our couplings, to say that we felt like an old married couple wouldn't be quite right, but in our moments of rest, lying sated side by side, staring contentedly into space, it often felt to me like we had been together all our lives. When I stopped to reflect on the perverse irony of what we were doing, it only incited my lust all the more.

They say older women are the most voracious, but I had never given it much heed. Until now. When it came to unusual positions and practices, Imogen seemed to have no inhibitions whatsoever, so long as they were carried out in a dignified manner. She hated filthy language. To her it was the height of vulgarity. The first time I got carried away and barked out some raving obscenity in the heat of the moment, she turned irate and reprimanded me as if I were a naughty schoolboy. That seemed to enflame something deep inside both of us. We carried on with the act, her scowling and slapping me, me whining and begging for mercy, until both of us exploded with a wicked, searing bliss the likes of which I had never experienced before. After that we rarely missed an opportunity to act out the skit of the mean, repressed termagant scolding the naughty little boy. Occasionally I felt she took it a little too far, cut a little too close to the bone, as when she made me say I was nothing but a frightened little brat hiding away from the big, bad world, at which point I had to remind her in no uncertain terms that I was a free man and could walk out of there any time I chose. These little outbursts of mine usually startled her, and she would bend over backwards to apologize if I had mistaken her playacting for any kind of affront to my manhood or independence. I always felt bad afterwards, pretended it was just part of the act so I could turn the tables and show her who was boss. She liked that too.

Accustomed as I was to banging no-good floozies and jittery whores, none of whom possessed an ounce of class, I always felt obliged to make a supreme effort on Imogen's behalf. I couldn't just please myself as I usually did. There were other considerations: our unusual friendship, her bereavement, her idealized conception of me, which I took pains to uphold. All of this helped me slow things down, pace myself, put her pleasure first. When I looked at her face, her eyes closed, her mouth open in pained-looking bliss, I felt a lot of things, not all of them charitable.

Sometimes I felt sorry for her. She was reeling from her loss, not behaving rationally. At other moments I felt a strange resentment, as if I had been lured to this from the very beginning, from the very first time she opened the door of her house to me. But that crazy thought was usually nullified by how damn good it felt gliding away inside her. She had been dreaming of this for a long time, and I aimed to deliver. It wasn't only for Walter that she had put all those blue-eyed blondes into the novels. They were for Eddie, too. And for herself. She wanted Eddie to fall for them. Time and again she had dangled them in front of him, but he never fell for the bait. He was always in control. Now *she* was the blue-eyed blonde, getting what she wanted at last. And I was Eddie King, *her* Eddie King, the one she had helped create. She had finally broken his will.

Poor old Walter, I couldn't help but think. A man not as strong as myself would have easily succumbed to complete domination by a woman like Imogen. Is that what had happened? Had she gradually pecked away at his manhood, driving him ever deeper into his fantasies of being a hardened, brooding detective, until he had nothing left of his own? How much of that supposed masterpiece he was working on was just bluster, a last ditch effort to reclaim his dignity? Of course I didn't voice any of these thoughts. For the most part we kept away from the subject of Walter, but it was always there, just beneath the surface, his spirit nearby, watching us. Not with disapproval, it seemed to me, but with a kind of amazed loneliness.

One morning at breakfast, I noticed she wasn't eating. She kept staring out the window. I asked her if anything was wrong, but she only shook her head. Eventually she said, almost in a whisper:

"I was out in the garden when it happened." She was gazing abstractly through the panes. Her eyes were absolutely still. I didn't press her. It was a good minute or so before she spoke again.

"We had eaten lunch as usual, around noon. Then he had gone back up to his study to do some work. At around a quarter after two, I heard a loud bang inside the house. At first I thought it was just a door slamming. But something about it wasn't right. It was loud enough to silence the cicadas, which were particularly noisy that day because it was so hot. I got up and made my way in through the conservatory."

She paused, eyes moving back and forth, reconstructing the scene.

"Our lunch plates were still on the table, right here," she said. "I had been eager that day to get back out to the garden, so I had left the dishes for later. Passing the table, I looked down at Walter's plate. I don't know why. On it was a small crust of bread and a peach pit. Somehow, at that instant, I knew he was dead. I could see every crumb, every fissure of the peach pit, the strands of flesh still clinging to the ridges, a tiny sliver of cheese, the dried red smears where the beets had lain. I could see every leaf and petal in the floral pattern around the rim of the plate. The strange thing is, even as I was rushing past the table, I remember thinking that I should have served pickled onions rather than the beets."

She turned and looked at me.

I didn't know what to say.

"I knew he was dead, but I was thinking about pickled onions."

I reached out and took her hand in mine.

After that first week our pace slowed. I loved lying in bed in the morning, watching her standing at her dresser picking out her slip for the day, choosing her dress at the closet door, the way she reached around behind herself to do up the buttons, conscious all the while of my gaze on her, holding her hairpins between her teeth while she arranged her hair. I would lie there, watching her, gradually succumbing to an inexplicable fear of losing her. However much I tried to rationalize it, telling myself that she wasn't going anywhere, the moment she left the room my heart would grow so heavy that I often found myself on the verge of tears, wanting nothing more than to have her back in my arms.

When she was asleep, I would lie beside her, gazing at her face, overwhelmed by the thought that somehow the indifferent universe had produced out of inanimate matter this amazing individual, and that I for some inexplicable reason was the one blessed to be with her for this brief moment in time. So many times I wanted to just open up and bare my entire life to her, tell her things I had never told a living soul. I didn't want any secrets between us. I wanted to know about her childhood, about what she was like when she was a girl. Where had she lived? Who were her parents? Was she good in school? What kinds of games did she play? When was her first crush? But she never wanted to talk about herself. Whenever I asked these kinds of questions she would just smile and say, "Let's not talk about the past, Eddie."

At the very least I felt we had to have the Walter issue settled once and for all. Not just full disclosure on how much she had really known about his stealing from me, but, also, the true state of their relationship at the time of his death. If she had still loved him, how could she be sleeping with me so soon after his death? There must have been some trouble in their marriage, which may have contributed to his suicide. But I didn't want to risk upsetting her by bringing it up. If I had learned one thing about Imogen Morris, it was that she had a wicked temper. As long as we worked it into our charades, we were fine, but I was always afraid of crossing the line, saying something that she could not forgive.

"I can't help feeling that it was destiny that brought us together," I said one morning as we lay caressing each other in bed.

"Eddie," she said in a tone that conveyed her doubts as well as her appreciation of the sentiment.

"I'm serious," I said. "I don't know what the hell I was before this."

This kind of talk made her uncomfortable, but I had to say it. I was done keeping everything bottled up inside. Where had that ever gotten me but alone? In retrospect I could see that there was more truth to those novels than I had been able to admit. Eddie King was a lonely, cynical, self-obsessed bastard, spending all his time trying to right the world's wrongs when there was more than enough rot inside himself to keep him busy for the rest of his life.

She didn't have any use for sentimentality. She recoiled when I expressed my feelings. That wasn't who Eddie King was. If he did have feelings he kept them to himself. She had lived so long with her husband's version of me that she couldn't brook any deviation from it. She wanted me to be that man. As long as I was silent and gruff, she was happy. The moment I started expressing my feelings she cringed. But I knew that beneath that tough, stoical exterior of hers she was a nurturing woman. It was in fact that combination of the hard and the soft, the mean and the sweet, in the same woman, that had me reeling.

26

ONE EVENING AFTER dinner, as we sat enjoying the fire, reading our respective books, I opened the next volume of the *Great Books* series to where it seemed to want to open, and a business card fell into my lap. It was white, dense stock, quality paper. "Eddie King, Private Investigator," it read in Helvetica, above the office address. It was one of the older cards. I turned it over. On the back, handwritten in black ink, were the words: *Tell him everything.*

Imogen must have sensed a perturbation in the atmosphere, for she raised her head and, concern wrinkling her brow, said: "What's wrong?"

"Nothing," I lied nonchalantly. "Just a nice poem."

"Oh?" she said. "Read it to me."

I looked down at the page and read aloud one of the poems there. I didn't hear a word of it.

"That was lovely," she said when I had finished. "Who is it by?"

"Hm?"

"The poem," she said. "Who is it by?"

"Oh. William Morris."

A strange, almost mournful expression came over her face as I said that name. It was only there a second. Then she smiled and asked me to read her another one.

The next morning, after breakfast, I told her I needed to go into town to get some paint samples.

"Can I go with you?" she asked, to my surprise. It was the first time since I had met her that she had expressed any desire to leave the house.

It took me a moment to find the right tone: "Actually, I've got some other things to do."

"I don't mind," she said. "I'll just wait for you."

I pretended to give it some thought, then replied: "Next time. I promise."

She smiled enigmatically, as if she had heard that too many times in her life. For good measure I kissed the back of her neck. A lie of a kiss. A kiss whose only purpose was to get me out of there.

Back in my office, I pulled the bottle and glass from the drawer and poured myself a drink. I took a sip and let it swirl around my tongue for a while before swallowing.

On the desk, where Detective Gallo had thoughtfully left it with the two checks he had fished from the trash, lay the old letter from Kathy Jerrell, back in its envelope. I pulled the letter out and read it again.

I read it a third time. I set the letter on the desk and finished my drink. Then I pulled the telephone over and dialed New Mexico directory assistance. I asked for the number of Pastor Glenn Jerrell on Futura Drive, Roswell. The operator gave it to me and put the call through.

A woman answered on the third ring. In the background children were shouting.

"Is this Kathy Jerrell?" I asked.

"Yes," she replied. She had a sweet voice, the sort of voice you hate to lie to. "Can I help you?"

"My name is Robert Justice," I said. "I'm a private detective."

All I could hear was the children. She covered the mouthpiece and told them to be quiet. They complied for a second or two.

Knowing that her first thought would be that something had happened to one of her kids or her husband, I didn't hesitate in telling her that Walter Morris, the novelist also known as Baxter Conway, had died last month.

"Oh . . . my . . . God," she gasped. I gave her a few moments.

"The reason I'm calling," I said, "is that I've had an opportunity to read the letters that you and Mr. Morris exchanged over the years, and I just have a few questions. Is this a good time?"

The line went quiet. Again she told the kids to settle down, a little less patiently than the first time.

"I can't believe it," she said. "I just wrote him a letter."

"You have nothing to be concerned about," I assured her. "I'm just trying to get a little information."

"Well I'm not sure I can help you," she said, her voice beginning to quaver. "We never actually met."

"It's nothing to do with you," I said. "I'm just trying to clarify something he mentioned to you in one of his letters. In the one dated August 2nd, 1998, you write that you'll regret it if he, meaning Walter, doesn't meet 'him.' I'm trying to find out who this 'him' is. You say, 'Tell him everything. It'll be such a weight off your chest.' Do you recall who you were referring to there?"

"I'm sorry," she said after a long pause. "I'm just kind of in shock here. Give me a second."

"Take your time."

The sound went muffled for about ten seconds. She barked something at the kids. When at last she released the mouthpiece the space around her was quiet. She asked me if I could repeat what I had read. I read it again.

"That was about his son," she said when I had finished.

At that moment, I was reaching for my glass. My hand never made it.

"His son?" I said as if the connection wasn't perfectly clear. "Are you sure about that?"

"Absolutely," she said a little too confidently, as if to make up for the slow start. "I remember it very well. He told me he had decided to try to make contact with a son that he and his wife had put up for adoption at birth. He was feeling very guilty about it. I always talked about my kids in my letters, and I think over the years it started getting to him. In that letter I was encouraging him to try to make contact."

"Do you know if he ever did?"

"No, I don't think so," she said. "If he did, he never told me."

"Did he tell you his name?"

"I don't think he knew it himself," she said. Then: "I don't remember. It was a long time ago. I would have to go back and look at the letters."

It hadn't occurred to me that she might still have the letters.

"I saved them all. God. I just can't believe it. He was such a great writer."

I allowed her a few moments to persist in that belief, then said:

"Is there any chance you could have a look through the letters again and see if there are any other references to his son?"

"Sure I could," she said. Then: "What exactly is all this about anyway?"

So I gave her a brief account of the suicide, followed by a story I had started concocting about thirteen seconds ago.

"In Walter's will he named his biological son as legatee to his estate, which includes all future proceeds from his novels. He also named this son as the beneficiary of a substantial life insurance policy. The probate process requires that he be notified. We need a name."

She bought it.

"Of course I'll look," she said. I gave her my number and asked her to call me if she found anything.

After we hung up I sat there for a while massaging my right earlobe with my thumb and middle finger, seeing in my mind a man in a black suit and fedora standing on the porch of an old house in Sunset Acres, a gun in his hand. Motive? Abandoned at birth? Hardly justification for premeditated murder. Resentful of his father's success? Unlikely. Trying to frame me? Why? A psychopath? Whatever the case, if this son really existed, I had a few questions I wanted to ask him myself. That wasn't going to happen without a name.

I considered various ways of asking Imogen outright, but in the end rejected all of them. She clearly hadn't wanted me to know that she had borne a child. Her fury would be all too predictable. And I wasn't feeling too charitable myself about her lying to me.

As I reached for the bottle, a line of poetry started running through my head. *Thoughts unsaid 'twixt Life and Death.* I poured myself a glass. *My fruitful silence quickeneth.* The glass paused halfway to my lips. I set it down. I got up and walked to the door and grabbed my hat and coat.

27

BUILT AT THE height of Brutalism, the County Public Health Building was a jumble of concrete blocks stacked four stories high, staggered side to side, streaked and stained filthy gray from decades of smog. As a symbol of the public health of the County, the building spoke volumes. All the floors above ground were presently vacant. Only Vital Records (pre-1980) was still here, down in the basement.

It was around 12:15 when I pulled into the empty parking lot behind it. I cut the engine and got out and made my way over to the service entrance on the west side and pushed the intercom button. A few moments later a man's voice I didn't recognize said, "Yes?" in what I could only assume was an ironic parody of some English butler confronted with a stranger at an unpropitious hour. Either this fellow had a peculiar sense of humor or he was a bit daft.

"I need to look at some records," I said.

"And you are?"

"Eddie King," I said. "I'm a private detective."

I heard a nasal snort, which may have just been him clearing his nose. A moment later the garage-style door slowly began to rise on its noisy chains and gears. When it had cleared the top of my hat, I stepped under it and into the enormous freight elevator. Nowadays it was the only way down. I pushed B. When the door had finished lowering, the elevator began its slow descent through the guts of the building.

Going down to Vital Records always gave me the impression that I was descending into an old black-and-white movie. During the war the building, or rather the previous one, had housed the Army Intelligence Service Language School. The basement, in addition to serving as a bomb shelter, was the Pacific Coast Headquarters for analyzing and interpreting the Census Bureau's information on Japanese Americans. That shameful collaboration helped put over a hundred thousand American citizens in concentration camps. It was at that time that the basement was outfitted with the banks of heavy-duty, gunmetal gray filing cabinets and all the other Army office furnishings that persist to this day. When that building was demolished to make way for this one, the basement wasn't touched. They left everything down there exactly as it was. Everything was battleship gray: walls, desks, chairs, fans, lamps. Even the water dispenser and punch clock were gray. Everything being the same colorless shade and tone, it was difficult to pick objects out from the background. At times it seemed as though the filing cabinets stretched away into the distance. At other times you felt like the walls were closing in around you.

As the elevator gently touched bottom, I raised the heavy gate at the opposite end and stepped out. A man I had not seen before was standing behind the counter. Only the knot of the maroon tie he was wearing under a charcoal sweater vest was showing, but amidst all that gray it stood out like a stoplight in heavy fog. He looked about ninety years old.

In his youth he must have been very tall, for even his severe stoop couldn't keep him under six feet. His face was striking: wispy gray hair parted ruler-straight atop a long, narrow cranium, a nose like the beak of a falcon, massive fleshy ears backlit by one of the bare bulbs in the low ceiling, oddly sensuous lips for a man, especially one his age, and the purest blue eyes I had ever seen, between which his bushy, permanently furrowed brows had gouged deep ravines. He could have been an old movie star from the silent era, or a retired five-star general.

"Afternoon," I said, approaching the counter. "Is Norman in?"

"You look the part," he said in a hoarse voice.

"Excuse me?"

He was gazing intently at my face, his heartbreakingly blue eyes darting here and there around my person.

"Do I know you?" I asked.

He smiled. There was something odd about this man. His disconcertingly blue eyes were only part of it. He reminded me of this actor my dad and I used to see all the time in these old sci-fi movies on TV on Sunday afternoons, movies he had grown up with and wanted to share with me. *Invasion of the Body Snatchers, The Atomic Kid, Creature from the Black Lagoon.* This one actor, who reminded me of a praying mantis, always seemed to be in every film, always playing the weird doctor or the mad scientist. My dad and I used to bet each other whether or not we would see him in the movie, and sure enough, he was always there. We would kill ourselves laughing every time he appeared on the screen. There was something of that same quality of the demented scientist hiding behind a mask of normality in this man's face.

"Is Norman here?" I asked again.

"He's presently occupied," he replied, still studying my face.

I eyed him back for a while then turned and grabbed one of the manila cards from the side counter and filled it out. I handed the card to the old mad scientist. He barely glanced at it.

"What's your relation to the deceased?" he asked.

"I'm a private investigator," I said. "I'm working for the mother."

As if merely humoring me, he asked to see my identification. I pulled out my wallet and showed him my detective's license. The ends of his long, bony fingers were bent with arthritis but otherwise admirably steady. Grinning to himself, he studied the license. He looked up at me.

"I'm afraid this license has expired."

"It's valid," I said. "There's a ninety-day grace period." In fact, this was last year's expired license, my current expired license having been lost with my other wallet when they blackjacked me.

He handed it back to me. "Do you have a letter stating your business relationship with the deceased's mother?"

"All I want is to have a look at a few records, for Christ's sake."

"You'll need the letter before I can accept your application."

"Application?" We stared at each other. "Look, man. Can we cut the crap? I've been coming here for years. I've never had any issues."

"My my," he said. "Tetchy tetchy."

"Send Norman over," I said.

"He's busy at the moment."

"Just tell him Eddie King wants to say hello."

He sighed theatrically and shuffled away, carrying his wounded dignity across his bowed shoulders. He disappeared behind a bank of filing cabinets.

A few minutes later Norman appeared. Norman was well past retirement age himself, but the County had retained him to administer the pre-1980 records. He camouflaged so perfectly with his surroundings, from his silver hair and sun-deprived skin, to his woolen tweed waist-coats and timeworn trousers, that I didn't realize he was directly in front of me until I heard him say, in his usual cheerful way:

"Eddie! What brings you down?"

He snapped into focus. We shook hands.

"Who the hell is that guy?" I asked in a low voice.

"Name's Whitner Bissell," he said. "He was some kind of B-actor, had a lot of parts in the fifties and sixties."

"You're joking."

"I wish I was," he said. "They'd had enough of him at the Natural History Museum, so they dumped him on me."

"What were some of the movies he was in?"

"I think he was in *The Manchurian Candidate*."

"Unbelievable."

"Do you know him or something?"

So I told Norman all about my dad and those old sci-fi movies.

"*The Manchurian Candidate*," I said, shaking my head. "My dad was obsessed with that movie. He used to go on about how all that crazy brainwashing stuff really happened. That movie freaked me out."

"I never saw it," Norman said. "The only one I've seen with Mr. Bissell in it is called *A Double Life*, from the late forties, I think. With Ronald Colman and Shelley Winters. He was the doctor in that one."

"Whit Bissell. I can't believe it. We were always trying to find out his name, but they always cut away to a commercial before the credits finished. He must be like a hundred years old."

"I'm convinced he's actually dead."

Whit Bissell. Working at Vital Records. I had to tell Dad.

"I just wish he'd stick to sweeping the floors," Norman said. "He's a royal pain in the ass." He glanced down at my card. "What do you got?"

I handed it to him. He read it.

"William Morris, eh? That's an old-fashioned name."

"I'm after the birth certificate," I said. "And if he's dead, the death certificate."

"That name kind of died out in the fifties," Norman said. "Death dates in the forties and fifties, we've got all kinds of William Morrises. But most of them were born in the late nineteenth century. Do you have a middle name?"

"I'm not even sure about the first name."

"Give me a few minutes." He took the card and made his way around the bank of filing cabinets and disappeared from sight. There was nowhere to sit, so I stepped over to the side counter and leaned my elbow against it. A little while later Whit Bissell came around the corner with a push broom and set about methodically sweeping the floor of the work area. He didn't look my way. I watched him shuffle to and fro with his broom, making artful little jabs into the corners, shaking the dust and fluff over his growing pile, working his way stoically around his little black-and-white movie set. Plenty of other actors have met worse ends than this, I thought.

At one point he looked over at me. A brief flicker of oddly touching vulnerability in his eyes told me he knew I knew who he was. He turned almost shamefully away. It was one of the saddest gestures I have ever witnessed.

Five minutes later Norman returned.

"It's your lucky day." He handed me the certificate. It attested to the birth of one William Joseph Morris, male, six pounds eight ounces, at Mercy Presbyterian Hospital, 11:20 a.m., March 24th, 1972. Attending physician, Chester Lee Wagstaff. I turned the certificate over. Above the baby's inked footprints and the mother's thumbprints were the mother's and father's names and dates of birth: Imogen Park Morris, June 11, 1943 and Walter Alexander Morris, December 7, 1941.

"No death certificate on file," Norman said, but my mind was elsewhere.

As I turned to leave I looked up and saw Whit Bissell looking at me. He was leaning on his broom, his hands joined at the top of the stick.

28

I WAS HALFWAY to the Department of Social Services when Walter Morris's date of birth began hovering before my eyes. *Dec. 7, 1941.* It seemed to be trying to tell me something. All my attempts to shoo it away were fruitless. It nearly made me run the red light at Roosevelt and MacArthur.

Passing St. Luke's, I recalled a certain passage in the Bible. I pulled an illegal U-turn at Pearl and headed down Harcourt back to the Regal Arms. A miraculous parking space was waiting for me directly in front of the door.

I took the stairs two at a time up to the fourth floor. Without bothering to close the door I walked directly to the lamp table and picked up that old secondhand Bible the vagabond had sold me. I opened the front cover and read the inscription. *To my son on your eleventh birthday. May you always be, above all else, a man of God. Love, Mother. December 7, 1952.*

I read it a few more times, just to be sure. Then, setting the Bible back on the table, I stepped over to the window and gazed out across the city, trying to get my mind around it. He must have picked some bum off the street and given him five bucks to pretend he was a Bible salesman. That was the easy part to comprehend. The real question was, Why? I could understand stealing my case files, but concocting this convoluted scheme to plant a Bible in my house—the Bible his own mother had given him on his eleventh birthday no less—that was pure insanity. Who knew what other demented little stunts he had pulled over the years. Of course it was possible that the Bible salesman was legit, that the date of birth was just another coincidence, that the Bible had belonged to someone else born on that infamous date. Possible, yes. But I was through giving a damn about possible.

Tossing the parking ticket into the street, I drove down to the Civic Center and parked in the employees' lot on Garfield and made my way into the Department of Social Services Building and up the stairs to the second floor. It smelled of stale cigarettes and broken dreams. Those were the words Conway had used in *King's Ransom* to describe the building. What did broken dreams smell like anyway? Probably moldy carpet. That day the Department of Social Services actually smelled like fresh paint. They were repainting the hallway on the second floor. Yellow ochre wasn't much of an improvement on mint green.

I asked the curvaceous brunette at the information desk which office handled adoption issues. She said number eight, down the hall, second to last door on the right. I thanked her and made my way down the hall.

In the adoption office a man and woman in their early to mid thirties, a handsome couple, were sitting side by side on the orange plastic chairs provided for the discomfort of the public. They were both wearing rather somber overcoats. Perhaps the coats were intended to convey their solid, middle class values. In the woman's lap, beneath her folded hands, lay a file folder an inch thick.

They looked up at me and smiled, perhaps thinking I was someone they were waiting to see. I nodded politely and walked up to the counter that spanned the width of the room, behind which, in a cluttered workspace, sat three women at their respective desks: a heavyset black woman, a middle-aged Hispanic woman, and an older white woman. None of them looked up from their computer screens as I approached the counter, though it was all but impossible that they hadn't registered my entrance. I waited. They feigned great absorption in their work. I took off my hat and made sure it made a sufficient thud as I set it on the counter to my side. At last the black woman looked up at me. She was wearing a fetching purple blouse.

"Yes?" she said with about as much enthusiasm as a plumber called out on Christmas morning. The other two carried on with their labors.

"My name is Eddie King," I said. "I'm a private detective. I'm seeking some information on an adoption."

The warmth of two intense gazes burrowed into the nape of my neck.

"Are you representing one of the parties involved?" she asked. I would have preferred she got up from her desk and came to the counter, if only for the sake of the expectant couple.

"Yes," I said, as quietly as I could. "The mother."

"What's the name?"

"The mother's?" I asked.

"The child."

"William Joseph Morris."

She typed it on her keyboard and stared at her screen.

"Date of birth?"

"March 24th, 1972."

She typed that. She then reached for the mouse and went through a series of movements and clicks as she watched her screen. When her hand at last was still, she turned and looked at me.

"That's a closed adoption, sir. The mother will have to come down here with the relevant paperwork, and we can look and see if the adoptee has signed the consent form. If he has, we can give that information out to her. If he hasn't, then you'll need to get a court order to unseal the records."

"Can you just tell me if he signed the consent form?"

"No, sir, I can't."

I picked up my hat and put it on my head. She was back at her work before I could thank her.

The couple made a good show of being absorbed in their own affairs as I walked past them on my way out the door.

It was about 1:30 when I stepped into the office. I hung my hat and coat on the rack and picked up the mail from the floor. The hospital bill had arrived. I didn't open it.

I stood for a moment at the side of my desk, staring down at the checks from Fletcher Enterprises. I bowed to fate and grabbed the checks and slid them into the middle drawer of the desk.

I sat down. It had been a while since I had studied the Silly Putty. I picked it up off the blotter and brought it close to my face and read it again.

I set it back down and hoisted the phone book onto the desk and turned to the B's. There were thirteen Brenner's, nine of them men who may or may not have been married to a woman named Ruth. Of the three women there was a Patricia, a Margaret, and an R. I pulled the telephone over and dialed R.'s number.

A woman answered. I asked for Ruth. Wrong number. I tried the same tactic going down the list of men's names. On the sixth call a woman replied:

"Speaking."

"Is this the Ruth Brenner who worked for the agency?" I asked.

She hesitated, wariness in her breath. She was about to say something, then decided not to. She hung up.

I took down the address.

29

MOST OF THE trees in Cedar Grove were older than the houses. The moment you crossed San Pablo Avenue north of the Aerotek plant it was like entering a primeval forest. Both sides of every street were lined with massive old oaks and cedars and walnuts and elms, their upper branches so thickly interwoven that cats and squirrels could travel from one end of the subdivision to the other without ever setting foot on the ground. Before it was Cedar Grove, it was an old-growth cedar grove. During the post-war aerospace boom the County, lobbying hard for the Aerotek contract, promised a new sector of housing for all the engineers and their families. As a gesture of compromise to the Joyce Kilmer Society, which was adamantly opposed to any development in the old cedar grove, the County promised to preserve as many trees as possible. To their credit, they did manage to retain every tree that happened to be standing within ten feet of the grid lines of the proposed street layout, which accounted for all the trees which seemed to have leapt out into the street. Every few blocks you encountered an enormous old oak or fig right in the middle of an intersection, a yellow band painted around its trunk, a sight that never ceased to amaze me.

Her address was 1919 Virginia Street. I took Rose off of San Pablo, drove six blocks down to Virginia, and hung a left. The leaves had started to turn. Thin shafts of sunlight angled down through the yellow and orange foliage, paving the street with golden cobbles. I rolled my window down and inhaled a heady draught of tree bark, chlorophyll, and rotting pumpkins. If I could choose anywhere in the city to live it would be in one of the sprawling ranch-style houses of Cedar Grove. Something about all that rectilinearity amidst the wild jumble of branches appealed to me. All those beautiful old LeSabres and DeVilles and Thunderbirds lazing in the driveways, not one of them with more than ten thousand miles on it, probably had something to do with it. Chalet blue. Starlight silver. Beaumont beige. Colors I yearned for as a kid but never came close to possessing.

It was about a quarter after two, and the only sign of life on the street was an elderly gentleman out for his constitutional in a smart tan blazer and a short-brimmed Panama. I pulled over to the curb in front of 1919 and cut the engine and sat there for a while reveling in the leaf-muffled silence. The house was tan brick with a two-car garage. The curtains in the wide picture window were open, a lamp shade illuminated within. A small patch of dappled sunlight lay like newly minted silver dollars atop the hood of the white '64 Impala in the driveway.

I got out and, buttoning my coat, made my way across the leaf-strewn yard. At the foot of the front door lay a black rubber welcome mat with "BRENNER" stamped in white caps in the middle of it. I rang the doorbell, a fine, leisurely three-tone chime, its final note slow to fade. The peep hole darkened. I held an amiable pose. She eventually got around to opening the door.

She was in her late sixties or early seventies, well-padded from head to toe. The thick lenses of her large, round bifocals magnified her eyes to nearly twice their natural size, which coupled with her relatively small nose and mouth gave her the look of a spooked barn owl.

She beheld me with suspicion from the safer side of the glass screen. The call must have put her on her guard.

"Good afternoon, ma'am," I said. "My name is Eddie King. I'm a private detective."

I held my license up to the glass in front of her face. She tilted her head back and took a long gander at it. The print was obviously too small for her to read, but she made a good show of it.

"I've already told the police everything I know," she said, her eyes returning to mine.

"I'm not sure what you're referring to," I said.

"You're not here about St. Jerome's?"

"No, ma'am," I said. "What is St. Jerome's?"

She gave me a dubious look. "The orphanage."

I put my license away.

"I wouldn't know about that," I said. "I'm trying to locate a man named William Morris. He was put up for adoption as an infant in 1972. As far as I know there was never any contact between the child and his natural parents."

I pulled the Silly Putty from my pocket and held it up to the glass. "I encountered your name among the father's possessions. It appears to be an impression from a newspaper article. I thought it might be a lead."

She squinted at it briefly, then, utterly baffled, returned her attention to me.

"I can't read that."

"It says you were a vital link between the agency and something else," I said, lowering the Silly Putty. "It's not clear what. It says you made a difference in people's lives."

That seemed to soften her.

"What did you say your name was again?"

"Eddie King."

She studied my face for a while, then she unlocked the screen door and opened it.

"Why don't you come in," she said. "I've got something on the stove."

I thanked her, removed my hat, and stepped in.

About three steps beyond the door I was bowled over by a powerful wave of déjà vu. The rust colored sofas, the heavy stone facade around the fireplace, the wood paneling at the back of the room, the blonde walnut shelves and cabinets with bottled ships and other dated bric-a-brac on them, the brass starburst clock, the vertically striped brown and tan curtains, the Harvest Gold table lamps with shades matching the drapes, the huge television console in a dedicated walnut cabinet, the bottle of Rolaids and the *TV Guide* on the brass and glass coffee table—everything was exactly as it had been at some other time, in some other life.

"Have a seat," she said. "I'll just be a minute." Even those words, her casual delivery, her mildly conciliatory tone, reverberated through me. Then, as before, she was walking away from me across the tan shag carpet, her beige polyester pants making the same scratchy sound, her broad, flat behind radiating the same sense of hospitality. Even the smells were uncannily familiar: a buttery aroma which I knew for a fact to be macaroni and cheese, a strange tonsily odor that seemed to be coming off all the brown in the room, the oily, lemony scent of furniture polish, and a certain faint musky fragrance, which I couldn't place but which was the most arresting of all.

I walked over to one of the rust colored sofas and took a seat, setting my hat beside me. That other man set his hat beside him too. As I sat listening to a spoon clinking against a pot, the déjà vu gradually faded. Only then did it dawn on me that anyone stepping into this relic of (or, heaven forbid, homage to) the 1970s would have felt like they were experiencing déjà vu.

She came back in, noticeably more relaxed, and sat down in the brown vinyl armchair facing me on the other side of the coffee table.

"Sorry," she said. "I didn't want my macaroni to burn."

"Smells good."

"When I first saw you," she said, "I thought you were an FBI agent. Or CIA."

I smiled. We sat in silence for a moment, then she said:

"I had so many babies. Two hundred and sixty-three, to be exact. Two or three to a room at any given time for nearly thirty years. They came and they went. Oh, such beautiful little people. Cast off like a change of clothes. You can't help but get attached to them."

I nodded.

"So you ran a kind of foster home here?"

"It was more than that. It was a real home for a lot of those kids. Some of those babies were with me for years before anyone claimed them."

"Was it here, in this house?"

"Yes." She turned her eyes towards the wall to my right and gazed at it for a while. "It seems so empty without them."

She looked at me. "Tell me again who you're trying to find?"

"His name is William Morris," I said. "He was born in March of

1972. His birth parents were Walter and Imogen Morris. I don't know the names of the adoptive parents."

"And why are you trying to locate him?" she asked. "Are the birth parents trying to reunite with him?"

"Actually, the father recently passed away," I said and proceeded to tell her the same story I had told Kathy Jerrell.

"What makes you think the baby was with me?" she asked.

"As I said, your name was mentioned in the article, and I thought it might be a lead."

"What article?"

I pulled the Silly Putty from my pocket again and held it out on my palm. "I'm afraid I don't know where the impression came from, but it seems to be newsprint."

"What is that thing?"

When I told her, she made a shooing motion with her hand, as if to bat away a pesky fly, and groaned. "I've seen enough of that stuff for one lifetime. That's one thing I won't miss, trying to get Silly Putty out of the carpet." She took the wedge and held it close to her face, tilting her head up and down to try to get it into focus.

"It's hard to read the backwards print," I said, sensing her mounting frustration.

"No wonder!" she exclaimed. "I thought I was really starting to go blind. Okay, now I see it's backwards."

"Shall I read it to you?"

She handed it back to me, and I read the text, offering my guesses at the broken words.

"It could be from the article they did on me," she said.

"Which article was that?"

"Oh, jeez, this was probably a good ten years ago. The paper did a piece on independent foster caregivers. They came and interviewed me."

"Do you happen to have a copy of it?"

"I'm sure I do somewhere back in there," she said. "I wouldn't have a clue where to look for it. There's so many old albums. That's one of my projects, put that room in some kind of order."

"Did you keep any records of the babies you took in?" I asked.

"All that stuff was subpoenaed for the case."

"What case?"

"The St. Jerome's case," she said as if it were common knowledge.

"I'm afraid I don't know anything about that," I said.

She grimaced. "Disgusting. What they did to those children. The director was running a child pornography ring out of the orphanage."

I crossed my arms and looked at her.

"I don't know how long it was going on," she said. "They were raided about two years ago by the FBI. He got thirty years. Keith Mannix is his name. You must have read about it in the paper. It was front page news."

It sounded vaguely familiar. Perhaps at some subconscious level I had already made the connection. It wouldn't have been the first time my intuition had had to wait for the facts to catch up to it.

"I'm sure other people were involved," she said. "All the records, dating back to the founding in 1932, were subpoenaed by the court. They came for mine, too. Who knows if I'll ever get them back."

She looked indignant, as if wanting me to share her personal affront, which I did to the best of my ability.

"St. Jerome's wasn't the only agency that used me," she said, keen to make it clear that she was in no way involved. "I was with Shepherd's Flock and Bright Futures, the Langley Agency, others I can't remember."

I nodded.

"Tell me," I said. "These albums you mentioned, do they have pictures of the babies you took in?"

"Yes, a lot of them do."

"Do you have dates in them?"

"No," she said. "But it's easy to tell when they're from."

"Would you be able to find one with pictures from the early seventies?"

"I don't know as that would be much good to you if you're looking for an adult," she said. "Do you have a picture of him?"

"No. But I'd like to have a look, if it's not too much trouble."

"Hold on," she said and got up from the chair and made her way back to the hallway and around the corner. While I was waiting for her, I grabbed the bottle of Rolaids from the coffee table and, for the hell of it, opened the cap and retrieved one of the tablets and popped it into my mouth. I chewed it and listened to her rooting around.

After a while I stood up and ambled around the room, looking at all the tacky odds and ends. I stopped before the bookshelf and perused the titles: *Better Homes and Gardens Fondue and Tabletop Cooking*, *More Joy: A Lovemaking Companion to the Joy of Sex*, *Angels: God's Secret Agents*, *The Total Woman*, to name but a few.

I was about to turn away when a certain combination of letters and layout snagged in my peripheral vision. Blow me if *Guttersnipe* wasn't staring me in the face, right there on the shelf beside *Shogun*. I pulled it out and opened the cover. An inscription on the title page, in blue ballpoint, read: "*To Ruth, a very special lady. Thanks for everything. Baxter Conway.*" Something cold and hard and about the size of a clenched fist slid down my esophagus into my stomach. The date beneath the dedication was "Aug, 1998."

"I'll be damned," I heard her say from wherever she was.

I stuffed the book into my inside coat pocket. "Did you find something?" I called out, quickly returning to the couch.

She came back into the living room holding a thick, powder-blue photo album. "I found the article," she said, taking her seat and opening the album on the coffee table. The clipping was loose, creased over where it had extended beyond the edges of the album. She handed it to me.

The date was June 8, 1998. The upper left-hand quarter of the page was occupied by an ad for the Chrysler PT Cruiser, a car that I detest for its pretensions of being something classic. The car was parked in some leafy urban utopia, at a three-quarter angle facing the viewer. On the near side a man and a woman were strolling hand in hand, the man's right shoe, raised in stride, about to make spatial, if not physical, contact with the leading edge of the grille—the vertical bands that I had mistaken for ventilation grating. The man and woman were dressed in the tastefully updated seventies apparel characteristic of late-nineties fashion, he with his bulbous toed shoes, flared trousers, and broad-collared shirt, she in a silky summer dress patterned in concentric ovals vaguely reminiscent of lava lamp globules. The ad was black-and-white, probably one of the last of its kind before all the dailies, even the cash-strapped *Herald*, had made the switch to color. The slogan at the bottom of the ad was one word: "Soul."

The article running along the right side of it was titled "Unsung Heroines Form Union." I found the paragraph that Walter had sampled; there wasn't much that I hadn't already gleaned from the snippet. I skimmed through the rest of the article, the gist of which concerned a group of local independent foster caregivers who, unhappy with their inability to bargain with either the State or the private adoption agencies, had decided to form their own union. I set the article aside, no more informed as to why Walter had taken an impression of it than before.

She was looking through the album, smiling sweetly at the memories it conjured. I leaned forward. From my vantage they were all upside down, pictures of babies and couples holding babies and some of toddlers and older children, taken with Polaroids and Instamatics and who knows what other devices, but it was immediately apparent from the colors blaring from the pages that we were in the 1970s. It wasn't just the clothes and the outlandish home furnishings in the backgrounds of the pictures. Even the photo processing chemicals of that era seemed to produce garish, saturated hues that instantly took me back to my own childhood, or rather to the images immortalized in our own family album: me on my yellow potty, me in the highchair with red goop all over my face, me in my orange and green Aquaman costume. Images etched into my brain with hydrochloric acid.

"I always asked the new parents to send me a picture once they got settled," she was saying. "I liked to see my babies with their new families. Not all of them did. Out of sight, out of mind."

She looked up. "What did you say his name was again?"

"William Morris," I said. "The father's name was Walter Morris. He was a writer. He wrote under the name of Baxter Conway."

"Baxter Conway?" she said with a startled look. "Not the detective writer?"

"Yes."

"Well why didn't you say so in the first place? Of course I remember him. He came to see me, God, years ago. He gave me one of his books." She turned towards the bookshelf and nudged up her glasses. "Signed it and everything."

Then she gave me a strange expression, a mix of dawning awareness and sorrow.

"Oh dear," she said.

"What?"

"He was looking for his son."

"Yes," I said. "I'm afraid he never found him."

"What do you mean he never found him?" she said. "I'm sure he did. He came here twice. We found the picture and the name and everything. Then he came back again, about a year later, to thank me. He told me he had found him. That's when he gave me his book. I wouldn't forget a thing like that. He was the nicest man. Who told you he never found him? The mother?"

"Yes."

"So you're working for her?"

"Not exactly," I said. "I've been retained by the lawyer handling the estate. The mother isn't interested in meeting the child. She doesn't wish to have any contact."

She frowned in thought.

"Do you remember the name they gave the baby?" I asked. "The adoptive parents?"

"Little Willie," she sighed, ignoring my question. "My heart went out to him. He was a tiny baby, so precious. How any mother could have given him up I will never understand. I had him, oh, about a month, I think. I cried when they left with him. I remember them well enough. Youngish couple, in their early thirties. She was real good-looking and knew it. An affected air about her. I don't recall much about the father. He didn't say much. They looked great on paper, but I had my concerns. It wasn't my decision. It was up to the agency. In those days it was much easier to adopt. If you were married, white, and had a job you pretty much had your pick."

"Do you remember the name they gave him?" I asked again.

"Hold your horses."

She turned to a page in the album.

"There they are. Oh, there's little Willie. Wasn't he gorgeous? Let's see here. These damn plastic things are so stiff. I can't get my fingers under them anymore. Can you pull it up? . . . Now. What's it say here? . . . *To Ruth.* Something *for all the* something *for little* . . . Can you read that? It looks like Robby to me. There's their names. Can you read it? Mr. King? Are you all right? Mr. King? . . ."

30

I HAVE NO recollection of the drive to Merino. That I drove is indisputable. They were my hands on the steering wheel. My knuckles were the same color as the cloud in the distance. The car was stopped at the curb, the engine off. Everything was still.

It took a while for my fingers to straighten after I pried them from the wheel. I got out. The sound of the car door shutting behind me seemed to lengthen as I walked across the yard, as if it were something caught on me, unraveling as I went.

At the sound of my entrance she turned startled from the television and, seeing it was me, smiled. The smile lasted about a second, then vanished altogether. Daisy, jerked to her feet by the whiff of my emotion, bared her teeth and unleashed on me for all she was worth. I walked straight past them both, into the kitchen and over to the cupboard where she kept her liquor. I grabbed the nearest bottle and a glass. My hands were too shaky to pour. I drank directly from the bottle and watched her come.

With every passive-aggressive step she took, a fresh wave of hatred swelled in my guts. Daisy was in the doorway, barking herself hoarse.

The TV was blaring ecstatic inanities. I gripped the bottle by the neck and poured fire down my throat and watched her come.

"Daisy!" she shouted. The dog turned, startled, was quiet for a few seconds, then turned back to me, growling defiantly.

The muumuu was greenish blue today, a bruise of nearly the same color in full bloom on her left shin. She stopped in the doorway and eyed me apprehensively.

"What's going on?"

I gave her a cold glare, then said, spitefully: "William Morris."

Her eyebrows rose, dipped, settled in an uneasy furrow. Her pupils dilated. Her body seemed to shrink under my gaze.

"What?"

"William Morris," I said again.

Her eyes pivoted to the bottle in my left hand, then back to my face.

"What the hell is going on?" Her voice was starting to crack.

I took another drink and stared at her.

"William Morris."

Her eyes were darting back and forth now. An innocent bystander might have thought it was confusion.

"Who is William Morris?" she asked, still desperately searching for some way out.

"I am."

What little color was left in her face evaporated. She gaped at me as if I were deranged.

"I know, Mom, okay."

That vile word, *Mom*, suddenly gutted of all meaning, hung in the air between us for a moment then dropped lifeless to the floor.

"What in God's name are you talking about?" she said. It was astonishing, the conviction in her eyes.

"Ruth Brenner?" I said with as much ridicule as I could freight into my voice. "Does that ring any bells? I've just come from her house. She showed me the picture of you and Dad holding me. It was your handwriting on the back of it. *Thanks for all the love you gave to little Eddie.*"

All she could do was shake her head.

"Mom. Don't." There it was again. That horrible word. Straight to the floor like a burst balloon.

"Do I need to spell it out for you?" I said, the anger rising in my voice. "You're not my mother."

"You've been drinking," she said sourly.

"Are you really going to stand there and lie to my face?" I said.

"I can't talk to you when you're like this." She turned and retreated to the living room. Daisy followed. I wasn't far behind.

"Forty years of lies," I fumed at the back of her head. "You've been lying to me for forty years. My whole life has been one big lie."

She slumped into her chair and reached for her pack of cigarettes. Her hands were so shaky she could hardly get the cigarette out, much less light it. I watched coldly as time and again her thumb missed the button of the lighter and the spark died. At last it caught and she brought the flame to the tip of her cigarette and sucked deeply.

"Why didn't you tell me?" I demanded. I was standing about ten feet away from her, off to the side. She refused to look at me. She was staring at the TV screen as if it were her only salvation.

"You're out of your mind," she said.

"Go get my birth certificate."

"Eddie, for God's sake. Who told you this asinine story? You're my son. I lost a quart of blood giving birth to you. That's the truth, so help me God."

"Go get the birth certificate," I repeated. "I want to see it."

She dropped the cigarette in the ashtray and got up in an indignant huff and set off down the hall. I took another drink. Daisy was cowering in the doorway to the kitchen. I flared my nostrils at her. She flinched and whimpered.

From the TV came sounds of joyous laughter. A man and a woman were sitting silently at opposite ends of a sitcom couch, doing nothing, staring blankly at the camera. Every few seconds a chorus of laughter would blast them, but they continued to sit unperturbed, which seemed to be the source of the hilarity.

My head was starting to spin. I looked around me. Everything in this house was false and ugly and shallow and brittle and stale. The sight of the debating trophy on the mantle made me want to vomit.

She returned with the birth certificate and shoved it at me on her way back to her chair. I had seen it plenty of times throughout my life. It stated, as it always had, that Edward Patrick King was born to Stella Ann King and Gerald Marcus King at 11:02 a.m. on April 16, 1972 at 5704 Baltimore Drive, weighing six pounds, eight ounces. The line for the attending physician was blank. The story which I had grown up with was that she was having a bath when the contractions came on so suddenly that she knew she would never make it to the hospital in time, so she stayed in the bath, and that's where I was born, in the very tub that years later I would bathe in myself. My father was on the rig that week. She gave birth to me all alone. I had heard this story so many times that it had acquired the heft and solidity of irrefutable fact. It was so vivid in my mind, me as a fetus sliding out of her into a bathtub full of blood, that it might as well have been a memory of my own.

The birth certificate looked authentic. That's because it was. It was an amended copy. They swap out the mother's and father's names, post-date it to the date of the adoption, and replace the name of the hospital with the home address. It's common practice with closed adoptions, a way of erasing all traces of the birth parents to protect the child. Perfectly legal. In my case no attending physician was named because for this "birth" there wasn't one, only a woman named Ruth Brenner. I was three weeks old when Gerald and Stella King adopted William Morris and changed his name to Edward King. The original birth certificate was in a filing cabinet at the Office of Vital Records.

I set the bottle on the TV and shredded up the birth certificate and tossed it to the floor.

"Eddie!" she shrieked.

It was her turn to go on the offensive.

"You ungrateful sonofabitch. You haven't done a damn thing for me since I moved up here. I don't know how many Christmases and birthdays and Mother's Days I've spent alone. Not even a call. What have I ever done to you? I was always there for you. When your father was off chasing every skirt in town, blowing all our money on drugs and guitars, I was there. Fifteen years of slaving away in that office so you could have a better life. Saving every penny so you could go to college. And you throw all your talent away on dead-end jobs and booze and whores. Who was the one who bailed you out every time you lost a job? Oh, then you come crying to me, begging for a loan, which you never pay back. You're just like your father. A no good, selfish bastard. Sometimes I wish I wasn't, but I'm your mother, goddamnit, and nothing is going to change that. Birth certificates don't mean shit."

She reached for her puffer and shot a defiant blast into her mouth. On the TV a bald man sitting in an armchair was laughing to himself. I stepped in front of the console, pulled my revolver from my shoulder holster and fired a round directly into the screen. A soft implosion followed hard upon the ear-splitting blast. An arc of pink electricity flared out from the sudden hole, through which a finger of black smoke lazily curled. For a moment the man in the armchair seemed to hover in the air before my eyes, like a genie from a bottle. Then he vanished. Mom screamed. A few panicked scrapes of toenail on linoleum were all that could be heard of Daisy.

It wasn't until the trailing whine of the concussion began to fade that I realized that the maniacal laughter I was still hearing wasn't coming from the TV. By then I was already out the door.

31

IT WAS AFTER eight o'clock when I reached the outskirts of San Calisto. The streetlights were just coming on, an unearthly tangerine glow, the gases not yet excited to the jaundiced yellow that would hang over the little seaside town until daybreak.

How I had managed to stay on the road was a mystery to me. For four solid hours I had seen nothing but images of Imogen before my eyes. Sometimes dressed, sometimes naked, sometimes filling my glass of wine. Each image an icepick through my heart. Around and around the thing I went, trying to find some way out. Mom was lying. I was certain of that. But she had sown enough doubt with her vehement denials to allow a tenacious little seed of hope to take root in me. Maybe there was something I was overlooking, some obvious explanation. Maybe there was a mistake on the birth certificate. Maybe Mom had had an affair with Walter Morris. I imagined every possible bypass. But they all led me back to Imogen.

I stopped at the first filling station and asked the cashier if he knew where Appian Way was. He didn't. I drove around until I found the

Domino's. The kid coming out with the pizzas gave me good directions.
I followed them, heading south onto the main drag (auto parts stores,
fast food restaurants, scuba gear rentals.) Past the A&W I took a right on
Oxbow Street and drove six quiet blocks to Appian Way, then half a
block to the Seabreeze Apartments.

The sign, in vintage cursive, was bolted to the stucco of the unit facing the street. I pulled to the curb and got out and made my way between
the buildings to the walkway skirting the courtyard. No hint of a breeze,
from the sea or elsewhere, was stirring tonight. A bone-jarring racket
echoing from the walls of the surrounding units was soon revealed to be
two kids scraping empty soda cans against the poolside pavement. The
hedges concealing them were in bad need of a trim.

His apartment, according to my address book, was 12B. If he still
lived here. The B's were on the second floor of the building to my left. I
took the staircase up and made my way to the opposite end accompanied
by the vacuous vibrations of primetime television, the clinking of silver-
ware against plates, the brisk clip of Spanish.

When I reached the door I stopped and stood before it, listening. It was
quiet inside. A light was on behind the orange curtain in the window to
the right. I looked back the way I had come. Through the gap between the
buildings, I could see my car parked out there on the street, comfortingly
black and solid. I lifted my hat and ran my fingers through my sweaty hair.
The scraping of the cans ceased momentarily, then started up again.

If not exactly my courage, I mustered up something and made myself
knock. I waited for half a minute. I couldn't hear a thing inside. I
knocked again, more forcefully, half dreading, half hoping he wasn't
there. It was another ten seconds before he hollered irately from somewhere back in the apartment:

"Who is it?"

"Eddie."

"Eddie who?"

I turned and looked back at the car. *Come*, it was saying. *There is nothing to be gained.*

I turned back to the door. "Eddie King. Your . . ." I clenched my teeth. "Open the damn door!"

An odd clicking sound accompanied his approach. The door opened a few inches, more than enough to reveal how much deeper he had sunk since I last saw him.

"Are you alone?" he asked, one solitary eye, his right, red-rimmed and lusterless, busy with suspicion. The wiry gray hairs of a beard concealed the lower half of his face.

"Yes."

He shifted to favor his other eye, trying to see around me.

"Did anyone follow you here?"

"Just let me in."

He studied me for another few seconds then stepped back and opened the door. I recoiled at the sight of him. He must have lost fifty pounds since I had last seen him. The most disturbing thing was the beard. Having never seen him with more than a shadow of stubble, it was hard to reconcile his familiar eyes and nose and forehead with that wild thicket of gray hair overgrowing his mouth and chin and neck. It was the beard of a castaway, a hermit, a madman. A cartoon beard. So shaggy and unkempt that the symbolism of it (hopeless isolation, social ostracism, mental imbalance) seemed to nullify its actuality as a beard, to nullify, even, the man it was attached to. That was how it struck me, not as something growing out of him, but something latched onto him, a parasitical organism sucking the life out of him.

He was in his maroon terrycloth bathrobe, untied, no undershirt, his saggy paunch hanging slack from his protruding ribs over a pair of navy blue boxers. At one time he had had trouble closing this same robe around his girth. A sour smell was coming off of him.

It wasn't until he moved to step back that I saw the prosthetic leg. Where his right leg below the knee should have been was a stainless steel cylinder, its hard plastic mount several shades browner than the skin above. The foot was a revolting little plastic flipper.

He grinned at the look on my face.

"I guess she didn't tell you about the leg," he said with that morbid pride of his. He stepped jerkily aside, eager to get the door closed. I stepped in, out of the way, my eyes riveted to the leg. He closed the door and turned and limped back into the apartment. I watched with a mixture of guilt and shame as the plastic foot swung along beside the real one under the drape of his bathrobe.

Like every other place he had lived, this one was crammed to bursting with his junk collection. Nearly every available surface was occupied by some kind of container—yogurt tubs, tin cans, Tupperware storage vessels, shoe boxes, prescription drug bottles, mayonnaise jars. During most of my childhood it had been scrap metal. Long after his acetylene torches had gone cold he had continued collecting every piece of junk that caught his fancy (weathervanes, carburetors, saw blades) believing that one day it would be just the piece he needed to complete a new sculpture. Year after year the piles in the back yard grew bigger, rustier, more contentious. After the divorce he had gotten into computers, long before the common man had any use for them. In those days he lived in a crush of circuit boards, disk drives, power supplies, monitors, scuzzy cards. The word that always came to mind when I thought of that period was "crater," not only because this was when he started living in his bomb-shelter-like dwellings, but because he was always using that word, as a verb, when his machines failed him: i.e., "The CPU cratered on me." In truth he was never really interested in doing anything on the computers. He just needed to be surrounded by parts of things, things in a transitive state. Nothing in his domain was ever fully assembled and functioning as it was intended to. All I wanted to do when I visited him on weekends was play computer games, but there was always something wrong with every machine. He finally gave up on computers when their innards became so minute that there was nothing left to disassemble.

"Have a seat," he said, motioning vaguely towards an armchair with a stack of magazines on it. I remained standing as he shuffled over to a chair at a round dining table and laboriously turned himself around to sit down.

"What happened to your leg?" I asked.

"Before or after they cut it off?"

I thought I detected a smirk, but it was hard to tell what was really going on behind the beard.

"Don't go swimming in a pool full of Mexicans if you've got diabetes," he said.

He picked up some unidentifiable little plastic object (it looked like a cylindrical bead) from a spread of them on the table and, after studying it for a moment, dropped it into one of several plastic boxes arrayed before him.

"How'd you find me?" he said.

"I had your address."

"I never gave you this address."

"Yes you did."

I was prepared to argue the point with the irrefutable evidence of an unimpaired memory, but he wisely chose not to press it.

"Just throw that stuff on the floor," he said.

I stepped over to a nearby shelf. Lined up on it, inside plastic tubs, were what looked like individual pebbles of gravel, segregated by size and shape and color tone: round grayish ones in one tub, oblong violet-toned ones in another, squarish white ones in yet another. On another shelf hundreds of prescription drug bottles (his own) were filled with tiny screws and nails and nuts and washers. Whereas with all his previous collections there had never been any clear order to the piles of junk, or rather whatever system there was had been known only to himself, now there seemed to be a disturbingly precise place for everything.

He picked up another one of the plastic things and, keeping his eyes fixed on it as he spoke, said: "So what's wrong with her?"

"Who?"

He raised his eyes and looked at me. "Your mother," he said. "Why else would you come all the way down here?"

"I came to see you."

His forehead creased, but he refrained from comment.

"You still a detective?" he asked after dropping the plastic thing into one of the boxes.

"I haven't been working."

"Join the club," he said then launched into a harangue against the Chinese that five minutes later had evolved into a disquisition on the dubious merits of desalination. He paused for breath.

"I'm not your son, am I?" I said.

Until that moment I don't think he had truly registered that another human being was in his midst. He looked startled, as if he had no idea who I was or why I was there. It only lasted a few seconds, then the dull medicated film slid back over his eyes. His gaze returned to his plastic widgets.

"What's going on?" he said without looking up.

"Just answer me," I said. "Yes or no. Am I your son?"

He raised his head.

"Why would you ask such a crazy question?" A nervous quaver tore at his voice. "What the hell did she say to you? If that woman was screwing around on me all those years . . ." He looked away, the vein on his temple throbbing. I stared at him. He refused to look at me.

"I know I was adopted," I said.

He shook his head in feigned indignation. At last he looked at me again.

"Who told you that?" he said. "Is that what she told you?"

"Just for once could you cut the bullshit. I know everything. I know about Ruth Brenner and the foster home. I know that my birth name was William Morris, that my parents were Walter and Imogen Morris, that I was born on March 24th, 1972, not April 16th. I've just seen the picture of both of you holding me, the picture you sent to Ruth Brenner thanking her for taking care of me. So you can drop the act. Just tell me the truth."

"Oh shit," he said and pressed his right palm to his forehead, rubbing it back and forth as he looked down, slowly shaking his head. In time his palm drew back, his fingers slid in to massage the point between his eyebrows. Then, still without looking at me, he braced his hands against the table and muscled himself up to standing. He limped four or five steps over to the bare wall to my right. There he stood, facing the wall, arms limp at his sides, for well over a minute. I have never seen a more pathetic sight. It was as if the shell of lies and self-delusions that he had been living in all his adult life had suddenly shattered and fallen away, leaving this shriveled-up old mollusk naked to the world, at a complete loss for how to go on.

At last he turned.

"When did it start?" he said.

"When did what start?"

"The paranoia. The weird coincidences. The déjà vu. The ecstatic visions. The heightened perceptions. The trip, Eddie. When did the trip begin?"

"Dad," I said, chopping the air with a rigid hand, determined to get through to him. "This isn't one of your damn conspiracies. Have you heard nothing I've said?"

His eyes were darting back and forth, making calculations, shuffling around the warped pieces of his paranoid jigsaw puzzle of reality. At last they settled on me.

"You may need to sit down to hear this," he said.

I remained standing.

He shuffled back to the table, closing his robe as he went, as if he felt that the gravity of what he was about to say required a corresponding measure of outward decorum. When he reached the table he planted his hands on it to lower himself, but apparently changing his mind he remained standing. His head slung low between his hunched shoulders, gazing intently at me from under his tilted brow, he said:

"Walter Morris was a CIA operative on MKULTRA from 1968 to 1973. He was a West Coast field agent with a special interrogations techniques unit. Their job was to pump unwitting subjects full of every drug they had at their disposal, and then watch us like lab rats, see if they could break down our identities, plant new ones in their place. Walter Morris was one of the people who tortured us on the rig. Ruth Brenner was the contact person between the agency and the field unit. We were out there for thirty-two days. They tried everything they had on us: LSD, mescaline, psilocybin, morphine, marijuana, sodium pentothal. There wasn't any prior consent. It was a total violation of the Nuremberg

Code. You ever heard of the Church Committee? The Rockefeller Commission? Frank Olson? Theodore Kaczynski? He participated in MKULTRA experiments at Harvard from 1959 to 1962. He was only sixteen at the time. Sirhan Sirhan was under CIA-induced hypnosis when he shot Robert Kennedy. Jonestown. Jim Jones was CIA. That whole thing was one big CIA lab. The Kool-Aid. They murdered Senator Ryan. It's all there on the internet. All the files are there. You can read it yourself. It's not a conspiracy theory. This shit really happened. Dulles was the one behind it. They wanted to create a Manchurian Candidate. That was their whole goal, to counter Soviet and Chinese advances in brainwashing techniques. Everyone thinks it ended in 1973. It never ended, Eddie. It's still going on, to this day."

The truly paranoid man is so intimate with every contour of the terrain of his demented inner landscape that without so much as batting an eye he can plant any seed of new information blown his way and watch it flourish at the speed of thought. At that moment, looking directly into his exhilarated eyes, I realized that in my headlong rush to hear the truth I had conveniently forgotten how utterly unhinged he was. Somehow I had deluded myself into believing that when confronted with the truth, face to face, he would have no choice but to confess. I had underestimated the depth of his infirmity.

"Walter Morris was not in the CIA," I said, determined to have my say before I left, if only for my own peace of mind. "He was a mediocre detective novelist." I took the copy of *Guttersnipe* that I had stolen from Ruth Brenner out of my coat pocket and held it up for him to see. "He also happened to be my biological father," I said. "He returned to Ruth Brenner twenty-six years after he and his wife, my real mother, gave me up to her, and he found out my adopted name. He named his detective after me. He spent twelve years of his life following me around, writing novels based on my cases. He was a coward. He never had the balls to face me. Now he's dead. Shot himself in the head with a snubnose .38. As for Ruth Brenner, she's an old frumpy woman who ran a foster home. You can carry on in your denial and your paranoid delusion, but those are the facts."

He heard me out, flinching here and there at the sharper edges, otherwise gazing at me with profound sadness, as if he were a helpless bystander at the final dissolution of his only son. He was quiet for a while after I had finished. Then, his eyes lowering to somewhere around my mid-section, he said:

"What's that?"

I looked down. Without realizing it I had taken the Silly Putty out of my pocket and was turning it around and around between my restless fingers.

"Nothing," I said.

"Let me see it."

"It's nothing." I put it back in my pocket.

He wouldn't relent. He came around the table, like a child fixated on some toy he can't live without. The sight of him limping towards me, his eyes riveted to my pocket, was so pathetic that I didn't have the heart not to let him see it. I took it out of my pocket and handed it to him. Until then I had always been careful when handling it not to touch the impression or deform its shape. I didn't care anymore. If he had regressed to such an infantile state that he wanted to play with Silly Putty, why should I stop him?

"Where did you get this?" he asked, staring fixedly at the impression, squinting like a jeweler through a loupe.

I didn't answer.

He shuffled quickly over to a bookshelf against the left-hand wall, on one shelf of which sat a pile of papers. Picking up a pencil, he started scribbling something, looking back and forth between the Silly Putty and the paper.

"This is it!" he exclaimed. "This is the directive. Do you know how long I've been looking for this? This is going to blow the lid off the whole thing."

Suddenly he turned pale. "Sonofabitch," he muttered. "They're onto me." He turned to me with fear in his eyes. "You've got to tell me everything? How did you get involved in this?"

"What the hell are you talking about," I said brusquely, thinking maybe I could scold him back to reality.

"The Agency," he said in a low voice. "The name of the rig was the St. Jerome. I need you on this, Eddie. It's not just about me anymore."

It was hopeless.

"The name of the company that owned the decommissioned oil rig was Poseidon Maritime," he went on, "a division of Fletcher Enterprises, headed by Gordon Fletcher."

It was my turn to go pale.

"He's CIA, Eddie," he said. "He's the head of the cell. The St. Jerome was his rig. House of Proteus. They're all CIA. It's still going on. They had Walter Morris murdered. Why do you think the police haven't arrested anybody?"

I was going insane. Either that or all of the acid he had dropped in the sixties had somehow warped my own brain cells, and I was having a bad trip. How else could I explain it? Where had he gotten Fletcher's name from? The House of Proteus? Had I mentioned those names to Mom?

"Gordon Fletcher is not in the CIA," I said with rapidly deflating conviction. "He hired me to follow his wife."

"He hired you?"

I was in no mood to repeat myself.

"Drop that job, Eddie," he said. "Drop it like a lead Zeppelin and get the hell away from him. He's a dangerous man. What did he hire you for?"

I didn't answer.

"It's the book, isn't it?" he said.

I stared at him. "What book?"

"The MKULTRA book. He wants to kill the book. There's only three of us left. Me, Michael, and Jack. Morris made contact with us after all these years. He said he was going to write a book exposing the whole thing. He had never been able to forget what he had done to us. It was all in his head, he said, and he needed to get it out. He was right here, Eddie, as close as you and me are. He told me everything, who was behind it. Three days later he was dead. He was murdered."

"He wasn't murdered," I said. I don't know why I persisted in arguing with him, in dignifying his insanity with a refutation. "It was suicide."

He shook his head. "It's still going on. They never shut it down."

He was staring bug-eyed at the Silly Putty again.

"This proves everything," he jabbered on. "Ruth Brenner was the link between the Agency and the unit on the Jerome. You've got to get out of here, Eddie. You're not safe. Get as far away as you can. Leave the state. Leave the country if possible. You have no idea how far their tentacles reach. They haven't gotten deep into you yet. I can see that just by looking at you. But it's only a matter of time."

I walked over to him, put my right hand on his shoulder, and with my left I picked up the piece of Silly Putty and squashed it in my fist, right before his eyes.

His howl of anguish followed me out the door, down the stairs, and across the lawn to the car. I could still hear it, hours later, miles from Appian Way.

32

AT A LONELY place called Dan's Liquors on the northern outskirts of San Calisto, I bought a bottle of Old Grand-Dad. A paranoid shiver ran through me at the sight of myself in the security monitor. I drove on, every now and then catching a glimpse of the moon-dappled water beyond the fields and trees and houses otherwise obscuring my view of the ocean.

I turned off the highway at the sign to San Calisto Beach and drove half a mile down the narrow road to a locked gate. I pulled over and cut the engine and grabbed the bottle and got out.

The gibbous moon was bright enough to light my way the remaining hundred yards to the parking lot. I opened the bottle and took a long drink as I walked, following the well-worn path around the restrooms and up onto the beach. The pale tail of the shore curved away to a point far off to the south, beyond which the beam from a lighthouse was wheeling monotonously over the ink-black water. I trudged through the sand, down to the crest of the berm. There I sank down and began to drink in earnest.

I didn't know what to believe anymore. Images of Imogen kept flashing across my mind, tugging upwards at my innards. I tipped the bottle back, listening to the ocean as I drank, the slow, steady crescendo as the incoming wave, having reached the end of its journey across the globe, gathered force and rolled over the outgoing one, rising to a thunderous roar as it struck solid earth, the high hiss as the water slid backwards across the sand to be sucked beneath the next wave, slowing molecule by molecule as it skulked out to sea until nothing remained of it but a ripple on the surface of the ocean, sculpted into a momentary mirror, angled precisely to reflect the light of the moon, which light was not of the moon at all but of the sun, having journeyed ninety-five million miles across the vacuum of space to collide with the dead gray dust of the moon, itself once a part of the earth, flung off by some cataclysmic collision and hurled into space only to be coaxed back into perfect equilibrium, leaving a gaping pit in the planet that in time would become the ocean whose rim I was presently sitting on, getting drunk, water wave and light wave meeting in a fleeting kiss whose only record was the pulse against the rods and cones of my retinas, subsequently translated into pure idea, pure illusion, the fiction that out there not far from me was something called water, atop which was sparkling something called moonlight, when in truth it was nothing more than matter and energy in a seemingly infinite number of permutations limited only by the dimensions of the universe, molded by the cells of my brain into metaphors of sorrow and confusion and loneliness, to be archived in my memory for future reference: that moonlit night when I sat on the beach and got drunk and railed against the cruelty of fate, a fate on a collision course with me since the birth or rebirth or endless rebirths of the universe, triangulating across space and time or some other unfathomable dimension to bowl me over and grind me into dust, myself nothing more than the flotsam of the collision of two bodies, themselves the flotsam of an endless chain of collisions, wave upon wave of lives rising out of and sinking into the earth, to produce me, a blink in cosmic time, a grain of sand on an endless beach, my own mother's lover, or just an unsuspecting lab rat in whose brain the novels of Walter Morris were nothing more than a hallucination, a guilt trip, a fever dream, the magma of my subconscious bubbling over in a bath of LSD.

The bottle empty, I hurled it out into the ocean. I watched as inch by inch the lip of the onrushing waves crept closer to the soles of my shoes. Suddenly a sheet of cold water slid under my ankles, startling me back to reality. I stood up. The beach tilted abruptly southward. I stepped northward to keep from falling, but the beach was faster than me. It sprang up like a catapult and smacked my whole length. I bounced and came to rest face down with a mouth and an ear full of sand.

The rumble of the ocean was deeper down here, the hiss sharper. I raised my head. Suddenly the lower half of me was engulfed in freezing water. I hollered and tried to stand up, but the weight of my wet pants dragged me back down. I managed to get up on my hands and knees just in time for another wave to slam into me. It tumbled me sideways, sucked me backwards, turned me over. Freezing salty water shot up my nose, down my throat. I hacked and heaved. The wet sand was dissolving beneath me, carving a cavity under my body as the water retreated. I was too preoccupied with trying to breathe to worry about moving. Another wave overtook me, propelling me forward, sucking me back. I clawed at the dissolving sand in a mounting panic to get clear of the waves. I must have made progress, because the next wave died at my knees. I dragged myself up the face of the berm, over the crest and at last onto the dry, warm sand. I kept crawling until the sound of the waves seemed far away. Then I collapsed and lay there panting and coughing for a long time.

When at last my breath was coming slow and steady, I closed my eyes. At some distant remove I sensed that I was cold and wet, and that I should try to do something about it. I decided to give it more thought after a little rest. I must have drifted off to sleep, because I awoke sometime in the night to a blood-red moon. So red that the sand before me was glowing like hot coals. I was freezing. Everything was still. No sound at all from the ocean. I raised my head. For a strangely enchanting moment I thought I was in hell. The ocean was on fire. The surface was heaving thickly, like lava, searing ingots of yellow light piercing slabs of molten iron and ruby red, all the way to the horizon. It was terrifyingly beautiful. The stink of sulphur hung densely in the air. The only thing lacking was the screams of the damned. I stared awestruck for as long as I could bear it, then I dropped my head and closed my eyes and prepared to be judged.

When I awoke again, the sky and the ocean were their usual misty morning gray. I was so cold I literally couldn't move. I concentrated on one agonizingly stiff limb at a time, eventually regaining some control of my body. It took about half an hour, but I managed to get up on my knees. After that I had to rest. It felt as though my entire mass was crammed into the right half of my skull, and it was pressing to get out.

Eventually I rolled over to a seated position. I was completely caked in sand, from the tips of my shoes to the shoulders of my coat. It was all over my face, encrusted in my hair. I started to wipe it off. I don't know why. It had probably saved my life.

Out of the mist a jogger materialized, a middle-aged man in black shorts and a white T-shirt, a brief hitch in his otherwise fluid stride the only indication that he had spotted me. He veered up the berm, into the sand, until he was standing before me, breathing deeply of health and vigor. Hands on hips he said:

"Hey, man, are you all right?"

He had a full brown mustache, cheerful cheeks, a bald crown. Somehow or other I knew he was a lawyer. It took everything in me to conjure up an affirmative little grunt and nod.

He studied me dubiously. "Are you sure?"

I nodded again. He wasn't convinced, but he wisely turned away and resumed his run, no doubt filing me away as just another homeless drunk on the beach.

I stayed put for a while, letting some of my mass drain from my brain. Somehow I conjured up the will to stand. The will preceded its fruition by quite some time. My head was spinning. I looked around for my hat, but it was gone, washed out to sea. Slowly at first, then with increasing assurance, I trudged back through the sand to the parking lot. At the restrooms I stopped and, leaning against the cinderblock wall, dumped wet sand from my shoes.

I hobbled the rest of the way up the road, the sound of the ocean gradually receding behind me. The sun had not yet breached the foothills. I doubted it ever would. I got into the car and sat there in a state of perfect stupefaction. *Never again*, I promised myself. The car was soon filled with the sour reek of my binge. I was not fit to drive. I pressed the ignition, put the heater on full blast, turned the car around, and drove back up the road to the highway.

33

IT WAS AFTER two when I reached Sunset Acres. The heat was stifling, billowing up in waves from the asphalt. There was a big, gaping hole in my head where my brain should have been. I got out and crossed the yard to the porch.

The door was locked. I cupped my hands to the window and peered in. She wasn't in the living room. I knocked again. I waited. Not a sound from within.

Wiping the sour perspiration from my upper lip, I left the porch and went around the side of the house and back to the conservatory. The yard was engulfed in the shimmering pulsations of cicadas, a strange, hypnotic sound, like ray guns in '50s sci-fi movies. The brilliance of the sunshine reflecting off the leaves and bark of the eucalyptus trees hurt my eyes. I peered through the glass of the conservatory. She wasn't there.

The back door was also locked. With a papery flutter where my heart should have been, I walked out to the shed and grabbed the ladder and carried it around to the front of the house. I leaned it against the roof of the porch and started up it. Halfway up I went woozy and had to stop. When it had passed, I carried on.

Three steps toward the study window a shingle gave way under my right shoe and broke loose. I lunged forward and caught the window ledge as the shingle slid down and disappeared over the edge. I kneeled there panting, waiting for my pulse to return to normal. When it became evident that it wasn't going to—if anything it seemed to be getting faster—I shoved the window up and climbed in.

The door was closed. I crossed directly to it, opened it and stepped out into the hall.

"Imogen?" I called out.

No response.

I walked down the hall to our bedroom. The strawberry finches paid me no heed as I stepped in. Her water glass was still on the bedside table. In all our time togther I had never known her not to take it down with her to the kitchen when she got up in the morning.

On my way down the hall I stepped into the bathroom, just to be sure. The sight of myself in the mirror gave me a shock. My face was as pale and bloated as a drowned corpse's. Overnight I had aged twenty years.

After confirming that she wasn't in my nap room, I went down the stairs to the dining room. All was still and quiet save the ticking of the clock. A quarter after two.

I went through the kitchen and out the door to the conservatory. The lunch things were still on the table: the loaf of French bread, the wedge of cheese, the jar of beets. Set for two. She hadn't yet cleared the dirty dishes. All that remained on the plate at my seat was a small crust of bread and a peach pit. The diffused sunlight was bringing out every little detail: the hardened pores of the bread, every ridge of the pit, the oil on the tiny sliver of cheese, the dried red smears of beet juice on the plate.

HEIR APPARENT

Back in the living room I told myself, despite all evidence to the contrary, that she must have gone out for a walk.

I had just taken a step toward the sofa when a gunshot rang out from upstairs. A single, emphatic report. Large caliber. So loud it set my ears ringing.

I reached for my revolver but it wasn't there. I rushed up the stairs.

An intense column of sunlight was radiating out of the partially open doorway of the study. The scent of burnt gunpowder hanging in the air. I paused at the door, listening, then, hearing nothing but my heartbeat in my ears, pushed it open.

No one there. I stepped in. In my earlier rush I hadn't noticed the neat stack of typing paper on the desk, about three inches thick. An old familiar dread came over me as I approached the desk, telling myself to just turn and walk away. In the end I couldn't resist the spare beauty of those four black lines surrounded by all that whiteness.

```
                        Heir Apparent


                           a novel


                            by


                       Walter Morris
```

I turned the page.

Chapter 1:

```
That morning when the cops came knocking, I was
dreaming that a man had shot me in the head. I
saw the flash. I heard the bang. But I didn't
feel a thing. Who this man was and why he wanted
me dead, I no longer recall.
```

I looked up from the page with the chilling sensation that she was watching me at that very moment, recording my every thought and action. A burst of sunlight flooded the room, so intense that at first nothing else could be discerned within it, and when, gradually, shapes did begin to return they were not what they should have been, not the planes and angles of walls and floors and shelves but something altogether more amorphous, no discernible edges at all, only what appeared to be translucent red jellyfish, slowly pulsing, no shadows, no edges, no corners, pulsing to the throb of my heartbeat, gently contracting, swelling, and above the thumping, or around it, another sound, a single high-pitched note, an E-flat, just within the range of human hearing, and then I saw it, floating in mid-air, a small dense, metallic object, drifting slowly towards the source of the light, pulling me along with it, everything within me contracting, expanding, flowing out into the light, no contours, no density, no differentiation, drifting for what seemed like an eternity, until gradually the light began to diminish, the thumping of my heartbeat to soften, edges, shapes, and distance to return, and I saw that I was floating in a sea of blood, rimmed by distant ice cliffs, and above it all two watery planets were shining down on me like enormous eyes, and they were full of love.